Praise for Cynthia D'Alba

An emotional, complex and beautiful story of love and life and how it can all change in a heartbeat.
    —DiDi, Guilty Pleasures Book Reviews on *Texas Lullaby*

Highly recommend to all fans of hot cowboys, firefighters, and romance.
    —Emily, Goodreads on *Saddles and Soot*

This author does an amazing job of keeping readers on their toes while maintaining a natural flow to the story.
    —RT Book Reviews on *Texas Hustle*

Cynthia D'Alba's *Texas Fandango* from Samhain lets readers enjoy the sensual fun in the sun […] This latest offering gives readers a sexy escape and a reason to seek out D'Alba's earlier titles.
    —Library Journal Reviews on *Texas Fandango*

[…] inclusions that stand out for all the right reasons is Cynthia D'Alba's clever *Backstage Pass*
    —Publisher's Weekly on *Backstage Pass* in *Cowboy Heat*

Texas Two Step kept me on an emotional roller coaster […] an emotionally charged romance, with well-developed characters and an engaging secondary cast. A quarter of the way into the book I added Ms. D'Alba to my auto-buys.

—5 Stars and Recommended Read, Guilty Pleasure Book Reviews on *Texas Two Step*

[..]Loved this book…characters came alive. They had depth, interest and completeness. But more than the romance and sex which were great, there are connections with family and friends which makes this story so much more than a story about two people.

—Night Owl Romance 5 STARS! A TOP PICK *on Texas Bossa Nova*

Wow, what an amazing romance novel. *Texas Lullaby* is an impassioned, well-written book with a genuine love story that took hold of my heart and soul from the very beginning.

—LJT, Amazon Reviews, on *Texas Lullaby*

Texas Lullaby is a refreshing departure from the traditional romance plot in that it features an already committed couple.

—Tangled Hearts Book Reviews on *Texas Lullaby*

[…]sexy, contemporary western has it all. Scorching sex, a loving family and suspenseful danger. Oh, yeah!

—Bookaholics Romance Book Club on *Texas Hustle*

Also by Cynthia D'Alba

Whispering Springs, Texas

Texas Two Step: The Prequel (digital only)

Texas Two Step

Texas Tango

Texas Fandango

Texas Twist

Texas Bossa Nova

Texas Hustle

Texas Lullaby

Saddles and Soot

Texas Daze

Single Title Novellas

A Cowboy's Seduction

Texas Justice

Big Branch, Texas (Kindle Worlds)
Kindle Format Only

Cadillac Cowboy (Hell, Yeah!)

Texas Ranger Rescue (Brotherhood Protectors)

Texas Marine Mayhem (Brotherhood Protectors)

THE MONTGOMERY FAMILY TREE

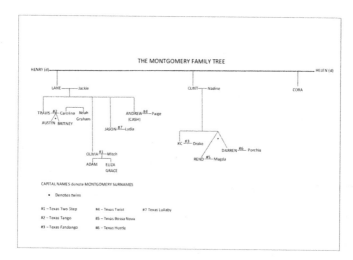

HENRY (d) —— HELEN (d)

LANE ——— Jackie   CLINT ——— Nadine   CORA

TRAVIS—#2—Carolina   Noah   ANDREW—#4—Paige
      *   Graham   (CASH)
AUSTIN BRITNEY
                  JASON—#7—Lydia

                                  KC—#3—Drake
         OLIVIA—#1—Mitch   DARREN—#6—Porchia
                                       RENO—#5—Magda
         ADAM   ELIZA
                GRACE

CAPITAL NAMES denote MONTGOMERY SURNAMES

  • Denotes twins

#1 – Texas Two Step   #4 – Texas Twist   #7 Texas Lullaby
#2 – Texas Tango   #5 – Texas Bossa Nova
#3 – Texas Fandango   #6 – Texas Hustle

TEXAS LULLABY

Whispering Springs, Texas

CYNTHIA D'ALBA

Second Edition

Texas Lullaby

by Cynthia D'Alba

Copyright © 2016 Cynthia D'Alba and Riante, Inc.

Second Edition 2017

Print ISBN: 978-1-946899-04-0

Digital ISBN: 978-1-946899-02-6

Cover Artist: Angela Waters

Updated Cover: Elle James

Editor: Heidi Shoham

Dedication

As this is the last book in the Texas Montgomery Mavericks series, I have so many people to thank. First, of course, to my editor Heidi (Moore) Shoham, who took a chance on an unpublished author seven books ago. She's been with me every step of the way.

To Angela Campbell and Sandra Jones, critique partners on many of these books...thank you from the bottom of my grateful heart.

To the D'Alba Diamonds. You ladies rock as my street team. You are always supportive and gracious with your time and reviews, reposts and retweets. You are a big part of my life, and I thank you for being there. A special shout-out to my Diamonds who took time to read the early chapters of this book and give me feedback on my twins. Thank you Delene Yochum and Paula Farrell. Your comments were very helpful.

To my husband, who has learned to wash clothes and

make his own dinner. Thanks, babe. Now, about the vacuuming and dusting....

And finally, to my very dear friend, Susie Wilson Williams, who asked me to use her granddaughter Ellery in a book. This one is for you. I threw in your daughter's name too!

Chapter One

"I'm worried about my sister. She and Jim should be here by now."

As always, the sound of his fiancée's voice made Jason Montgomery's heart swell with love. He leaned over and put his arm around the back of her chair. "I'm sure they are just running behind schedule. It was probably tough for Meredith to get her and Jim and those three kids packed and on the road."

Lydia Henson rested her head on Jason's shoulder, tiny wisps of her brunette hair tickling his cheek. The scent of lilacs and lavender from her perfume swirled around him. He inhaled, letting the intoxicating aroma fill his lungs.

"You're probably right." Lydia chuckled. "Between my sister's kids and all the Montgomery children, there are going to be a lot of short people running around at our wedding tomorrow."

The excitement in her voice when she spoke of children drove a stake into his gut. By accepting his marriage proposal, she'd accepted not having a family. His adamant stand of not wanting children was a well-known fact, and something that wouldn't change.

"And that doesn't bother you?" he asked.

"What? Rumbustious kids at our wedding and reception? Of course not." She looked into his eyes. "I love my nieces and nephew. And I adore all the ones on your side. But you and I aren't cut out to be parents, and I've accepted that. I knew when we started dating that you didn't want children. And I appreciate your being so bluntly honest about it. The long and short of it is I'd rather spend my life with you and no children than spend my life with anyone else…period."

"I love you." He leaned in to kiss her but was interrupted by someone banging on a water glass with a knife. Resting his forehead on hers, he sighed and then looked in the direction of the noise. Dressed in a gray suit with a blue tie, his brother, Travis, stood directly in front of the head table where Jason and Lydia were sitting, a wide grin splitting his face.

Travis lifted his water glass. "To my brother and his soon-to-be wife. Caroline and I wish you all the happiness we've found."

Twenty glasses filled with wine, water or iced tea were lifted in a salute, along with shouts of well-wishes.

Cash, Jason's youngest sibling, stood. "I second that. And I have to say, it's about time you made an honest man out of my brother, Lydia."

Jason playfully elbowed Lydia. "Yeah."

Lydia laughed along with the rest of the Montgomery clan, as well as her parents. At three years, it had been a long engagement.

Jason looked around the room at all the Montgomerys gathered for tonight's wedding rehearsal dinner. He was the last single adult Montgomery male. All his siblings had married, as had his cousins. If the smiles and contented expressions were any indication, marriage agreed with all of them. He was looking forward to joining their married ranks.

And now the next generation of Montgomerys had begun arriving. He adored his nieces and nephews. There wasn't much he loved more than spoiling them rotten and handing them back to the parents to straighten out. But he'd known for years that fatherhood wasn't in his future.

Every woman he'd ever dated had been sure she'd be the one who'd change his mind, sure that Jason would want children with her. It didn't work that way, at least not for him.

He'd long ago accepted his fatherless future. If any woman could have changed his mind, it would have been Lydia Henson. However his siring children, or rather *not* siring children, was based on biology, not emotion, something no woman could alter.

And it was something he'd never shared with anyone for any reason, not his siblings, not his parents, not even Lydia. Since she and his sister-in-law were the main medical care providers in town, he'd also made sure nothing appeared in his chart here. He loved his small town, but information that could be considered juicy had a tendency to find its way into the gossip mill. News of his infertility could make him the object of pity or jokes, neither of which was acceptable. So far, his past medical diagnosis had stayed in Austin, where it had originally been made.

He glanced over at the love of his life. She was as beautiful tonight as she'd been ten years ago when they'd met. Maybe she had a few lines around her eyes that hadn't been there, but she'd earned those honestly with laughter and smiles. Her chestnut-brown hair was coiled into a fancy twist right now, but later, he'd pull out the pins and let the thick waves wrap around him. As Lydia chatted with his mother, her jade-green eyes flashed with happiness and contentment.

He'd met Lydia back when he was in law school and she'd been a medical resident. He and his date had been brought into the emergency department after a car accident. Hell, right now, he couldn't even remember what his date's name had been that night. The minute he'd laid eyes on Dr. Lydia Henson, he was a goner.

But not so for the good doctor. Her hours at the hospital had been ridiculously long. Residency and then establishing her very successful private practice had taken a toll on their relationship. Needless to say, they'd had their ups and downs over the years they'd been together.

Then, last September, they had parted ways over the issue of children—her for, him against. In a moment of frustration, he told her she should go find a man to marry who wanted children. He'd been more than a little shocked when she'd agreed with him and walked away. He'd been sure they were done. And for a while, they were. But they hadn't been able to stay apart.

The rustle of Lydia's dress jerked him from his memories. She shoved her chair back and stood. "I know the bride isn't supposed to give toasts at her own rehearsal dinner, but what the heck. It's my wedding, right?"

"You go for it," Jason said with a pat on her cute butt.

"To Mom and Dad. You were always there for me and Meredith. You moved us to military bases I've never heard of in countries I'd never heard of, but what a great life you gave us. My sister is late, as usual, but if she were here, I know she'd be stomping her feet and lifting her glass in agreement. I love you both."

She turned to face Jason's parents. "To Lane and Jackie. You welcomed me into your home from the first day Jason brought me there. You've made me feel like family." She turned to face Travis and Caroline at the front table. "And thank you to Travis for marrying Caroline and keeping my great partner in town."

Travis lifted his water glass in acknowledgement and Caroline grinned.

Then she looked down at Jason and smiled. "My life hasn't been the same since you were carted into my emergency department all those years ago. I love you. I can't wait to spend the rest of our lives together."

Lydia lifted her glass. "Ladies, to the men we love."

The women in the room stood, tapped their glasses together and drank before retaking their seats.

Jason rose. "Well, hell. How am I supposed to top that?"

The gang chuckled.

"I'm not going to try." He looked at Lydia. "You are my love. My life." He leaned down and kissed her. "Now that my brother's broken tradition and started all the toasts before dinner, I suggest we eat this wonderful meal so we can get to the desserts."

Jason sat and Lydia leaned over. "We've killed as much time as we can waiting for Meredith and Jim." She glanced toward the two empty seats and back to him. "Maybe the kitchen can hold their food in a warming area so it'll still be edible. Think I should call her again?"

"It's only been a couple of hours since y'all spoke. It's a good what? Four- or five-hour drive down from

Wichita? They were making good time. I expect them to walk in any minute."

"You're probably right. I haven't seen Levi since he was born. I bet he has grown so much."

Hearing the pleasure in her voice as she spoke of her new nephew dug a pit in his gut. Raising children had been a major point of contention between them. He wished things were different for him, for them, as far as children went. But things were what they were, and he'd given up childish things like wishing for the impossible when he had been ten.

Some things were just not meant to be. His fathering children was one of those things. He had been blessed with parents who'd been wonderful role models for how to raise a family and it sucked that his option for biological children had been taken from him. Still, he'd rather others believe him too selfish to have kids than have to tolerate their pity if they discovered his gun wasn't loaded.

They finished the salad course and still no Meredith and Jim. The wait staff removed the salad plates and set thick filet mignon before each guest. Jason had just cut into his when a waiter handed him a note.

Jason.
Meet me outside. Now.
Mark Singer

Jason frowned as he read it. What could the sheriff want with him?

"Everything okay?" Lydia asked.

"Singer is outside and wants a word with me. Probably can't make the ceremony tomorrow and wants to wish us well. I'll be right back."

The Whispering Springs county sheriff was standing in the hotel hall just outside the private dining room. Hat in hand, Singer wore a serious expression that did not change when Jason held out his hand.

"Mark. Good to see you. What can I do for you?"

Singer shook Jason's hand. "I hate to do this to you tonight, but I'm afraid I have some bad news."

Jason braced himself for whatever the sheriff had to say. "Okay. What's the problem?"

"An accident report from Gainesville came across the wire an hour or so ago. No names, just location. State police called me about five minutes ago to notify the family." Mark slid the brim of his hat through his fingers as he turned it. "I'm sorry, Jason. It's Lydia's sister and her family."

"How bad?"

"I don't have all the details, but it's bad. I was told to find the family and get them as quickly as possible to the North Texas Medical Center. I thought it might be better if you could bring them out here instead of me delivering bad news in front of the whole group."

Concern and apprehension dug dual trenches through his gut. For a man who didn't wish for things, he hoped that *bad* meant a broken leg or two and nothing worse.

"Lydia is going to be crushed."

Mark nodded. "Yep. I know how close she is to her sister."

"Wait here. I'll get them."

Jason headed back into the reception, his heart chugging like a freight train.

"What was it?" Lydia asked as he neared her chair.

Jason hesitated, fully aware that he was getting ready to blow apart the world of the woman he loved.

"The sheriff needs to see you and your parents outside for a minute."

She frowned. "Why?"

Jason shook his head. "Mark can explain everything."

Lydia rose slowly as realization formed in her eyes. "It's Meredith, isn't it?"

He hated being the one to break her heart with bad news, but he loved her enough to give her an honest answer. "Yeah. I'm sorry, babe. Go get your parents and take them out. I'll be right there."

A shadow fell over her face as she nodded.

She quietly took her parents out the side door but their actions, however subtle, did not go unnoticed by the rest of the Montgomerys.

"What's going on?" Lane Montgomery asked.

Jason blew out a long breath and then squatted down between his parents' chairs. "Something has happened to Lydia's sister. A car accident. Don't know how bad. Singer was sent here by the state police to find the family."

A loud cry came from the hall. Jason rose and hurried out. Lydia's mother clung to her, weeping in noisy gasps. Her father stood at rigid attention, his military background evident in his posture.

"I'm so sorry," Singer was saying. "I don't have a lot of information beyond what I've provided."

"Can you fill me in?" Jason asked.

"Drunk driver hit their van a little ways outside of Gainesville. Report I got was that the husband was dead at the scene. The wife and kids have all been taken to North Texas Medical Center. I don't have any information on their condition."

Those dual trenches were now deep caverns trying to cut him in half. If he felt this way, he could only begin to imagine what Lydia and her folks were going through.

Jason raked his fingers through his hair. "Damn."

"I know." Singer's solemn expression said everything.

"What can we do?" Jason's father asked.

Jason whirled toward his parents, unaware until now that they had followed him into the hall.

"I don't know. Not yet. I guess the first thing is we need to find out how badly Meredith and the kids are injured."

"Let me get Caroline," Jackie said. "Maybe she can call up there for the family. Lydia is too upset. Caroline will understand all the medical jargon to translate for the rest of us."

Jason nodded. "Good idea. In the meantime, I need to talk to Lydia."

Jackie headed back into the reception, and Jason went over to where Lydia stood with her arms around her mother's waist to support the older woman.

"Let me," he said, slipping his arm around her mother. "Come on, Ida. Let's find you a place to sit down."

"My baby," she wailed. "And her babies."

"I know, I know," he said in what he hoped was a calming tone.

Jason's dad was standing beside Larry Henson, his arm around the older man's shoulders. It was clear Larry was trying to remain strong for his family, but the shaking of his body and his ashen face said that the news was taking its toll.

The doors to the private dining area opened and various Montgomery family members flowed out into the hall.

Ida's body went limp in a swoon. Jason tightened his hold, and Travis hurried over to sweep Mrs. Henson up into his arms. "I've got her," he said. "See to your bride."

Jason found Lydia near the entrance to the dining room. His sister-in-law Caroline had her arm around Lydia's shoulder as they talked. He crossed to his fiancée, put his arms around her and hugged her close.

"I'm sorry, babe."

"I know." She gave him a quick hug, took in a shuttering breath, stiffened her spine and stepped back to continue her conversation with Caroline. "Neither of us are great at throwing around our weight to get what we want, but I really need you to do that now. Call and badger everybody until we know what's going on."

This woman, his Lydia, was in full doctor mode, barking out orders, expecting others to do what she said. Since her brother-in-law had died, he had to assume the accident had been quite catastrophic. He worried about Meredith's condition. He suspected Lydia of having the same fears.

Caroline stepped over to the side and began dialing numbers.

Jason's brother-in-law, Mitch, gripped Jason's shoulder. "Whatever Olivia and I can do, just ask."

Jason nodded. "I know. Thanks."

It didn't take long before Caroline handed her phone to Lydia. The conversation between Lydia and the hospital was one-sided, but Jason didn't need to hear both sides to know that what Lydia was being told was not good. He didn't understand many of the medical terms he heard, but the stricken expression on Lydia's face said more than words.

She clicked off the phone and looked at him. "I have to go."

Jason nodded. "Okay. When?"

"Now. I'm not sure Meredith will make it through the night."

"I'm so sorry, honey."

"I know. Me too." For the first time since she'd gotten the news, a large tear rolled down her cheek. "I think I'm going to lose my sister." Her whispered statement almost brought him to his knees. If this were any of his family...

He pulled her into a tight embrace and ran his hands up and down her back. "What can I do?"

"Get me to Gainesville as fast as possible."

"No problem." Stepping back, he searched for the one person who could get them there the fastest. "Mitch," he called.

Mitch nodded and hurried over.

"Lydia and her folks need to get to Gainesville ASAP."

Mitch nodded. "I'll notify the airport to get my plane ready to fly. It's only a four-seater, so——"

"No problem," Jason said. "I'll stay here, take care of a few things and then drive up as soon as I can."

Lydia groaned. "The wedding." She looked at Jason, sorrow pulling deep creases in her face. "I'm sorry, Jason, but there's just no way."

"I know. It doesn't matter." But it did. Disappointment punched him in the gut, not that he would begin to show it. Of course they couldn't get married while her sister, and maybe her nieces and nephew, fought for their lives. She would always associate her wedding date with one of the worst days of her life, not the kind of memory he wanted for her.

"Yeah, it does matter, but this is why I love you so much," Lydia said. "You get it."

"Get your parents. You all should change into something more comfortable than what you're wearing. Five minutes won't make a difference," he added when she tried to object to taking time to change clothes. "You may be there a few days."

"You're right. You're right. I can't think right now."

"I'll drive you home to change." He kissed her and then waved his mom over. "Mom."

Jackie said something to Larry Henson and then walked quickly to where Jason and Lydia stood. "What can I do, honey?"

"I'm going to take Lydia home to change and grab an overnight bag. Mitch is getting his plane ready to go so he can fly them up there tonight."

"Good idea."

"Can you and Dad help the Hensons get into something more comfortable for travel? Oh and maybe an overnight bag for them? Lydia and I should be back here in about fifteen minutes. I can pick them up and drive them to the airport."

"Of course."

Jason stopped her as she turned to leave. "And, Mom, we need to notify as many people as we can that there won't be a wedding tomorrow."

Jackie Montgomery didn't waste time asking questions about the cancelation of the wedding. She nodded and hurried off.

The silence on the drive to Lydia's house was broken only by her irregular breathing and quiet sobs. Once there, Jason stood in the living room and waited for her to change clothes. In under five minutes, she was back out dressed in scrubs and carrying a duffle bag.

"Ready. Let's go."

"How did you do that?"

"The duffle bag? Already packed. It's my emergency bag for when I'm called to the hospital and have to be there overnight."

Her parents were standing in the hotel drive with his parents when he pulled up. After loading them into the car, he hugged his mother.

"Thanks, Mom."

"Of course, honey. With all the Montgomerys working tonight, we'll get everyone notified about the postponement."

He noticed her wording. Postponement, not cancelation. He hoped that's what it was.

THE TIRES OF MITCH'S PLANE KISSED THE TARMAC AND then settled down. The small plane taxied to the hangers and Mitch cut the engines.

"Stay here," he ordered before jumping out.

Lydia knew nothing about flying except to buckle in, so she didn't know what Mitch was doing outside. She heard doors opening and closing and she assumed he was getting her duffle bag out. Her parents hadn't wanted to pack anything. Their only concern had been getting to their youngest daughter.

She jumped when her door opened.

"The car Jason ordered for you is here. Let me help you guys out."

The car's driver was loading her bag into the trunk. She helped her parents exit the plane and into the car. She turned and hugged Mitch before she followed her parents into the limo.

"Thank you."

"Not a problem. You call us and let us know what's going on. We'll all be praying for your family," Mitch said and hugged her tightly. "Get going."

She had decided that wearing her doctor persona

might get her and her parents access where simply being the sister might not. She strode into the hospital lobby with the brashness of a general leading an attack, her shell-shocked parents following in her wake.

"I'm Dr. Henson. Where is Meredith Hardy?" she demanded at the information desk.

The older woman, who must have been used to demanding doctors, nodded. "Hold on a sec, Doc. Let me look." The information volunteer scrolled through a list of names on her computer screen and then said, "Ah. Here she is. ICU. Do you know your way?"

"No. Directions please." Lydia had never snapped orders at staff like this before, but she feared that loosening the tight control she had on her emotions would send her spiraling into a crying jag.

"Certainly, Doctor, although it's quite past visiting hours."

"Do I look like I'm here for a visit?" Lydia shot back.

"No, ma'am. Down the hall behind me. Take a left."

Lydia gave a short nod and headed in the indicated direction. "They're with me," she said over her shoulder, gesturing for her parents to follow.

She'd expected an argument at the nurses' station about seeing her sister, but they seemed to be expecting her.

A nurse sitting at the station rose. "Dr. Henson. The front desk let me know you'd made it. I'm Kelly, Mrs. Hardy's nurse."

"Excellent. Fill me in."

"Multiple broken bones and contusions. Bleeding into her brain. Ruptured spleen and left kidney. She went straight to surgery upon arrival. Both organs were damaged beyond repair and have been removed. We were able to get her abdominal bleed under control.

However, her blood pressure has remained erratic. She's unconscious and unresponsive to stimuli. Right now, it's her head trauma that has us concerned. It was fairly severe. Would you like to see her?"

Lydia nodded and then looked at her pale-faced parents standing in the door to the unit. She turned her gaze back to the nurse. "Do you know anything about the children that were in the accident with her?"

The nurse nodded. "Three little miracles, if you ask me."

"What do you mean?"

"They are fine. I think one of the girls has a small cut on her cheek that required stitches, but other than that, and being scared and shook up, they are fine."

"They're here?"

"Yes. Social services were called since they were unattended minors."

"Can you get someone to take Mr. and Mrs. Henson to see their grandchildren while I assess Meredith's condition? I'd like to be able to prepare her parents before they see her."

"I'll see to it."

Lydia entered her sister's room, pretty sure the staff realized that she was there more in a family capacity than physician. She appreciated their allowing her access to her sister and the records.

Meredith lay on white sheets, the color a marked contrast from her gray tones. A ventilator manually pushed air into her lungs, the rhythmic swoosh of the machine blending in with the beeps and tweets from the other mechanical devices keeping her alive. Multiple bags of IV fluids dripped into different veins on Meredith's body. An empty blood bag hung off one of the IV hooks.

For a couple of minutes, Lydia stood frozen in place, observing her sister. Meredith's arms were fully extended, her hands rotated toward her body. Decerebrate posturing. She'd seen it before, a sign that the outcome would probably be fatal. The nurse had been correct. The damage to Meredith's neurological system was serious.

As she gazed down on her sister, the medical tenet about doctors not treating family members had never seemed more pertinent. Lydia gasped in a small, hiccupping breath and stepped to Meredith's bedside.

"Hey, sis. You're not supposed to be here." She touched Meredith's hand. Cold. Rigid. Lifeless. "Mom and Dad are here," she said. "We need you, sis. Your kids need you."

There was no response, and really, she didn't expect one. She and her parents would have to say their goodbyes, because Lydia knew Meredith was not coming back.

A code was called over the loud speaker, and nurses in the area jumped into action. Lydia looked around but saw nothing in the ICU that would suggest a patient in immediate distress. Her gaze caught that of a nurse on the phone who was nodding while speaking. As soon as she disconnected the call, the nurse came into the room.

"Dr. Henson."

"Yes?"

"It's your father. He collapsed and has been moved to the emergency department."

All the thoughts in Lydia's head fled as she tried to process this new information. "What happened?"

"I'm not sure. But your mother has asked for you."

"I don't know where I'm going. Can someone direct me?"

Lydia hurried back to the lobby, took a right turn and followed the arrows to the emergency room. She found her father resting on a hospital stretcher, an oxygen mask over his nose and mouth, a bag of IV fluid flowing into a vein.

"What the hell happened?" Lydia asked.

Her mother twisted her fingers. "I don't know. One minute we were standing there looking at the babies and the next he grabbed his chest and collapsed on the floor."

It could be something as simple as an anxiety reaction to something as serious as a heart attack. Even as she had this thought, a lab tech entered.

"Need to draw some blood," he said.

Lydia stepped back to allow the tech room to work. Seven tubes of blood later, the tech left. There wasn't much Lydia could do right now, not for her sister or her father, and she hated her sense of powerlessness.

She was torn. Should she stay here with her father or head back upstairs to her sister? And what about her nieces and nephew? She needed to check on them too.

She desperately wanted to find a corner where she could let everything go and cry.

She desperately wanted Jason here. Everything was better when they were together.

"How are the children?" she asked her mother. The question served two purposes. First, she was worried about the kids, and second, the question would refocus her mother's attention.

"The children?" her mother said with a glazed expression. "Oh, they're fine. They were asleep when we were there." Ida's expression changed to one of panic. "Oh, Lydia. What are we going to do if Meredith dies?"

Wasn't that the million-dollar question.

Chapter Two

The next four hours would go in Lydia's memory book as pure, total hell. Her father had had a mild heart attack. Three of his heart vessels needed stents and he was adamant that he wouldn't have surgery done right away. He insisted on seeing his own doctor in Florida first. Nothing Lydia, her mother nor any doctor told him could sway him off his hard stance.

Meredith's condition continued to worsen, so Lydia got her mother up to the ICU for a short visit. Whether that was a good idea or not, Lydia wasn't sure. But since she knew Meredith would not recover, she felt her mother deserved to have one last chance to talk to her youngest daughter.

The children woke up crying for their momma and daddy. Their wails of fear and despair ripped at Lydia's heart like tiger claws, leaving gaping wounds she feared would never heal.

When she was ready to drown in the storm of all her family problems, Jason, Travis and Caroline found her sitting in pediatrics rocking baby Levi back to sleep. The rocking was soothing to her and the baby, but seeing three pillars of support walking in was as if she'd been tossed a lifebuoy during a raging storm. She clutched Jason's arm when he neared.

"You're here," she said.

"Of course I am. I'll always be here. I'm sorry it took so long to get to you. There was an issue with Mitch's plane when he got back, so we drove." He pulled her up out of the rocker and held her and the baby tightly against him. Her eyes shuttered closed in relief.

"What can we do?" Travis whispered.

"I don't know where to begin." She filled them in on Meredith's rapidly failing condition, her father's heart event and refusal for immediate surgery, and the abject terror her nieces were going through. If there was anything fortunate tonight, it was that her nephew, Levi, was too young to understand more than dirty diapers and empty tummies. The entire time she spoke, she continued to sway with Levi.

"Do you want me to check on your sister?" Caroline asked. "Make sure nothing has been missed?"

Caroline had a much stronger background in emergency medicine than Lydia. Before marrying Travis and settling in Whispering Springs, Caroline had been much in demand as a contract physician for trauma centers.

"Would you?" Lydia asked. "I've read her chart, but I can't think of anything they've missed or that should have been done that wasn't, but trauma is more your expertise than mine."

"Of course." Caroline gave Travis a peck on his lips. "You can't go with me to ICU. Make sure your phone is on and I'll catch up with you later." After getting directions, Caroline headed off toward ICU.

"Travis, can you check on my parents? I need to look

in on Ellery and Annie. I can't let them wake up again and be so scared. If you can talk my dad into surgery, I'd be in your debt."

"Sure. Where do I need to go?"

Lydia gave him directions to her father's room and he headed out.

Once he was gone, that left her alone with Jason. "Thank you for coming."

"You don't have to thank me. I wanted to be with you. I hate it took so long."

"Doesn't matter. You're here now." She carried the sleeping seven-month-old to the crib and lowered him into it. He wiggled a little at the sudden loss of her body heat but didn't wake. Lydia was thankful for the small favor.

For a couple of minutes, she held on to the crib rail and watched him sleep.

"He's a good-looking kid," Jason noted.

"Yeah. I can't believe how much he's grown."

His broad hand covered the back of her neck and he began to massage the muscles here.

"What did you do about the wedding?"

"Postponed. With all the Montgomerys working the phones, it didn't take long for the notification to spread. Lots of well-wishes for you and your family."

Glancing over at him, she smiled. "I know you told them, but make sure your family really knows how much we appreciate their help." A hiccup rattled her and then, because there was no way to stop them, a volley of tears overflowed her eyes and trickled down her cheeks.

"Oh, babe. I wish I could do something." Jason slid his hand off her neck and down her back in comforting strokes.

"Meredith isn't going to make it," she whispered. "I

haven't said that out loud, but I know it. I can't find a way to tell my parents. Mom is so frantic over Dad that I don't think she realizes how bad Meredith is. In her mind, Meredith is hurt but she'll be okay. She won't, Jason."

"Dr. Henson?"

She and Jason turned toward the voice. A pediatric nurse stood in the doorway. "I'm sorry, Dr. Henson. ICU called. You're needed there."

Jason took her hand and squeezed. "Come on," he said. "I'll go with you."

When they arrived at the ICU, they found Caroline, Travis and both her parents waiting for them. Her father looked up at her from his wheelchair, his ashen face a reminder that he still faced his own medical challenges. Her mother clung to Travis's arm, his strength most likely the only thing keeping her upright.

"What's going on?" Lydia asked.

Caroline put her arm through Lydia's. "Meredith's doctor is here. He wants to talk to the family."

Lydia had had talks like these before, only it had always been her delivering the bad news rather than being on the receiving end.

She nodded. "Where are we meeting him?"

Meredith's nurse walked up. "Come with me. We have a family room for you."

Lydia took her mother's arm while Jason pushed her father's wheelchair into a small conference room. She braced herself and then realized it wasn't her she was worried about bracing. It was her parents. This was not going to be easy.

Her mother had already started crying. So had her dad.

Dr. Harrington entered and sat. "Dr. Henson. Mr.

and Mrs. Henson. Mr. Montgomery. It's times like these that make being a physician hard." He sighed. "I'm sorry, but Mrs. Hardy died about five minutes ago. It was too sudden for us to gather you to say your goodbyes."

Ida Henson gasped and slumped against Lydia. "No. No. Not my baby."

Larry Henson sobbed into an already soaked handkerchief.

"She never regained consciousness. Take some comfort in the fact she felt no pain."

Hot, salty tears leaked into the corners of Lydia's mouth. She could taste them on her tongue. An odd realization came over her. She'd delivered death notifications to families before, but she'd never thought about what came next.

Jim had been an only child with no living parents. Wherever Meredith was buried, he should be with her.

And the children. Years ago, when the twins were born, Meredith had made Lydia swear to take the kids if anything happened to her and Jim. Lydia had agreed, but then both women had laughed at the ravings of a new mother. And now Lydia was faced with the prospect of raising three small children.

Her parents were in their mid-seventies, long past the age of being able to keep up with toddlers. Plus, her father's heart event tonight clearly signaled that she couldn't look to them for help.

And then there was her fiancé, the man who'd been adamant about not wanting the responsibility of raising children.

She was on her own.

Suddenly overwhelmed with the enormity of the task facing her, she slumped in her chair and allowed the tears to flow.

How Lydia was able to hold it together for the forty-eight hours after her sister's death was a question she would probably ask herself for the rest of her life. Because she was the only family member who could realistically take the children, and because of the prior agreement with her sister, they were released into her care.

Since she and the children would be living in Whispering Springs, she persuaded her parents to bury Meredith and Jim there so that the children would be able to visit the graves as needed to understand the concept of death. Jason's parents immediately volunteered to arrange for the burial sites at Greenwood Cemetery, right outside the city limits of Whispering Springs.

Caroline sweet-talked Larry Henson into having one of the stents done in Dallas. She and Travis drove Lydia's parents down to Baylor and got Larry checked into the hospital there. And while Lydia was relieved her father was getting the stent he needed, she also felt a modicum of relief at having one less problem to deal with.

The children were almost more than she could handle. Ellery and Annie, the three-year-old twins, cried almost non-stop on Sunday while they were in the hotel waiting for Meredith and Jim's bodies to be released. Levi was a dream baby. He ate and slept, unconcerned by the chaos going on around him.

Jason was the lynchpin that held them all together. He rented a van to get them home. He brought food when they were hungry. Bought clothes for the kids to wear. Held Lydia at night when she could take no more.

However, the guilt of leaning so heavily on Jason ate at her. It wasn't fair. The man was putting up a good front, but he had minced no words in expressing his disinterest in parenting. She would have to find a way to do this without him. However, for now, she would take whatever help she could get from wherever it came.

Monday, the bodies were released for burial. Eternal Rest Funeral Home arrived to transport them back to Whispering Springs. As they were packing up the hotel room, Lydia's cell rang.

"Dr. Henson," she answered.

"Is this Lydia Henson?" a female voice asked.

"Yes."

"I'm trying to reach Meredith or Jim Hardy. Your number was given as an emergency contact."

The emotional stab came in hard and fast, gutting her so quickly it made her drop to the edge of the bed.

"Who is this?" she asked.

"Naomi. We have Jasper here for boarding. The Hardys usually pick him up first thing on Monday morning, but we're getting concerned since we haven't heard from them. Do you have another contact number for them?"

"Jasper? Who is Jasper?"

At the mention of Jasper, Ellery and Annie began jumping around the room shouting, "Jasper. We're going to go get Jasper."

Lydia put her finger to her lips, which did little to slow down the two girls.

"Their dog," the woman on the phone replied.

"Meredith and Jim had a dog?"

"Yes. A golden retriever. Now about reaching the Hardys? Can you help?"

"Hold on a second." Lydia stood. "Jason, I need to step outside for a minute to finish this call."

"No problem," he said, tucking both girls under his arms to swing them. "I've got this." The two girls giggled and shouted as he tossed one and then the other onto the bed.

The hotel room door snicked closed behind her.

"Meredith and Jim were…" she paused to swallow against the lump growing in her throat. "Meredith and Jim were killed this weekend in a car accident." A flood of tears gathered again in her eyes.

"Oh my God. I am so sorry for your loss."

She sniffed. "Thank you."

"I hate to ask, but what do you want to do about Jasper? We can keep him until you pick him up."

A dog. The last thing she needed was a dog. She opened her mouth to ask if it was possible to find him a new home, but the sounds of Ellery and Annie laughing echoed in her mind. They'd already lost so much. How could she take away their pet too? Maybe having Jasper with them might help a little. It certainly couldn't hurt.

She sighed. A dog and three kids.

"Can you hold on to him until I can get there?"

"Of course."

"Thank you. We'll head up there today." Besides, they had to go to the house and get clothes for the kids.

The house. How would she be able to take care of cleaning out the house and selling it? Once again, she was swamped by a tidal wave of all the responsibilities she'd just inherited. Her stomach threatened to return her minimal breakfast of toast and coffee.

"Today or tomorrow. No hurry," the woman was saying. "Again, I am so sorry for your loss."

Lydia leaned against the door to their suite, running

the various options of getting to Wichita and back to Whispering Springs. She didn't see any way possible to do everything they needed to do and get home in one day.

The door behind her opened, sending her stumbling backwards. Jason caught her before she fell.

"Sorry about that," he said. "You about ready to head home?"

She sighed heavily. "I have to go to Wichita first."

"What? Why?"

"Seems there's a dog I have to pick up."

"Ah. Jasper by any chance? The girls have been talking about brushes and toys ever since you mentioned that name."

She nodded. "Look, would you mind terribly if I took the van? We can rent you another car to get you home. As long as I'm headed to Kansas, I might as well pick up clothes for the kids."

"Hell, yes, I'd mind." The remark snapped like a flag in a heavy wind.

"I just, well, you've been awesome, but these are my problems, not yours."

His eyebrow shot up. "Problems?"

"No, no. That's not what I meant." She rubbed at the headache forming at her temples. "I don't know what I'm saying. I'm just a little overwhelmed at the moment."

The twins shoved their way between Lydia and Jason.

"Are we getting Jasper?" Annie asked.

"I love Jasper," Ellery said.

"Jasper. Jasper," Annie said, jumping up and down.

Lydia caught Jason's gaze and saw his determination. She wouldn't be driving to Wichita alone.

They decided that taking the girls to the house to

pack might be too traumatic. Instead, they checked in to a hotel and Jason volunteered to babysit while Lydia did what she needed to do. The girls thought staying in a hotel was grand fun, especially since there was a pool.

The house was so quiet with only the sound of a ticking grandfather clock to break the silence. The sense of loss and grief swamping her was like nothing she'd ever experienced. She went to the master bedroom and sat on Meredith's bed. The room and everything in it smelled like her sister.

She put her head on Meredith's pillow and wept.

WITH ANNIE AND ELLERY DANCING WITH EXCITEMENT around his knees, Jason paid for a couple of new swimsuits and two sets of arm floaties. Even though the girls told him they knew how to swim, he did know better than to trust a couple of three-year-olds for accurate information.

The young gal working in the store had flirted with him the entire time the girls had been picking out new suits. Once they were paid for, the store clerk volunteered to help Annie and Ellery get dressed for swimming. Jason gladly took her up on her offer as his arms were full of a wiggling Levi.

The hotel advertised a small, indoor kiddie pool, one of the reasons he'd chosen this place. The girls giggled and pranced and twisted around like they had ants in their pants as they all walked down to the pool area. The kiddie pool was maybe six inches deep where the kids walked in and might have been two or two-and-a-half feet at its deepest, but that was about it, thank goodness. He pulled a lounge chair closer and let the girls wade in the water. Within seconds, they were laughing and splashing each other.

Levi pushed against Jason's chest, wanting down. He didn't have a suit for the baby. Heck, he didn't have one for himself. He hadn't even thought about Levi wanting in the water.

The baby began crying…loudly. Jason knew Levi wasn't hungry and his diaper wasn't dirty. The only thing he might want is the water.

Jason sighed, pulled Levi's shirt over his head and took off his shorts, leaving him dressed only in his diaper. He put a towel on the concrete where the pool was the shallowest. He sat on the towel and sat Levi in the water, whose diaper quickly sucked up water and doubled in size. Levi gurgled and splashed, a glob of drool dripping from his toothless grin.

"Uncle Jason," Ellery said. "You should come in too."

Jason chuckled. "I forgot my swim suit. I can't."

"Levi doesn't have on one," Annie said.

Oh, yeah. Jason could picture his explanation to the cop who would arrest him for getting into a kiddie pool wearing only his briefs. "But officer, Levi didn't have on pants either."

"That's true," he said. "But I like sitting here watching you guys play."

The girls lay in the water, practiced swimming like someone named Ariel, whoever that was, and had a floating contest. Levi, on the other hand, loved hitting the water with his palms, effectively throwing water droplets on Jason. Before long, Jason's shirt was fairly damp. He didn't mind. In fact, he was getting quite a kick out of watching them play.

He checked his phone for the time and to see if he'd

missed a call from Lydia. Almost five p.m. and no call. That made him a little nervous. Sure she was fine, he nonetheless would have appreciated her checking in. He didn't know how long to let the girls swim or what to do about dinner.

At close to six, the girls were wearing down. He'd taken Levi out of the pool and gotten him redressed without getting squirted. A real accomplishment, in Jason's opinion.

"Uncle Jason. I'm hungry," Ellery said.

"Me too," Annie echoed.

"Me three," Jason answered, which made the girls giggle. "How about we go back to the room, get cleaned up, and I'll have dinner delivered to the room."

"What are we eating?" Ellery asked. "I want chicken."

"Me too," Annie echoed.

"I think we can do that. Get on out of the pool and let's get you wrapped up in the towels."

Damn, he was tired. The kids were cute and funny, but they were energy vampires.

Back in the room, he ran a tub of water and put both girls in there, along with a tired and cranky Levi. He let the girls play a little while he took a wash cloth to Levi and then got him out. Keeping an eye on the twins in the tub, Jason put Levi in a fresh diaper and his pajamas and then sat him in the portable crib the hotel had supplied.

"Be right back, buddy," he said.

Levi began to cry.

"Yeah. I know how you feel," he whispered and handed the baby a bottle, which Levi tipped up immediately and began sucking.

Back in the bathroom, he did a cursory bathing of the girls and got them out and dressed in their pajamas.

He settled them on the bed with a movie and called room service. Then he collapsed into a chair. Where was Lydia?

The sound of the door lock popping jerked him awake. Good Lord, he'd fallen asleep in the chair. He quickly ran his gaze around the room. The twins were still engrossed in the movie. Levi had finished his bottle and was now standing in the crib watching his sisters.

A bronze-colored long-haired dog preceded Lydia into the room.

"Jasper," both girls shouted and jumped off the bed.

"We missed you," Ellery said, her arms wrapped around the dog's neck.

"Yeah. Missed you," Annie repeated.

"Hi," Lydia said as she pushed three large suitcases through the door.

"Hi, yourself," Jason said and heaved himself out of the chair. "I was getting worried."

"Sorry. It took a little longer than I thought it would. The girls do okay?"

"We went swimming," Ellery announced.

"You did?"

Both girls nodded.

"Yeah," Annie said. "Uncle Jason bought us new bathing suits."

Then with that announcement, both girls ran to the bathroom and came back carrying the wet swimwear.

"Wow," Lydia said. "Those are cute."

"Yeah, and he let us swim in the deep end."

Lydia's eyes flew open wide and she snapped her head from the twins to Jason. "The deep end?"

"Yeah," he said, a grin threatening to break out as he teased her. "The deepest end of the pool."

She glared at him. "How deep was the deepest end of the pool?"

"I'm not sure. Maybe two feet. Could have been as deep as two and a half."

She smiled, and it was so good to see that on her face after the terrible weekend. "I see." She looked at the twins. "Very daring."

They nodded.

"Okay then, go put your bathing suits back in the bathroom and let's talk about dinner."

To the girls' utter delight, Jasper followed them into the bathroom. In a minute, the sound of a dog drinking from the toilet echoed into the room.

"Just tell me the water was clean," Lydia said with a sigh.

"Freshly flushed. I promise."

A knock at the door had Lydia spinning around.

"I've got it," Jason said. "We ordered chicken fingers for dinner."

"Yay," the girls shouted.

The headache that'd been threatening to break out all day finally pushed through and Jason flinched at the noise. Lydia must have seen his expression, because she hurried over to the girls to quiet them down and then to pick up Levi who'd started crying.

Between the two of them, they got the girls fed and into bed over their whiny objections. Levi, who was turning out to be an easy baby—thank God—ate and fell asleep almost immediately. Jasper climbed onto the bed with the girls, curled up and went to sleep. It was close to nine when the room finally fell quiet.

Jason took Lydia's hand and led her into the small living room area of the suite. They both collapsed on the sofa.

"I was getting worried about you," he said

"Afraid I'd run off and leave you with the kids?" she asked with a smile.

"Nope. I've seen you with them. You're a natural mother."

Her face flushed. "No, I'm not. I'll never be able to replace Meredith."

"Then don't try. Just be you, and they'll love you."

She shrugged. "Thank you for taking care of them this afternoon. Without them underfoot, the packing went pretty fast."

He put his arm around her. "How are you doing? It's been a hell of a couple of days."

"Not so good. I miss my sister." She twisted on the seat until she was facing him. "I can't believe she's gone." Her eyes grew shiny with tears. "I can't do this," she whispered.

"Yes, you can. You're strong and brave. Your sister knew you would love her kids as much as she did. She trusted you."

Tears rolled down her face. "I want to curl up in a corner and stay there until this nightmare is over."

"I know," he said and pulled her snuggly against him. "I know." He kissed the top of her head. "Just take it a day at a time. And if that's too much, an hour at a time. You'll come out on the other side, just like they will. You'll see."

She sniffed and settled her head on his chest. His shirt grew wet with her tears, but that was okay. She could lean on him. He loved her.

He could give her the support she needed…for now.

Chapter Three

Late the next day, an exhausted Lydia, Jason, three kids and one very large dog pulled into the drive at Lydia's house. Never had her own place looked so good. Except, now that she studied her cozy little abode, how in the world would she, Annie, Ellery, Levi and one very large, very hairy dog fit into her two-bedroom, one-bath home? At least the backyard was fenced for Jasper. Thank goodness for small wins.

"Are Momma and Daddy here?" Ellery asked.

The question was a direct hit to Lydia's solar plexus. She drew in a deep breath and turned around in the passenger seat until she could see the girls.

"No. Remember I told you that your momma and daddy had gone to heaven to live with the angels?"

Ellery looked at her mulishly. "I don't want them to go live in heaven. I want them to live with us." Her bottom lip stuck out in a pout.

"Me too," Annie said, her mouth striking the same pose.

Me three, Lydia thought. "I know, sweetheart."

Both girls started crying, which woke Levi and got him on a crying jag.

She cut her gaze to Jason, who was watching her. He lifted one eyebrow in question and she shrugged.

This was too hard. How was she ever going to do this?

She forced herself to open the passenger door. "Come on. Let's go inside and get ready for bed."

"I don't wanna go to bed," Ellery wailed.

"Me neither," Annie echoed.

Drawing in a deep breath, Lydia climbed out of the car. Jason did the same on the other side.

"Can you get Levi? I'll get the girls."

"No," Ellery said obstinately. "I want Uncle Jason. I don't want you."

"Me too," Annie said.

"I've got them, Lydia. You get Levi and the dog."

By the time she got Jasper leashed up and Levi unbuckled from his seat, Jason and the girls had disappeared into her house.

As Jasper pulled her toward the porch, she tightened her hold on Levi and let her mind run through their sleeping options. For tonight, the girls could sleep either with her in her bed or she'd have to make a pallet of blankets on the floor. The second bedroom was where she kept her recliner, a desk and a desktop computer, not to mention the stacks of medical journals she swore she would read one day. She'd need to get a couple of twin beds for there. That solved the future sleeping arrangements for the girls, but where was she going to put Levi? She needed another bedroom. And probably another bathroom.

When she'd bought this house, she'd thought it a temporary stop before she married Jason and moved into his large, five bedroom, thirty-six hundred square foot house. She'd once asked him why he had such a huge house when he didn't want children. He'd replied that he'd gotten a steal of a deal on it, something just too good to pass up.

At first she hadn't believed him, sure that his protest of not ever wanting children was a ploy by a single guy to keep women at arm's length. But over the years they'd been together, he'd never once wavered, and they'd had plenty of heated discussions on the subject.

The bedrooms at his house now held his office, a personal gym, a guest room and a storage room. He certainly hadn't had any trouble converting those extra bedrooms into usable space.

House hunting wasn't, or hadn't been, high on her to-do list. She might need to readjust her priorities.

Her home had been pretty much a mess when she'd left for Gainesville last Friday. She dreaded facing it. However, she walked into a spotless living room, not a dust bunny in sight. She also noticed her furniture had been rearranged. Her first thought was that someone had broken in, but why would thieves redecorate?

She frowned and turned in the circle, effectively wrapping Jasper's lead around her knees.

"Here. Stop turning," Jason said. "Give me Jasper and I'll turn him loose in the backyard."

"Okay." She did, but she was still confused.

"Aunt Lydia. Come see," Ellery said, grabbing hold of Lydia's pant leg.

"Come see what?"

"Our new beds."

New beds? She followed a skipping Ellery down the short hall to her office. The office was gone. The desk, computer, chair and all the magazines had disappeared.

In their place were two adorable twin beds with frilly pink bedspreads. A matching curtain framed the only window in the room.

"What does this say?" Annie asked, holding up a white envelope.

"I don't know. Let's see."

"Here," Jason said, walking up beside her. "Give me Levi."

She happily passed the sweaty and heavy baby over and took the mysterious envelope to open. It was addressed to Ellery and Annie Hardy. Inside was a brightly colored card.

Welcome to your new home, it proclaimed in big letters.

The inside was signed by every person in Jason's family. At least she was pretty sure everyone had signed it, but she'd have to wait until the tears in her eyes subsided to be able to read the writing clearly.

"It says welcome to your new home," she said. "It's from Jason's mom and dad, his brothers and sister, his cousins and his uncle and aunt." She looked at Jason. "I believe your family might have done a little home remodel while we were gone."

"Seems like," he agreed. "It's very pretty," he said to the girls. "I love it. Don't you?"

"Yay," they both said.

"I can't believe they did this," Lydia muttered. "I'm so…"

"Hey," he said. "My family adores you. Of course they'd do anything to help."

"Still…this is…wow. I'll write every one of them thank-you notes. I'll owe free medical care to them all for the rest of my life."

He chuckled. "We already get free medical services."

"Whatever. You know what I mean."

Knowing that the hours in the car combined with spilled food meant the girls had to have baths before bed, Lydia said, "Why don't we find the bathroom so you two can take a bath? Doesn't that sound like fun?"

"I don't want to take a bath," Ellery stated flatly. She crossed her arms over her chest.

"Me neither," said Annie and assumed the same defiant stance.

"Are you kidding?" Jason asked, widening his eyes as though surprised. "I can't imagine that Ariel would turn down a chance to get wet, can you?"

"No," they each replied slowly.

"So why would you?" he asked.

The girls looked at each other and it appeared some form of nonverbal communication passed between them.

"Okay," Ellery said. "But I want you to bathe me. Not her."

"Me too," said Annie.

Jason passed Levi to Lydia. "Seems I've been ordered into service."

She smiled, but her heart was breaking from the girls' words. They didn't want her. They wanted Jason. They didn't like her.

Battling against another round of useless tears, she brightened her fake smile. "Great. Get to work then."

The three of them marched down the hall with Levi and her following. Jason got the water filling the tub while the girls undressed, only helping them when required. Ellery and Annie climbed into her tub and sat.

"Okay, this time I want to see some washing behind those ears. I'm pretty sure I can see french-fry dust and catsup back there," Jason said, sounding stern but making the girls giggle.

Lydia turned her back and rolled her eyes. She watched him help the girls wash while she gave Levi a sponge bath in the large bathroom sink.

How could this man not want children? He was a natural with them, unlike her, who was floundering and making mistakes at every turn.

"I need to set up Levi's Pack 'n Play so he has somewhere to sleep tonight."

She'd found a portable crib slash playpen in Levi's room and added it to the pile of clothes and diapers she'd packed.

"Can't believe the folks wouldn't have thought of something for him too," Jason said.

"Yeah. You're probably right. You okay in here?"

"Absolutely. We're good, right, girls?"

"Yes," they answered.

Since she'd already discovered that her office had been converted to a bedroom for the twins, she headed to her room wondering if there were changes there also. Sure enough, there was a new crib erected in the corner where there had been a dirty clothes hamper. As she'd found in the living room, her bedroom was spotless. Even the fan above her bed shone with its freshly cleaned blades.

She put Levi in the crib with a pacifier and waited the sixty seconds it took for him to fall asleep. Man, she envied him. Some nights it took her hours to shut down her brain and drop off. Since Friday, her sleep had been comprised mostly of short naps with bad dreams.

The giggles of two little girls and the booming laughter of a grown man resounded down the hall. She hurried toward the sound, needing the break from her gloom.

The next day, she took the girls and Levi to her office

to show them off and make sure the staff was aware that she wouldn't be in the rest of the week. The rest of the week? As she'd spoken the words, the reality of how much her world had changed hit her again. What would she do with the children while she was at work? And what about the nights and weekends of being on-call? Who would take care of them if she had to go rushing into the night?

She thought about asking her parents to move to Texas to help her, but they were in their seventies. As her father's recent heart issues had reinforced, neither of them were in the best of health. Besides, they'd done their job raising Meredith and her. It wasn't right to ask them to take on raising another set of young children.

The funerals were scheduled for Thursday. She and her parents decided that the children were too young to understand what was happening at the funeral and made the decision to not bring them. Magda Montgomery, Jason's cousin-in-law, volunteered to sit with the children at Lydia's home and Lydia grabbed that lifeline.

Magda arrived early, about nine a.m. The funerals weren't until one.

"Magda," Lydia said as she opened the door in response to Magda's knock. "You're early."

"I know, but I thought it might be a good idea if I spent some time with the girls before you left, so they'd know I was an okay person."

Lydia blinked. "Of course. What a good idea. I should have thought of it myself."

"Plus," Magda continued, "with me here, you can get dressed without a lot of interruptions."

"Thank you again. You're so thoughtful."

Magda smiled. "I want to tell you again how very sorry I am about your sister and her husband. If she was as wonderful a person as you, then she was special indeed."

Lydia teared up. "She was so much more than I can ever hope to be. So funny. So smart. And you can't believe how organized she is."

She is. As she'd uttered the phrase, reality gave her a solid punch in the gut. Her sister was, not is.

She shut her eyes and drew in a stuttered breath. A pair of arms encircled her.

"You'll be okay," Magda whispered in Lydia's ear. "Whatever you need, all you have to do is ask."

"Thank you," Lydia whispered back.

The twins took to Magda like a long-lost friend. The three of them sat cross-legged on the floor of the girls' room and played dolls. Lydia felt comfortable that she could leave and the girls wouldn't miss her.

She met her parents at the B&B where they were staying. Her parents had aged a decade since Friday. The creases in her mother's face were deeper and more pronounced than Lydia could remember. Her father's shoulders were slumped as though carrying five tons on each side. Until that moment, she'd let the idea of having them move to Texas from Florida continue to float to the top of her options. But one glance effectively erased that.

A black limo from the funeral home picked them up thirty minutes before the start of the service. Her father was recovering from his stent so her help was required getting both of them into the backseat of the limo. She'd asked Jason to meet her at the mortuary, not wanting her parents to feel pressure to put on a good front for him. She realized now it wouldn't have mattered if he was with them or not. Her parents were walking shells of their former selves.

As sad as Lydia had thought herself before, the magnitude of her grief was endless as she sat through the funeral and then rode behind the hearses to the cemetery. Jason's mother had picked out a couple of beautiful plots under a spreading oak tree. Lydia might have given cremation more serious thought had it not been for the children. They needed a place to help them remember their parents, except for Levi. He would never know how wonderful his mother and father were. How excited they'd been when he was born. And the memory of Meredith and Jim would fade for the twins too, replaced by more recent events in their lives.

And that made her sad.

I'll bring them to visit, she promised Meredith as she watched the casket being lowered into the ground. She would regale the kids with stories of growing up with their mom and all the funny things she'd done. They would remember their mother, even if the memories were the ones Lydia gave them.

When the funeral was in the rearview mirror, Lydia sent her parents' home to Florida. Her dad needed to recover and see a doctor down there about the other stents he would require. Her mother needed to be with the group of women friends she had. Both of her parents had excellent emotional support systems around them in Florida. In Texas, they would look to her to provide that support, and frankly, she didn't have any left to give.

Friday evening, she was standing in the kitchen heating soup and cheese toast for dinner when Ellery can busting into the room.

"Guess who's here? Uncle Jason," she said before Lydia could venture a guess.

"Where is he?"

"Levi was crying so he went to see what was wrong."

Lydia turned off the flame under the soup and jerked the cookie sheet with the cheese bread from the oven.

"Why didn't you come get me when Levi started crying?"

Ellery shrugged. "I don't know."

"You know I can't hear him when I'm back here."

"No, I didn't."

"I told you that when I'm in the kitchen, I can't hear Levi."

"No, you didn't."

"Yes, I did." She felt foolish arguing with a three-year-old, but Ellery and Annie had to learn to listen to her.

Ellery's bottom lip quivered. "No, you didn't," she screamed. "I want my mommy."

Lydia dropped to one knee. "Come here, Elle." She pulled the crying child into her arms. "I'm sorry. Don't cry."

The little girl's tears were like acid dripping directly onto Lydia's heart.

"Hey," Jason said from the doorway. "What's going on back here?"

Ellery shoved out of Lydia's arms and ran to Jason. Wrapping her arms around his knees, she said, "I wanna go home. I want my mommy."

Lydia looked up into Jason's eyes and then shut hers with a slow shake of her head. *This is too hard, Meredith. Why did you leave us?*

Pushing herself to her feet, Lydia pressed her lips into a semblance of a smile. "Hey, you. I wasn't expecting to see you tonight."

Jason walked toward her, Ellery riding on his leg with each step. "Got done early. Thought I'd see how it was going." He dropped his gaze down to Ellery and back up. "Where's Annie?"

"Oh, crap. I don't know. Elle, where's Annie?"

"With Jasper."

"And where's Jasper?" Lydia asked.

"In the front yard."

Her heart momentarily stopped. The front yard? The unfenced, open-to-the-street front yard?

"Shit."

"That's a naughty word," Ellery announced. "You can't say that."

"Did you come in the front door?" Lydia asked as she hurried past Jason and Ellery. "Did you see them?"

"I did, and I didn't see them anywhere."

Holy hell. She hadn't had her sister's children for a week and she'd already lost one.

Lydia raced out the front door calling Annie's name. The small yard was empty. "Maybe we should call the police," she said.

Jason picked up Ellery and sat her in a rocking chair on the porch. "Do not move," he said and followed Lydia down the steps. "No police yet. Let's look for a minute."

They walked around to the corners of the house calling Annie and Jasper, all the while keeping an eye on Ellery, who hadn't moved from the chair.

"Have you been in the backyard yet?" Jason asked.

"No. Ellery said the front yard."

"Little girls can get confused."

"Maybe." She bounded up the steps. "Stay with Elle. I'll go look."

She ran through her house like she was moving with weights tied to her ankles. Her heart slammed against her chest. Her lungs didn't want to inflate. In the kitchen, she slid to a stop at the backdoor and jerked it open.

"Annie? Jasper?"

A *woof* came from the back corner of her yard. She raced out and through the fresh spring grass. In the far corner, Annie was curled up asleep, the big dog sitting beside her.

"Good boy," she whispered to Jasper, stroking down his back. Tears of relief trickled down her face. "Good boy."

She carried the sleeping child into the house.

"Where was she?" Jason asked. He and Ellery were standing in the kitchen.

"Backyard, not front. I'm going to let her sleep for now. I can always reheat the soup later."

"Ms. Ellery and I will set the table for dinner, okay?"

Ellery nodded.

Lydia got Annie settled in her bed, sans shoes and dirty socks, but she elected to ignore the girl's clothes for now. She pulled the sheet over Annie's tiny body and whispered a prayer of thanks.

When she returned to the kitchen, she stood in the doorway observing the scene in front of her. Ellery stood on a chair beside Jason, who'd relit the burner and was stirring the pot of homemade chicken noodle soup.

"And so," he was saying, "we never ever touch this stove without an adult being with you, okay? We wouldn't want anything to ever happen to you."

"Like what happened to Mommy and Daddy?"

Lydia's heart cracked.

"Well, not like that," Jason said. "But this fire can hurt you, and you're too special a little girl for us to let anything bad ever happen to you."

"Okay."

"So tell me again. What are you not supposed to do?"

"Touch the stove."

"That's right. You hungry?"

Ellery nodded.

"Okay. Hop down and scoot the chair back to the table." He turned around with the saucepan in his hand and noticed Lydia. "Hey, beautiful." He lifted the pot higher. "I've got soup."

"I'm starved," she said. "You too, Elle?"

"Yes. I'm starved."

Jason ladled soup into three bowls, two large and one small, while Lydia loaded the cheese bread onto a plate and into the microwave to heat.

After dinner, Ellery wanted Jason to give her a bath and then read her a story, which was fine with Lydia. She still had to feed Levi and bathe him. Annie woke up before Lydia had finished feeding Levi and wanted her dinner right then. Lydia gave Levi a cracker to bang on his high chair while she put some soup in a bowl. She set a couple of pieces of cheese toast beside it.

Annie was generally a good-humored child. Most of the times when she acted out, she was following Ellery's lead. Now, she climbed onto a chair and ate her soup while Lydia finished feeding Levi a mixture of peas and carrots, some pureed fruit and pureed turkey. He'd already drunk four ounces of formula before dinner. At this rate, the kid would be eating her out of house and home by the time he was three.

"You done eating?" she said to Annie, who nodded.

"You want to take a bath with Levi tonight?"

Annie nodded.

Thank goodness.

Annie joined Ellery, who was already in the tub

under Jason's supervision. When she set Levi in the tub with his sisters, he promptly peed, which set the girls into fits of giggles. Jason's expression made her start laughing.

"It's okay, big guy," she said to Levi. "Everybody pees, isn't that right, Uncle Jason?"

"Yeah, but not in my bathwater."

The girls thought that was funny too.

Lydia opened the drain and ran a supply of fresh water into the tub. It didn't take long since there hadn't been much to start with.

Levi loved the water and gurgled and splashed with joy.

Ellery and Annie played with a couple of boats and fish she'd picked up at their house. They dunked the boats and made the fish swim in the water.

Lydia blew out a long breath. Jason's large hand covered the area between her shoulder blades, the comfortable touch making her want to be absorbed into the warmth. Her sister would miss all this. She would never see her babies grow to school age children and then teens—heaven help her—and finally adulthood. It was so unfair.

"I know what you're thinking," he whispered into her ear.

She ventured a quick glance away from the kids over her shoulder into the eyes of the man she loved so much. "What's that?"

"That you can't wait to get me alone."

She chuckled and turned her gaze back on the children. "Yeah. How did you know?"

He kissed her neck. "A man just knows these things."

And that made her laugh.

Chapter Four

As the weeks passed, Lydia struggled to get a grasp on her time-management skills, and as soon as she had, or thought she had, one of the kids would do something that would throw a monkey wrench into the schedule.

She'd quickly discovered there was no way for her to return to work yet. The children were too fragile to be left with strangers, when in reality, she was little more than a stranger to them too.

Many nights, Jason came over to help with dinner and bedtime. By the time dinner, playtime, baths and storytelling were done and all three children were in bed, Lydia wanted nothing more than to climb between the sheets herself. The idea of sex was the furthest thing from her mind. She could probably lie there while Jason did all the work, but there was no way to work up any enthusiasm for participation on her part. He swore he didn't mind, but he'd joked—or claimed he was joking—that this was why he hadn't wanted children.

She was on her third week of trying to learn how to

juggle all the balls, such as folding clean clothes during the twins' thirty-minute nap, when her cell chimed. Stretching across the mound of clothes, she looked at the caller id. A lifesaver. Caroline Graham-Montgomery. A real adult to talk to.

"Hi, Caroline."

"How are you doing?" her partner asked. "How are the children?"

"We're all hanging tough for now. This is going to be an adjustment for all of us."

"Ellery and Annie are only about a year ahead of Austin and Britney. I can imagine what you're going through. Obstinate, bossy and whiney, and at the same time, so cute you think your heart is going to bust. Right?"

"Yes. Exactly. Some days I'm pretty sure the girls hate me." She said that expecting Caroline to offer up some soothing words. Instead, Caroline burst out laughing.

"Yeah, they probably do, or think they do at that exact moment. Don't worry. They forget pretty quickly."

"But your kids aren't like that," Lydia protested.

That made Caroline snicker noisily. "Wrong. My two are just like that. Britney announced last night that I was mean and she didn't like me anymore. She only loved her daddy. And then she climbed into his lap."

"That's horrible," Lydia said with a gasp. "What did Travis say?"

"He told her that if she wanted cowgirl boots, she'd better be nice to her mother because he had no intention of going shopping."

Lydia chuckled. "And?"

"And Miss Priss decided I wasn't the horrible ogre

she said I was. But she still marched out of the kitchen and went to her bedroom to play."

"Did you follow her?"

"Shoot, no. If I give in to her threats and blackmail at this age, I can only imagine what a horrible teen she'll grow in to. I know Travis and I can afford to give our kids anything they want, but that's not going to happen. They can't act in any fashion they please. I know they're only two, but I think consistency is the key to raising them right, or that's what Travis and I have decided. I'm not trying to tell you what to do with yours. Not at all."

"Slow down, Caroline. I'd appreciate any advice you have to share. I mean, we both went through the same human growth and development classes and learned all the theories about raising children, but holy moly, theory and practice are so different, you know?"

Caroline laughed. "I do. To change the subject, have you and Jason talked about resetting your wedding date?"

The idea of taking on a wedding right now was more than Lydia could handle. Plus, her life was so different than the last time Jason had asked her to marry him. She wasn't so carefree and unencumbered now. She was carrying the exact baggage Jason didn't want.

"Nope. No discussions. Right now, I can't even think about it."

"I totally get it. I remember bringing the twins home. I'm glad Travis was here to help. Don't hesitate to call if I can do anything."

"Well, since you asked..."

"Shoot. What do you need?"

"At some point, I need to come back to work. I need to talk to adults. I need to not cut anyone's food but my own."

Caroline laughed again. "What can I do?"

"I don't know how to juggle all my balls. How do you do it all?"

"Are you kidding? I don't do it all, as you say. I have Travis and Mrs. Webster to help. Jackie comes over the minute I call. In fact, Jackie and Lane have been taking Austin and Britney one weekend a month so Travis and I can be alone."

Lydia sighed. "Sounds wonderful."

"Oh, you bet. I get to sleep until eight or nine on Saturday and Sunday."

Lydia chuckled. "I bet his parents imagine wild weekend sex for you two."

"Personally, I don't care what they think we're doing over here on those weekends. Wild orgies. Sex swings. Who cares? All I know is I don't have to wipe a butt that isn't mine for two whole days."

Lydia howled with laughter and then quieted quickly when she remembered the sleeping kids. "That's hysterical."

"What I'm trying to say is that I am in the same boat as you except I have help with rowing. Don't try to row and steer all by yourself. You have lots of friends who would love to give you a hand. All you have to do is tell us what you need."

"I guess I need someone to help with the children so I can go back to the office. I haven't figured out how to take on-call yet, and I hate I'm leaving you in such a lurch there."

"It's been quiet, so that hasn't been a problem. Bringing on Paige as a nurse practitioner was one of the smartest decisions you ever made. I mean, I realize she's married to my husband's brother, so I might be a little prejudiced, but she's smart as a whip and the patients love her. She's taken night call for me a few times. You know a lot of those after-hour calls are medication refills or medical questions or things that don't constitute an emergency. We're covering for you for now, but I admit, I'm looking forward to having you back in the office."

"You're lucky to have Mrs. Webster to keep Austin and Britney so you could go back to work."

"And don't forget Jackie and Lane for backup."

"Right. Like I said, you're a lucky duck. I need a Mrs. Webster in my life."

"I talked to your parents at the funeral. Have you thought about asking them to move to Texas? It might be a win-win for all of you. Your mom could give you some time off and give you a chance to keep a closer eye on them at the same time."

"I know and I've thought about it. But—"

"But you want to do this without their help."

"I want to do it without *requiring* their help. Mom would push herself too hard. Dad is still not back to tip-top shape and won't be for a while. Every time I talk to her, I tell her how great things are going. She's got enough to worry about without my adding to her plate."

"So we need to find you a babysitter, right?"

"Daytime, for now, if you and Paige can continue with the night calls."

"I'll make some calls and get back to you."

"Thanks, Caroline. I wasn't kidding when I told Travis I was so glad he married you for my benefit."

Her friend laughed.

"I'm hungry." Ellery stood in the door rubbing her eyes.

"Me too," Echo Annie said.

Lydia glanced at the clock. Almost four. "I gotta go, Caroline. Thanks again."

"Don't forget to call if you need anything. I mean it."

"Thanks." Lydia dropped her phone on the pile of unfolded clothes and turned to the girls. "How about I make you some triangle sandwiches?"

Lydia had fond memories of growing up eating sandwiches with Meredith that their mother had cut into shapes. Neither she nor Meredith cared what was between the bread. It had been the various shapes that had drawn them in.

She got the girls set up with their individual plates of tiny peanut butter sandwiches on the floor in front of a movie and went to check on Levi. He was waking up when she entered. When he saw her, his face lit up with a bright smile. Her heart swelled so large she was sure it would explode.

"Hey, Little Man. You're awake. I bet your college tuition that your diaper is wet or dirty. Want to take that bet?"

He laughed and clapped his hands. It didn't matter what she said to him. It was all in her tone, and apparently this kid believed her to be the best thing ever. If only the other two did.

And, yes, his college tuition was safe since he knew better than to take her bet. She put on a fresh diaper, shirt and shorts and carried him to the living room where his sisters were both enthralled with *The Little Mermaid* movie running and didn't notice when Jasper snuck a sandwich triangle off a plate. The dog looked up at her with a goofy open-mouth smile. Oh well, the girls would be hungrier at dinner.

She got one of Levi's bottles out of the refrigerator and his greedy little hands reached for it. As he pulled the nipple into his mouth, she felt the tug deep in her gut.

Thank you, Meredith, for trusting me with your children. Thank you for showing me what I would have missed if I had married Jason.

JASON HUNG UP THE TELEPHONE AFTER A LONG conversation with the Hardys' probate lawyer. Thankfully, Meredith and Jim had been responsible enough to have wills prepared during Meredith's pregnancy with Levi.

About two weeks after the funeral, Jason had brought in Lydia's mail and found a letter from Samuel Wood, Esq. When he'd shown it to her, she'd been standing in the kitchen, Levi hanging off her hip, her hair in a disheveled knot that had begun on the top of her head but was seriously listing over to one side, a streak of what he suspected was Levi's spit up from breakfast or lunch staining the back of her shirt, and bags under her eyes that could have been mistaken for shipping trunks.

"Do you want me to follow up on this?" he'd asked.

"God, yes," she'd said. "Please."

He and the Kansas attorney had played phone tag for a couple of days until they'd finally made an appointment to speak on Saturday, when both of their offices would be quiet. The Hardys had provided well for the children. There were million-dollar life-insurance policies for both of them. At Jim and Meredith's ages, those had probably been easy to secure. The odds had been in the insurance company's favor of not having to pay those. Now, that two million would certainly help with the expense of raising the children and paying for any college they wanted to attend.

Lydia had been appointed as executor of the estate

as well as guardian for any minor children, meaning Ellery, Annie and Levi. The Hardys had another couple who'd agreed to raise the children in the event Lydia couldn't. He suspected she wasn't aware of that. He made a note to send a private investigator to check out this other couple before he mentioned them to Lydia. Depending on the PI's report, they may or may not be a viable option for Lydia to consider.

Their house in Wichita was in an up and coming neighborhood where sales were quick. The house had a mortgage, but if the information Wood had provided was accurate—and Jason had no reason to think otherwise—the house should sell for more than the outstanding balance, depositing another nice nest egg into the children's account.

There was a stipulation that Lydia could have anything from the house and a request that Meredith's wedding rings be held for the children, should any of them want them.

Wood had done an excellent job with the will. Jason could find nothing that'd been forgotten or mishandled. The next step was to empty the house and get it ready to sell, unless Lydia had other plans for it. He couldn't imagine that she would want to move to Wichita and live in it. That seemed far-fetched. Selling it would be the logical step.

However, since the children had come to live with her, she'd changed. She wasn't nearly as predictable as she'd been, not that he was complaining, because he wasn't. It was just that she'd always been the consummate professional. He'd never seen her as the nurturing sort, but this new role of mother to three orphans had opened up a new side to her, a maternal element he hadn't realized existed in her.

He also realized, even if she hadn't yet, that she needed help. He'd been looking for an opening to broach that subject with her, but so far, it hadn't happened. She hadn't had a minute away from the children since she'd taken them in. And that needed to change also.

He placed a few calls and put some plans into action. Then he stood and pulled his keys from his pocket. Today, he would have to make an opening for that discussion.

The first thing he noticed when he pulled into her drive was that grass had begun growing and needed to be cut. The weeds in her flower beds seemed to have sprung up overnight. He looked down at his khaki shorts and nice polo shirt. He was not dressed for yard work. Maybe tomorrow.

The sound of a children's movie seeped through the door. He smiled and knocked.

"I'll get it," a little voice said.

"Don't open that door," Lydia yelled. "That's dangerous."

The door flew open and Ellery and Annie stood there. "Uncle Jason," they both cried.

"I told you not to open the door," Lydia said, marching up behind them.

"But it's Uncle Jason," Ellery explained.

"But you didn't know that, did you?"

Ellery's face took on a stubborn expression before she held up her arms for Jason to pick her up. Annie did the same. He lifted both girls into his arms, one on each side of his body. Jasper had followed the family to the door and was now on the porch butting Jason for a scratch.

"Good afternoon, princesses. Have you both been good today?"

Both girls nodded in the affirmative.

"Actually, we've had a nice day," Lydia said. "Come on in. Jasper, come on."

The dog wandered into the front yard and lifted his leg on the only tree out there. As soon as Lydia called his name again, he bounded up the stairs and into the house.

Jason carried both girls into the living room and set them back on their feet. There were two spotlessly clean plates on the floor.

"Looks like I missed snack time."

Ellery and Annie looked at their plates and then Ellery narrowed her eyes at Jasper. "Jasper ate my sandwich."

"Mine too," Annie said.

"Bad dog," Ellery said.

"Bad dog," Annie agreed.

Jason chuckled. He couldn't help it. The bad dog was lying on his back, all four legs in the air. Lydia rolled her eyes.

"Welcome to chaos," she said.

"Girls, I need to have a talk with Lydia. Want me to start your movie over?"

He did and the kids sat down to watch a movie he was sure they'd seen no less than a million times.

"Come on in the kitchen. You want some wine? A beer?" Lydia said.

"A beer would be great. I'll get it."

Lydia put Levi into his high chair and got out some baby food jars. "I'm going to feed him while we talk. Okay?"

"Sure. Let me do it," he said.

"You don't have to, Jason. I know this isn't your scene."

He frowned. "Not my scene?"

"You know, babies and bottles and diapers. I get that."

"Lydia..."

"No, no. Really. I get it."

He turned Levi's highchair until it faced him. "I swear, Levi. Women are so complicated. Trust me."

Levi gurgled, a drop of drool running down his chin.

"Exactly," Jason said. "That's what I'm talking about."

Lydia laughed and shoved the baby food and spoon over to him. "Knock yourself out."

He would never admit it, but feeding Levi was a little scary. He'd never fed a baby like this. When he'd had the kids for the day, feeding Levi had consisted of handing him a bottle and letting him handle it from there. This... this was totally different. But law school had taught him to fake it until you make it, so he jumped in, uncapping the jars.

He sniffed the first one. It didn't smell bad at all. Strained prunes. Yeah, that didn't sound so great. Still, he put a little on the spoon and held it up to Levi. He opened his mouth like a baby bird, and Jason deposited the icky-looking mess in there. Levi immediately spit it out, splattering Jason's clean polo.

Risking a glance at Lydia, he found her resting her chin in the palm of her hand, her elbow on the table, and the cutest grin he'd ever seen on her face.

"Let's try that again," he told Levi.

This time, the prunes stayed in, even if a little oozed from the corners of his mouth. Levi slapped the high-chair tray and grinned.

"I've got a surprise for you," he said, spooning in another bite.

"Yeah? What's that?"

"How would you like a babysitter and a night off?"

She straightened. "I don't know. These kids are just getting used to me. I'm not sure about bringing a stranger into my home."

He shoveled another tiny spoonful into Levi's mouth. "Not a stranger. My parents."

"Oh, Jason. That's so nice but I—"

Before she could finish her sentence, the doorbell rang.

"I'll get it," Ellery yelled.

"Good God. That girl is going to let in a serial killer one day." She sighed. "Don't open the door until I get there," she called back. "Not that she'll listen to me," she added, standing and hurrying out of the room.

Jason had a good idea who might be at the door. When he heard his father's booming, deep voice talking to Ellery, he knew he was right. Now, if Lydia didn't kill him for arranging this without her permission…

"Hi, honey," his mother said.

"Look who's here, Jason. It's your parents," Lydia said, although he was pretty sure her voice was coming through gritted teeth. She glanced at his mother. "I am so sorry that the house is such a disaster. If I'd known you were coming, I'd have—"

"Hush," Jackie said. "I raised four children in a tiny ranch house. I know it's impossible to keep a meticulous, or heck, even a kind-of-clean house with kids." She went over to Levi. "You must be Levi," she said, tickling the baby under his chin. "I'm Mimi. That's what all the kids call me."

Levi smiled and purple-tinged drool ran down his chin.

"Hi, Mom," Jason said.

Jackie turned toward Lydia. "How in the world did you get him to feed a baby? No one else ever has."

"Stop it, Mom," Jason said, embarrassed at his mother's comment. "Maybe no one ever let me before. You ever think of that?"

Jackie rolled her eyes. "Right."

Lane came around the corner with each girl holding on to an index finger. "Did you see these two beautiful ladies I found in the living room, Mimi?"

Jackie smiled. "I did." She squatted to their level. "I'm Mimi. Now which one of you is Annie and which one is Ellery?"

The girls released Lane's fingers, ran over to Lydia and hid their faces on her thigh.

"They're a little bashful around strangers," Lydia said. She dropped to one knee. "This is Annie," she said as she patted the back of the girl dressed in green. "And this is Ellery."

Ellery wore a white top with obvious food stains on the front.

"Girls, these are Uncle Jason's mom and dad."

The girls looked at Jason, who smiled back at them and then to his parents.

"Yep," he said. "My mom and dad. They have been wanting to come meet you forever."

"That's right," Jackie said.

Lane held out his hands to the girls. "They were taking me to their bedroom to see it. Do you want to come along, Mimi?"

"I sure do," Jackie said.

The girls looked at Lydia.

"It's okay. You can go," she told them.

Ellery grabbed Lane's left finger and Annie his right, and the four of them left the kitchen.

The minute they were gone, Lydia dropped into a chair. "What the hell? I can't believe you invited your parents over here. Good God, Jason. Look at this place. Dishes piled in the sink. A pile of clothes on the sofa. I haven't run a vacuum in days. Dog hair is probably covering every surface. I am so pissed right now."

The last sentence was said with such a fierce growl that Levi's chin began to quiver and then he began to cry.

"Oh, baby," she said to Levi, patting his back. "It's okay."

Jason swallowed. He'd known she'd probably be upset, but he'd underestimated her ire. Before the children had come, Lydia had been flexible, ready to go with the flow.

"Look, babe, you need a break. You've been here twenty-four seven for weeks. Mom's been bugging me nonstop to let her come over to see the kids or get you to bring them to their house. Nonstop. I swear. I can only take so much nagging."

Lydia's lips tightened into a hard line. "Nagging?" she finally said. "So nagging works with you? How about I nag you to get your ass out of my house. Better yet, I'll nag you to get the hell out of my business."

Jason lifted a spoon of—he stopped to read the jar label. Pureed turkey. Yum?—to Levi's mouth, which opened immediately for the food.

"Sorry. You can't scare me off."

"I'm. Not. Trying. To. Scare. You. Off." Each word was said with exact pronunciation. "I'm telling you that I don't need you, or anyone else, to rescue me."

"Good. I'm not trying to rescue you," he said, putting air quotes around the last two words.

"You are really pissing me off right now."

"Okay." He pulled on his in-the-courtroom calm composure. She was beyond exhausted. He'd bet every dollar in his wallet that her shoulders were a rock garden. This situation wasn't healthy for her or the children.

He wiped Levi's face with the wet cloth on the table and then fed him another spoon of something that looked disgusting but must have tasted fine.

"Lydia. I love you. You know that. Do you think for one minute I'd do anything that I thought would hurt or embarrass you? Of course not," he added before she could say anything. "But these children have been through so much. Uprooted to a new house. New adults taking care of them. The most important people in their young lives gone forever."

"I know," she said, her voice tense enough to cut solid wood.

"What I know about children won't fill a thimble, but what my mother knows about kids would fill this house and overflow into the streets. She's the one who pushed me to get you some time off. Time to recharge your batteries so you can be a better mother."

The word mother felt so foreign rolling off his tongue when talking about Lydia. It wasn't something he'd ever expected to call her.

She slumped back in her chair, not defeated, but weakening.

"Mom and Dad want to stay here this evening. Let me take you somewhere special. Somewhere that will put some sparkle back in your eyes."

"If this is about sex…"

He laughed. "I wouldn't say no. I've missed holding you, but, no, this isn't about sex. This is about you. You've known me for a long time. Can't you trust me?"

She sighed. "But the house—"

"Is fine," he completed. "Go take a shower. Put on some shorts and a T-shirt. Don't worry about make-up or anything like that. It's just a little Lydia time. Okay? We'll be back before you know it."

She hesitated and he went in for the kill, just like he did anytime he saw a weakness in the courtroom.

"Lydia. Trust me."

"I will kill you at some point for letting your parents see my house like this."

"Accepted," he said with a grin. "Go. Get ready."

After she left the room, he looked at Levi. "I'm telling you, man. These females are tough, you know? But don't you worry. I'll teach you all the tricks."

Spit dribbled off Levi's chin, and somewhere deep inside Jason, a powerful emotion tugged at his heart.

He'd lived the past ten years knowing that children weren't in his future. He'd accepted that reality, built his life around it, made sure everyone around him knew it. He had never allowed himself to want children. Never allowed himself to daydream about being a father. He'd told—no, convinced—himself that being an uncle would fulfill any nurturing urges he might have.

Except now, fate had dropped three children into the life of the woman he'd been ready to spend the rest of his life with, which posed huge questions.

Did he want to spend the next eighteen years—minimum—raising children that he'd been sure he didn't want?

How could three tiny people get wedged into his heart so fast?

Chapter Five

L ydia was embarrassed, humiliated and beyond pissed off at Jason. Not only was her house a total wreck, but she couldn't remember the last time she'd washed her hair. His parents would think her a horrible substitute parent. They probably were feeling sorry for the kids having to grow up with her as their only adult.

But they were here. The damage was done. They'd seen what her life had become...a collection of dirty dishes, messy diapers and little girls who rarely minded her.

She so sucked at this parenting thing.

As she made her way to her bathroom, voices trickled out of the girls' room. She tip-toed up to the door to see what was going on.

Lane was in the floor. The girls were trying to figure out how to clip barrettes and bobby pins into his chopped hair. Jackie sat on Annie's bed, giving them suggestions on the best way to fix Papa's hair. The girls looked happy. Lane and Jackie were wearing grins and flushed faces.

"Everything okay here?" she asked from the door.

"Aunt Lydia. Papa wears barrettes in his hair," Ellery said.

Lydia nodded. "So I see. You look quite festive, Lane."

"Thank you," Lane said. "I've been looking for a couple of new ladies in my life to help style my hair."

Jackie snickered.

"If it's okay with you two, I'm going to jump in the shower. Jackie, you might want to check on Jason. He and Levi are flying solo."

She nodded but didn't get up. "I will…in a minute. It won't hurt him to be alone for a couple of minutes."

Lydia's heart picked up a little. She'd never say it aloud, but it made her nervous to leave Levi with Jason. This was a man who'd made his interest, or rather lack of interest, in childrearing crystal clear, so his nurturing center probably didn't exist, even if he did feed Levi tonight. Sure, he'd taken care of them for a day, but that'd been an emergency situation, one he hadn't been able to walk away from easily.

"Are you sure? Maybe you could go check?" Lydia said.

Jackie waved her off. "Go on and get dressed. We're all fine." Her gaze met Lydia's. "We're all fine. So are you. We've got you covered."

Lydia turned away before Jackie could see the tears that welled up in her eyes. "Damn it," she muttered as she swiped at her eyes. She was simply tired.

The entire time she was in the shower, she expected the door to come slamming open with some emergency. One of the girls had gotten hurt. Or Levi had aspirated. Or maybe the house was on fire. But nothing happened.

The hot water felt like heaven, as did her scalp when she rinsed away days of grime.

Her only problem was after she was out and dried, she realized she'd forgotten to bring any clothes with her to the bathroom. She wrapped her damp towel securely around her and peeked out the door. The hall was clear. She threw the door fully open and made a dash for her bedroom.

"Oh, good," Jackie said when Lydia walked in. "You're here. Would you mind if I gave Levi his bath tonight?"

Lydia startled at finding Jackie in her bedroom, but of course, it was Levi's room too.

"I'm sorry," Jackie said. "I didn't mean to scare you. I thought you saw me when you walked in."

"I didn't, but no biggie. Sure, you can bathe Levi, but you don't have to. I can clean him up."

Jackie narrowed her eyes in a threat. "Don't you *dare* take this baby away from me. It's the only baby I've got to play with right now."

Laughing, Lydia headed for her closet. "Hey. You two don't mind me. I don't want to get between true love."

As she stood in her closet and dressed, she listened to Jackie talking and cooing to Levi, who was giggling. Granted, she didn't know a lot about babies outside her medical training, but she knew Levi was the definition of a good baby.

The clean hair, fresh shorts, clean polo and sandals made her feel better. However, she still wasn't keen on leaving the children. What if something happened? Her sister had trusted her. Wasn't leaving them a violation of that trust? Maybe just having the time to shower and dress in peace was enough. She'd thank Lane and Jackie and let them go home.

Jackie and Levi were gone when she stepped back into the bedroom. Lane and the girls were not in their bedroom either. A mild panic seized her. Where were the children?

She raced into an empty living room and then into the kitchen. She skid to a stop. Lane, Jason and the girls were sitting at the table. Jackie had Levi sitting in the kitchen sink, water splashing every surface.

"Hi, honey," Jackie called. "Lane was hungry. I hope you don't mind. I made him and the girls some hot dogs."

"I helped," Ellery said.

"You sure did," Lane said.

"I fed Jasper," Annie said.

"All by yourself?" Lydia asked.

"Yes."

Jason caught her eye and pointed to his chest and then to Annie. Ah. He and Annie had fed Jasper.

"Well, you girls sure are helpful."

Their faces lit up with smiles at her praise.

"We brought the girls a movie for after dinner. Something titled *Frozen*. I've been assured by Caroline that they will love it and you will come to hate me because they will watch it over and over."

Lydia chuckled. She might not have had children before now, but even she knew about the song "Let It Go".

"Well, I'll just have to let it go, right?" Lydia joked.

Jackie grinned at her. "Exactly. Now, I think Jason has some plans for tonight."

Panic hit her again. "I don't know. I really appreciate you coming over and letting me get a shower, but—"

"No buts," Jackie said. "Lane and I aren't exactly newbies at this, you know?"

Lydia walked over to Jackie and lowered her voice. Little ears had long hearing ranges.

"Look, Jackie, I really thank you, but I'm not sure the girls are ready to be left with strangers."

"Really?" Jackie tilted her head toward the table.

Annie had crawled into Lane's lap and was feeding him a chip.

"They lost their parents," Lydia said. "I don't want them to think I'm leaving too."

"Honey, you're not going to be gone that long. If there's a problem, we'll be on the phone to you jiffy quick. I promise. Don't make a big deal out of leaving. Just walk out the door. Don't give long hugs and goodbye speeches. That's what confuses them. By the time they realize you're gone, we'll be watching *Frozen* and eating the cookies I have stashed in the car."

"You have cookies stashed?"

Jackie grinned. "A grandmother's prerogative."

"But—"

"I'm not their grandmother? Semantics, my dear. Now go. We'll see you in a couple of hours."

Lydia hesitated. This was such a bad idea.

"Go," Jackie repeated. "We'll all be fine."

Lydia felt pushed out of her own house. She knew Jackie and Lane meant well, but still…

Jason stood and walked over. "Ready?" He glanced at his watch. "We have to be somewhere in twenty minutes."

"Where?"

"It's a surprise."

She was definitely surprised when Jason wheeled into the Eden Spa. Known for its upscale clientele and impeccable service, not to mention pricey massages and facials, Lydia had never been here. Oh, she'd wanted to, but somehow it'd never worked out.

"The Eden Spa?" she said to Jason when he shut off the engine.

"For once in your life, can you please let someone else be in charge for a little while?"

"Yeah, I can do that."

"Well, thank God. Now let's go. We're almost late."

And heaven knows, the man couldn't abide being late. Good thing he didn't have children.

But on the other hand, he had no idea what he was missing.

The aroma of fresh eucalyptus greeted them in a posh lobby. Soft new-age music drifted from hidden speakers. Cushy chairs and sofas were placed in such a way that privacy was assured, if one wanted privacy.

Jason stepped up to the curved desk. A blonde smiled warmly at him...too warmly, in Lydia's opinion. She couldn't blame the girl. Jason was an extremely handsome man. Last fall, when he'd put himself in a bachelor auction to piss her off—which it did—there had almost been a riot among the women to win the date.

"Good evening, sir. My name is Brandi. How may I assist you?"

That was the question the blonde asked Jason, but Lydia heard all the nuances in the woman's tone that clearly conveyed her interest in Jason. A twinge of jealousy pumped through her veins. She pressed her lips together and interlocked her fingers to keep from doing something silly, like latching on to Jason's arm.

"Good evening," Jason said, his smile a little too bright, adding a lump of coal to the green flame already burning in Lydia's gut. "I have an appointment for two. Jason Montgomery."

"Oh, yes. Mr. Montgomery. We are so pleased to have you with us this evening. Your room is ready. If you would follow me, please."

The blonde, whose name tag spelled Brandi with an I, stepped from behind the desk. "This way."

She twisted her hips as she walked toward a doorway.

Jason reached back and took Lydia's hand. "Come on. I think you'll enjoy this."

"Is this Mrs. Montgomery?" Brandi with an I asked.

"No. This is Dr. Henson," Lydia replied. *And I know fifteen ways to poison you and no one would ever know.*

Jason chuckled. The cad.

With a sexy sway, Brandi with an I led them down a hallway until she came to an open door. Gesturing she said, "In here. Your massage therapists will be right with you."

Inside the dimly lit room sat side-by-side massage tables. Faint music filtered into the room. Soft, glowing electric candles sent dancing shadows up the walls. Above the tables, the ceiling was hidden by draped material, sort of how Lydia always pictured a sheik's harem room.

"Take off as much as you feel comfortable with," Brandi said. "You can leave on your underwear if it makes you more comfortable."

"No problem," Lydia said.

Jason nodded.

"Excellent. Once you are ready, please lie on the tables face down. Mr. Montgomery, I will be your massage therapist for the evening."

Of course she will. Lydia would have bet Brandi with

an I would be rushing from the room and changing the schedule if she hadn't been assigned to Jason. Hussy.

"Dr. Henson, your therapist is Rebecca."

Brandi closed the door.

Lydia looked at Jason. "You scheduled a couples' massage? Who are you and what have you done with Jason?"

He laughed. "You told me I needed to try new things."

"Yeah, but I was talking about changing Levi's diaper."

He laughed again. "Come on. Let's do this."

Never one to be shy of his body, Jason stripped out of his clothes quickly, hanging them on the hooks provided. Of course, he had every reason to be proud. Lydia took a minute to look at him. It'd been almost a month since she'd seen him naked, not that she had any trouble pulling up the vision when she needed.

He was broad shouldered with a sculpted muscular chest and a rocking body that narrowed at the waist and hips. A dark line of hair ran down his flat stomach until it joined with a thick thatch of coarse pubic hair. His cock stood erect and grew longer under her gaze.

"This might not be the best time to be looking at me like that," he said.

"Oh. Sorry. Just admiring the scenery."

He chuckled. "Hand me your clothes and I'll hang them next to mine."

She did and, as they crawled onto their separate tables, said, "You know that girl is out there changing the schedule so she can do you."

"What girl?" His frown puckered.

"Brandi," she replied with exasperation. "You know, the one who was eating you up with her eyes."

"Are you jealous?"

"No." *Yes.*

"Honey, I don't see any other women when you're in the room. I only have eyes for you."

"So when I'm not around, you do have eyes for other women?"

He just laughed as someone rapped on the door.

"Ready?" a voice asked.

"Ready," Jason answered.

Lydia rolled her face to the side to see Brandi reentering the room along with an attractive brunette. "Dr. Henson, this is Rebecca."

"Good evening, Dr. Henson," Rebecca said. "If at any time you feel discomfort or pain or if you need me to press harder or softer, don't hesitate to speak up."

Lydia nodded. "Okay."

"Take a deep breath," Rebecca said.

Beneath the opening in the face cradle of the table, Rebecca waved her hand. The aroma of lavender filled the small cavity. Lydia drew in a deep breath and blew it out slowly. She felt her body growing heavier and sinking into the mattress as she relaxed.

Under Rebecca's strokes, muscles tight with knotted tension gave up and released. Lydia moaned and sighed as different areas of her body received the attention they so badly needed.

When Rebecca began on Lydia's legs, one of Jason's thick fingers touched the back of Lydia's hand. She turned her hand over and Jason linked his fingers with hers.

Take that, Brandi with an I.

The massage lasted a full seventy minutes. When Rebecca stepped away from the table, she said, "I hope you enjoyed that."

All Lydia could do was moan. "It was awesome. Thank you."

"Take it slow getting off the tables," Brandi said.

"Will do," Jason replied. "Thanks. It was great."

"Anytime, Mr. Montgomery."

The two ladies excused themselves.

Lydia sat up and looked at Jason. "Anytime, Mr. Montgomery," she said with a roll of her eyes.

He laughed. "Hey. I wasn't jealous about your therapist."

"Because mine was a woman. Next time, I will have some hunky guy do me."

Jason pressed her against her table, their naked bodies flush. "You need to be done? The only guy who's going to do you is me." He lowered his mouth to hers. She parted her lips and he swept his tongue into her mouth, moving and touching everywhere.

She groaned and pressed against him, her sex throbbing. She wrapped her leg around his waist and then stopped.

Crap.

She lowered her foot back to the floor and pushed him back. "So not the place for that."

He groaned. "I know. I know."

They got dressed, albeit slowly. Because of all the oil, Lydia's feet slipped forward in her sandals with each step as they walked back to the lobby. Jason held her hand the whole way, only releasing it to pull his wallet out to pay the bill.

"Here you go, Dr. Henson." Rebecca handed her a glass of water. "I'm sure you already know this, but drink a little more water tonight."

Lydia smiled at the soft-spoken woman. "Will do. Thank you."

"I hope you enjoyed it."

"I did."

"Wonderful. I hope I see you again."

Lydia decided to drag Jason out of there before Brandi could do her sales pitch to get him to return, preferably without Lydia.

She got into the car with a long sigh.

"Good?" he asked.

"Oh, yeah."

"Ready to head home, or do we have a little time?"

"I don't know. Can I call your parents?"

He punched a button and a phone ringing came from the speakers.

"Hello?"

"Hi, Mom. Lydia is worried about the kids."

She slugged his arm. "I'm not worried," she said into the car microphone. "I just wanted to make sure everything was okay."

Jackie chuckled. "We're all fine. Levi conked out about thirty minutes ago. We got through *Frozen* once and then Lane and the girls took Jasper into the backyard to teach him how to play fetch."

"Did they cry when I left?" Lydia's heart pounded hard against her chest. She wasn't sure what answer she wanted.

"Not really. Annie whimpered a little. Ellery pouted, but all that lasted about five minutes. Once the movie started, they got over it."

"I'm not sure if I'm insulted they didn't miss me too much or relieved."

"Relieved," Jackie said. "Trust me. Be relieved."

"I thought we'd stay out a little later, Mom, if all is okay."

"Sure. You kids have fun. Your dad and I have it under control."

"Thank you, Jackie," Lydia said. "I guess I needed to get out more than I thought."

"Happy to, dear. See you two later. Have fun." She hung up.

"You heard my mother. She said for us to have fun."

Lydia twisted in her seat to face him. "Did you have something specific in mind?"

He grinned and lust hit her like a bolt of lightning. "Well, I was thinking we should finish what we started a couple of minutes ago."

"Without Brandi with an I?"

Chuckling, he leaned across the console. "Definitely without Brandi with an I." He kissed her. It was deep and wet and that one bolt of lust turned into a rainstorm.

He pulled back. "What do you think?"

She licked her lips, drew the taste of him into her mouth. "I'm wondering why we're still sitting here in a parking lot."

JASON'S HEART, AND HIS SUV, WERE RACING AS HE tore through Whispering Springs to get to his house. Never one to count chickens before they hatch, he'd nonetheless put clean sheets on his bed and vacuumed his bedroom. There was no reason for him to be feeling such nervousness about tonight. He and Lydia had made love hundreds of times.

But tonight, Lydia was not the same woman she'd been a couple of months ago. Abrupt changes, like deaths of loved ones, did that to a person, changed them, made them reevaluate their own lives. He reminded the nervous quiver in his gut that she was still Lydia...still the woman he loved.

On the other hand, the tension in his spine had him antsy, as though he were with someone new, a different woman that he'd never been with before.

He pulled into his garage and shut off the engine. He noticed she was twisting her fingers together. He laid his hand over hers.

"You're nervous."

She shut her eyes and sighed. "I know. It's silly." Their gazes locked. "We were supposed to be an old married couple by now. Instead, it feels like we're starting over somehow." She shook her head. "That sounds so stupid."

He squeezed her fingers. "No, I understand. You've been through hell and back in the past month. There's no pressure here. I can start the car and head back to your house if you want."

"Seriously?"

She sounded so hopeful. Disappointment nibbled at his pride.

"Sure." He reached to restart the car, but she grabbed his hand.

"Wait! I didn't say I wanted to go home."

She smiled.

He smiled back.

He let her get into the house before he attacked, pushing her up against the wall, running his hands down her body, over her breasts, cupping the sweet flesh of her ass.

"My God, Lydia. I've missed you," he whispered in her ear before running the tip of his tongue around the edge.

She rolled her head to the side, exposing the soft flesh of her long neck. He sucked her ear lobe between his lips and nibbled. She shivered and arched her groin firmly against him. As hard as his cock was, her sighs and moans and thrusting pumped additional blood to the region. The head of his dick pushed at his waistband, trying to find more room to expand.

He slid his mouth to her neck, licking and nibbling his way down until he came to the juncture of her neck and shoulder. She moaned as he bit the thick tendon there. And then his hands were everywhere, on her breasts, her waist, her butt and back to her breasts. Slipping his hands under her shirt, he pushed it up until he came to her bra, and he pushed that up too.

"I need you," he said in a low voice and sucked her nipple into his mouth.

She cried out and began ripping at his clothes, shoving and unzipping him.

He unfastened her bra and tore it down her arms, letting it fall to his kitchen floor before pulling her shirt over her head and tossing it away. Her full, luscious breasts heaved with her breathing. The sight ripped through him like a tornado. He leaned over and drew her flesh back into his mouth and pinched and tugged the other nipple to full erection. Then he moved his mouth to that breast and used his fingers to roll the first.

Lydia wrapped one leg around his hip, bringing her hot center against his rigid shaft. She began to rock against him, letting out a throaty grunt with each movement.

Damn. He was going to come in his shorts at this speed.

He sucked her breast roughly as he shoved his hand down her shorts and into her panties. She was slippery and hot. So wet. So ready for him. He pushed a finger up her. The sound of her groan almost did him in. He pulled it out, added a second one and thrust both fingers firmly in her. As he moved his fingers in and out, her hip thrusts became harder and faster, her breathing faster. Her head rolled back as her mouth gaped.

And then she cried out, her channel milking his fingers as she climaxed.

He stopped and waited for her to come back to him.

She sighed and smiled. "Thanks. I needed that. I'll never look at your kitchen the same way again."

He laughed and pulled his hand from her shorts. "Shall we adjourn to my bedroom?"

LYDIA SNATCHED HER BRA AND T-SHIRT OFF THE floor. "I'd say lead the way, but I think I'll race you instead."

Knowing his house as well as her own, she took off at a run, laughing as she rounded the door of the kitchen and charging for the stairs that led to the second floor. Behind her, Jason's heavy footsteps were gaining ground. Catching him off-guard was the only reason she had any lead at all. He was bigger, taller and faster than she.

She took the stairs two at a time, but before she could take a step toward his room, she was swept off her feet into his arms. She laughed, throwing her arms around his neck.

"I've caught you fair and square," he said. "Now you're my prisoner."

"I'm so scared," she said and began nibbling on his neck.

"No hickeys, wench. It's too hot to cover them with a shirt and tie."

He never should have said that. Never one to resist a dare, she bit his neck and sucked the salty flesh into her mouth.

"Now you've done it," he threatened.

He tossed her onto his bed, where she landed on her back with a soft bounce. He landed on top of her, pinning her flat. She looked up into his crystal-blue eyes and every cell in her body sighed with pleasure. There wasn't a jury in the world who could rule against him once he hit them with his hypnotizing gaze.

No wonder Brandi with an I had wanted to climb him today. Any woman would love to have Jason Montgomery. She had him for now, although in her gut she knew the end would be coming. There was only so much time he could keep up the pretense of enjoying the children. And she had to put the children first.

Threading her fingers into his hair, she pulled him down for a kiss. She wasn't as frantic for release as she'd been five minutes ago. He'd been kind enough to take the edge off, so to speak. For a few minutes, they took pleasure in rediscovering the insides of mouths, the backs of teeth, the tingles that came from the perfect bite at the right strength.

Then she slid her hands under his shirt and shoved it up.

"Off," she said between kisses.

He sat up long enough to pull the material over his head and toss it across the room. When he lay down on top of her, his hot, muscular flesh heated her breasts, made her arch her back in an attempt for more contact. She moved her shoulders, loving the rough texture of his chest hair on her sensitive nipples.

He slid his hand under her butt, hiked her up so that his rigid shaft pressed firmly against her. She separated her legs, wrapped them around his thighs and pushed her pulsing center to that delicious length of firm flesh.

"I've missed you," he said. "I need to feel you surrounding me. Taking me deep inside you."

"Me too, babe," she said. "So much."

With quick fingers, both of them were naked within a minute. When he went to lie on her, she pushed him back onto the mattress.

"No hickeys on your neck, but you never said I couldn't suck anywhere else."

She enclosed her fingers around his long, thick dick, loving the way it was velvety soft but granite hard at the same time.

"Well," he gasped out. "That's true."

She smiled, sliding her hands down to the base and back to the head. She loved his penis, loved the power her hands had to bring him to his knees…and better yet, the way her mouth could totally wreck every ounce of self-control this polished man had ingrained in his soul.

When she lowered her mouth over the head of his cock, he held his breath. She ran her tongue around the cap, sucking in the salty liquid from the slit. Closing her lips, she slid him deeper into her mouth. He groaned and knotted the sheets in his hands.

Slowly, she pulled back her head, letting the chilly air of the room cool the wetness she'd left on his shaft. He quaked below her. Power surged through her veins.

She took him deep again, deep enough to hit firmly at the back of her throat, and slid him out again, stopping to run her tongue around the rim of the head.

"Fuck," he muttered in a gravelly voice.

She popped him out of her mouth of a noisy suck. "Patience. We're getting there."

He grabbed her head and pushed her back down on him. She took his length in between her lips, let him set the pace. He thrust roughly and as deeply into her mouth as he could get. Wrapping her fingers around the base, she worked his shaft in gliding movements in time with his hard attack on her mouth. She let him have his way for only a minute or so, knowing him well enough to realize he would not last long at that pace.

If he had any idea how aroused she got giving him a blowjob, he'd probably drop his pants every time they were in the same room.

He grunted with his strokes. His breaths came in short gasps. He pulled her hair hard, held her so tightly she would have had to rip out her hair by the strands to get away.

God, she loved this.

Her center throbbed and ached. Musky fluid tickled as it ran from her and down her leg. He jerked her mouth off him.

"Stop. Don't move," he said, his eyes shut, his chest heaving. In a minute, he opened his eyes. "Damn. That was close." He smiled. "This show was almost over before the main event."

"Now that would have been a crying shame."

She sat up, threw a leg over his waist and straddled him, her opening poised over his cock standing at full attention. He grabbed her hips and tried to push her down, but she just laughed.

"I'm the one doing the riding, cowboy."

"Then get on with it. I'm dying here."

Reaching between her thighs, she held his cock and

seated herself fully up to the hilt. He hissed and thrust up.

Yeah, this wasn't going to last long for either of them.

She started riding him, pushing up and down from her knees. Leaning forward, she changed the angle so that every time she hit full depth, her clit would have contact with his pelvis. Her strokes became faster, his thrusts harder. A powerful tension rose from her toes, through her legs and up to her gut. She swallowed and slammed against him, pounding her rigid nub. And then she was soaring over the edge. Waves of erotic pleasure swept through her. She cried out, her head dropping back, her gaze up as she rode the crest again.

He grunted and then groaned. Digging his fingers in her hips, he held her motionless as he drove up into her, finding his own release. Powerful jerks from his cock rattled her insides.

She fell onto his chest and both of them gasped for oxygen. His hands stroked up and down her back.

"I love you so much," he said. "So very much."

"I love you too."

They lay there, connected and together as one. Lydia let out a long sigh and rested her cheek on his chest.

"What do you want to do about our wedding?"

His question startled her. She froze, her heart, which had finally returned to a normal rate, shot back into the dangerous range. How could she marry him now that she had three children? Could the man have been more adamant about not wanting a family? He didn't want one...ever. Not even kids of his own. How could she expect him to accept another couple's children to feed and clothe and house?

Ellery, Annie and Levi were her blood. Her family. She'd loved them before, but now? She'd thought she'd known what love was, but what she felt for these three children defied adjectives. She would die for them. Kill to protect them. Give up anything that might hurt them, even the love of her life.

Jason had been great with the kids thus far, but his interactions had been for limited times only. He hadn't seen the fits, the screams, the hysterics over cutting the sandwiches incorrectly—according to whichever twin happened to be screaming about it. He'd never had to deal with the heart-wrenching cries of two little girls who wanted their mommy and daddy.

And Levi was starting to cut teeth, a painful process for him and anyone around him. She wasn't looking forward to that.

She loved Jason and she knew he loved her, but she worried he was acting out of obligation. He had asked her to marry him and she'd agreed, but that was before her entire world had taken a ninety-degree turn. Was it possible that he was merely being the honorable man she knew him to be and standing by the commitment he'd made, even if he wanted nothing more than to run?

How could she bring three children into a marriage with a man who'd always held firm that he didn't want children? How was that fair to him or to the kids? Hadn't the children been through enough upheaval and uncertainty?

Plus, she was still learning how to be a mother. There were some days when she rocked motherhood and lots of other days when she felt completely overwhelmed. The need to return to her job hung heavily around her. She needed time to adjust to the reality of being mother and doctor before she could think about adding the role of wife to the mix.

She simply could not take on anything else right now.

She couldn't marry him, not now. There were too many unanswered questions, too many ways this could go horribly wrong.

She realized he was looking at her, waiting for her answer. She sighed. "I don't know. I can only take it one day at a time."

Chapter Six

They sat in the drive of Lydia's house. The light from her living room lamps glowed through the windows across her darkened porch.

"We've been gone for hours," she whispered. "They're going to know what we've been doing."

He chuckled. "I'm pretty sure that was their plan when they offered to babysit."

They climbed from his SUV and walked up to the porch hand in hand. But she released his before she opened the door. Tonight had been a great break from learning how to be a mother, but now it was back to reality…her new reality.

The television was playing low as they entered. Jackie was sitting on the sofa, flipping through today's newspaper. In the rocker, Lane sat holding a sleeping Levi. There was an empty bottle on the coffee table, which she noticed had been cleaned of all the sticky mess usually there. The clean clothes that had been piled up were folded in stacks at one end of the sofa. Other than the whispered dialogue from the television, the house was shockingly quiet.

"We're back," Lydia said, stating the obvious.

"Did you have fun?" Jackie asked. "I bet all that tension is gone."

Lydia's mind flashed to the hot sex before remembering the wonderful massage that had preceded it. "Oh, the massage," she said. "Yes, it was wonderful."

Lane chuckled as though reading her mind.

"I see you've got the little man. Has he been any trouble?"

Lane shook his head. "Not too much. He was a little cranky earlier. Jackie thinks he's cutting his baby teeth."

"Oh, poor Levi. I noticed that earlier today. That's not going to be fun."

"For either of you," Jackie interjected.

Lydia leaned over to give Levi a kiss on the top of his head. He smelled like baby powder and innocence.

When she straightened, Lane said, "Doesn't this old man get a kiss too?"

Lydia chuckled and kissed his cheek, which was so different than kissing Jason's face. Lane's skin was tough and rough from years of running a ranch. His five o'clock shadow, which would better described as a nine o'clock beard, scratched her lips.

"Where are the girls?" she asked.

"They went to bed about an hour ago. They were tired, so I decided to give them their baths and read them a book. I think we might have made it to page five before they both conked out," Jackie said.

"Thank you. I really appreciate it."

"I enjoyed it." She patted the sofa. "Come sit down and tell me all about Eden Spa. I've been dying to go there. I hear it's really froufrou."

Lydia laughed as she sat. "It's really nice. It smells like fresh eucalyptus when you walk in. Lots of soft music and lighting."

"Sounds just like you, Jason," his dad teased.

Jason leaned on the hall doorframe. "Don't knock it until you've tried it."

"So the massage was as good as advertised?"

"I don't know how it's advertised, but I was like melting ice when Rebecca was done. I wanted to ooze off the table into a puddle on the floor. But get Jason to tell you about *Brandi*."

His mother arched an eyebrow. "Brandi?"

"Oh, she had it bad for your boy," Lydia said. "Good thing I was there. She might still be rubbing on him."

Jason's cheeks flushed as his parents laughed.

"She wasn't that bad," he said.

"I didn't say she was bad, but you have to admit, she was hot for you."

He waved a hand down his body. "Who wouldn't be?"

She giggled and realized it'd been a long time since she'd felt like her old self.

A scratching noise came from the hall.

"Where's Jasper?"

"He was in with the girls." Jackie started to rise.

"Stay, Mom. I'll let him out."

In a minute, a streak of reddish-blond vaulted into the living room and onto the sofa between Lydia and Jackie.

"What are you doing?" Lydia scolded. "You know you aren't supposed to be on the furniture."

Jasper's tongue lolled out of his mouth. He dropped flat and then rolled onto his back for someone to scratch his belly. Jackie immediately did.

"Hmm. I see what's been going on."

Levi let out a loud fart and shifted in Lane's arms.

"I think that's my signal to hand him over," Lane said.

Lydia chuckled, stood and lifted Levi onto her shoulder. "I really thank you both for tonight. I don't think I could have left them with anyone better. And believe me, it was hard to walk out that door."

Jackie and Lane stood.

"We understand," Jackie said. "I thank you for trusting us with your precious children."

Jackie kissed Lydia's cheek, as did Lane.

"Come on, Grandpa. It's past your bedtime," Jackie said.

When they were gone, Lydia looked at Jason. "Thank you. I needed tonight more than I realized." She indicated Levi with a tilt of her head. "I've got some dirty work to do. Can you lock the door when you leave?"

Jason's head snapped back. "Oh. Okay."

"Thanks, babe," she said and stepped up to give him a kiss. "I enjoyed tonight."

JASON TURNED THE LOCK AND SHUT THE DOOR AS instructed, or more like ordered. He'd planned on staying over, but it was clear from Lydia's comment that she didn't have the same expectations. For a little while this evening, he'd seen the woman he'd fallen in love with —funny and sexy and so hot in bed she melted him every time.

As he drove away, he wondered if he was losing her

to another man, a much, much younger and smaller man who was getting a clean diaper at the moment.

The next day, he went to see his brother Travis. He needed to ride some of his stress away and his brother always had a horse or two that needed the exercise. He pulled up to the house in time to see Travis chasing a naked Austin out the front door. Jason climbed from his car with a grin stretching his mouth wide.

"Come back here, you little hellion," Travis hollered.

Wearing only a pair of cowboy boots, Austin screamed with laughter and raced down the stairs toward Jason. "Unca Jason. Help."

His nephew slammed into Jason's legs, and Jason leaned over and lifted the two-year-old into his arms. Austin wrapped his arms around Jason's neck and clung, pressing his little lips into Jason's neck as he laughed.

A pain hit Jason, so hard and so deep it almost dropped him to his knees. Sometimes life sucked, and his wonderful nephew was a hard reminder of that. It wasn't so much that Jason had made a firm decision to never father children. He hadn't. That decision had been taken out of his hands when he was twenty. Now it was easier for him to say he didn't want kids. He'd said it for so long and so loud that even he believed it most of the time, until moments like this, and the one yesterday when he'd fed Levi. Those hurt.

"What are you doing to my favorite nephew?" Jason demanded, which made Austin giggle. "And where are his clothes? You making him go naked all the time?"

Travis stopped and grinned. "Yep. We took away all his clothes and now he only gets cowboy boots to wear."

Austin wiggled to turn around. "Don't want a bath."

"Too bad, cowboy. Your mom says you get a bath because you stink."

"I don't stink."

Jason made a major production out of sniffing his nephew. He jerked his head back, rolling his eyes in a dramatic fashion. "Good Lord, boy. When was your last bath? You smell like one of the horse stalls."

Austin giggled.

Actually, he smelled like a sweaty little boy, and right now, that smelled like heaven.

"Come on, cowboy." Travis held out his arms. "Let's go."

"No. I want Unca Jason to do it."

"You heard him, Travis. I'm the cool one now."

Travis chuckled. "More power to ya, bro."

The brothers headed for the front door only to be met by Travis's wife, Caroline.

"There you are," she said to Austin. She held out her arms. "Come here."

"You talking to me?" Jason asked. "I mean, I'll come with you, but it's kind of rude to do this in front of your husband, isn't it?"

Travis growled, which made Austin giggle.

"Nice try, Counselor." She wiggled her fingers at Austin. "Come on, Austin. Your private pool awaits."

Austin allowed Caroline to take him, and then she kissed Travis. "Thanks for giving a good chase."

"Hey," Jason protested. "I'm the one who caught him."

"She's not allowed to kiss other men," Travis said with a deep voice.

Caroline laughed, leaned forward and kissed Jason's cheek. "Thanks." She left with a wiggling Austin, who was trying to escape from his mother.

"A bath?" Jason asked. "This early in the day? Won't the kid be stinky and filthy by bedtime?"

Travis snorted. "That's your idea of children? Stinky and filthy? No wonder you never wanted any. But, yeah, he'll need another bath before bedtime. Caroline's taking the twins over to Olivia's. She's hosting something called a trunk show...maybe? I think that's what it is. Something to do with buying winter clothes for the kids on the cheap. I don't know. I don't ask too many questions."

"Hmm. I wonder if Olivia invited Lydia."

"No clue. If she didn't, it's only because she didn't think of it. We're not used to thinking of Lydia with children."

"Think I should call Olivia and ask?"

"You can if you want to. I have no idea what the protocol is with these things."

"I don't either. Screw it. I'm going to call."

"Follow me to the kitchen. I need another cup of coffee."

"Sure."

Jason dialed his sister's house as they walked.

"Hello?" Olivia's husband, answered her cell phone.

"Mitch? What are you doing answering Olivia's phone?"

"It's a madhouse over here. I don't even know where my wife is at the moment."

"What's going on?"

"That damn clothing thing she's doing. There are stacks of crap everywhere."

"I don't guess you know if she invited Lydia to this today, do you?"

"Hell, I'm pretty sure she invited the entire county to our house."

Jason paused, feeling nosy for pushing the issue, then asked, "Can you find Olivia and ask?"

"Sure. Hold on."

Travis pointed to the coffee maker. Jason nodded and Travis set a fresh mug in the single-serve machine and pressed start. The machine hissed and steamed. In a few seconds, the aroma of heaven filled the room.

"I'm back," Mitch said into the phone.

"Great. What did you find out?"

"She did and Lydia's coming. That help?"

"Yup. I'm over at Travis's. Want to come here? I thought I might take one of the horses out for a while."

"God, yes. Be there shortly."

After disconnecting, Jason shoved his phone in his jeans pocket.

"Feel free to invite people over to my house, bro," Travis said.

Jason shrugged. "It's not people. It's Mitch."

Travis laughed. "I'm just pulling your chain. You really want to ride today?"

"Yup. That's why I'm here. I need to clear my head. You mind?"

"Of course not. I always have horses that need exercise."

Halo M ranch, and specifically Travis, was known for the excellent cutting horses raised and trained here. Halo M supplied horses to many of the local ranches, riding clubs and tourist trail-ride outfits. Because of the reputation Travis had built for quality horse flesh, the ranch's stud business had quadrupled over the past couple of years.

The brothers sat at the kitchen table, talking spring training for the Dallas Cowboys and their chances for the Super Bowl next year. Both their heads jerked toward the door at the knock on the doorframe.

"Hey," Mitch said. "I met Caroline going out as I was coming in. She said to head on back."

"Coffee?" Travis asked.

Mitch shook his head. "Olivia had me up at the crack of dawn. I'm pretty much coffeed out. What are y'all talking about?"

"Cowboys," Jason said. "Think they'll make the Super Bowl next season?"

After a spirited discussion on the most current NFL rule changes, the guys headed down to the stable area. Travis picked out three horses he assured them needed some exercise and they headed out. They took off in the direction of the original Montgomery homestead founded by Jason and Travis's great-great-grandparents.

As they neared the ranch where their brother Cash lived, Jason asked, "Do you guys mind if I stop by and see if Cash is around?"

"Nope," Travis said, turning his gelding toward the house Cash had recently rebuilt.

The three men rode into the yard and were met by a yapping mutt.

"Hey, Buster," Jason called down to the dog. "Where's your owner?"

Buster danced around the horses, who didn't react to the barking, hyper dog. Another testament to Travis's horse skills.

"Buster," Cash yelled. "Stop all the barking." Cash appeared at the backdoor dressed only in a pair of jeans.

"We come at a bad time?" Jason asked.

"Nope. Paige just left for something at your sister's house. Something to do with clothes. I don't know."

"Let me guess," Travis said. "You don't ask."

"You know it. I learned a long time ago to choose my questions carefully. God knows, I didn't want to get dragged into some girl thing."

The three men laughed.

"What's up?" Cash asked.

"I wondered what your schedule looks like these days."

After a successful career as world champion bull rider, Cash had settled back in Whispering Springs and had opened his own construction and building rehabilitation company.

"I've got a couple of small projects going, but nothing major. I promised Paige we'd take a long vacation in June, so I'm trying to clear my work calendar before then. Why? What's up?"

Jason swung off his horse. The other guys did the same.

"I wanted to talk to you about Lydia's house."

Cash frowned and then nodded. "Okay. Y'all want to come in? Better yet, let's go to the lanai. Want some water? Cokes?"

"Lanai?" Travis hooted. "Woo-hoo. Fancy, bro."

Cash gave him a one-finger salute. "Bite me."

The other guys laughed.

"I'd love a Coke," Jason said.

"Yeah, me too," Mitch echoed.

"Okay. Come on."

The four men walked into the kitchen and left carrying glasses of fizzing soft drinks. Jason, Travis and Mitch headed through the dining room out to the covered deck at the side of the house. Cash detoured to grab a shirt and then joined them.

"So this is a lanai," Jason said. "I would have called it a covered deck."

"Basically the same idea. I just like the word lanai," Cash said.

That made Travis snicker again. Cash rolled his eyes at his brother.

"So what can I do for you, Jason?" Cash said.

"I might be overstepping, but Lydia's house is way too small for her and all the children. Levi has to sleep in her room. She's lost her office to the girls' bedroom. Between all the toys and a sixty-five-pound puppy throwing hair everywhere, it's hard to walk in there. I was thinking about adding on a new bedroom and fancy bathroom for her. Maybe add a sitting area so she can have her office back."

"I don't get it. Why do that? Your house is big enough. After you two get married, she won't need that house. Seems like a waste of money," Travis said.

"Yeah, that's the thing," Jason said. "I'm not sure how long that's going to take or even if we will get married now."

Cash leaned forward. "Seriously?"

"Yeah. She broke that little bit of news last night."

"Wow, bro. Sucks," Cash said.

"Give her time," Mitch said. "She's had it rough lately. I don't blame her. I'm sure her head is about to spin off her shoulders."

"I know," Jason said. "I know. It'd be so much easier on her if she moved in with me."

"Have you talked to her about that? Moving in to your bigger house?" Travis asked.

Jason blew out a long breath. "No. I thought about it, even started to say something to her about it, but with her hesitation about rescheduling the wedding, I can't see her agreeing to move into my house."

"Maybe she isn't looking for the easiest path," Travis said. "Maybe she's looking for what's right."

Jason frowned. "What do you mean?"

"You've made no secret of the fact you never wanted kids." Travis held up his hand when Jason started to speak. "I'm not judging you. Raising kids isn't for every-body. It's a hell of a lot of work."

"Yep, it is," Mitch said. "And it's exhausting."

"But it can be fun too," Travis said. "Some folks just see the work and miss all the fun stuff that goes on."

"I know all that," Jason said, brushing his hair back off his forehead. "I do. It's just that…never mind. It's impossible to explain." He looked at Cash. "Anyway, I was wondering if you had time to add on to her house. Her yard is big enough to accommodate the add-on. But it sounds like my timing sucks."

"Not really," Cash said. "Paige and I don't have any vacation plans in stone yet. It's only May. Even if Paige insists we leave in early June, which doesn't sound like my wife at all, I'd have four weeks to do it. Bring in a little help and shoot, not a problem. Let me talk to Paige tonight, okay?"

"Great. Thanks."

"One thing," Mitch said. "You haven't mentioned Lydia wanting this. You have talked with her about this, right?"

"Um, no. It just came to me this morning."

Mitch laughed. "Take it from the man who bought a ranch as a surprise for a woman he was trying to impress, this is risky. Your sister was a hard nut to crack. My little surprise-the-woman-with-a-house almost went sideways fast." He shook his head and chuckled. "I was lucky."

"Hell, man," Travis said. "You were desperate."

"Yeah, that too," Mitch agreed.

"I've got to do something to show Lydia that I'm all in."

"But are you?" Travis said. "Do you really realize what you're taking on?"

Jason shrugged. "I think so."

"Well, think more," Travis said. "This is a huge step. The potential to land on your ass is enormous."

"I'm sure Paige will be happy to do whatever she can to help Lydia," Cash assured. "Even if we need to postpone our trip for a while. As long as Lydia's onboard."

"Great. Thanks," Jason said. Now all he had to do was get his fiancée's approval.

And figure out if she was still his fiancée.

Easier said than done.

Chapter Seven

"**A**re you crazy?"

Lydia's reaction to his idea of adding on to her house was not going well.

"I can't build on to this house." She bent down to pick up a couple of dolls and set them on the sofa side table. "Look at this place." She swept her arm around. "Can you imagine the mess? It'd be worse than it is now."

In Jason's opinion, which he would not offer, the house couldn't be much more of a disaster than it was now. However, he suspected his appraisal would not be received well.

"Look, Lydia. It's that or move in with me. You have to have more space."

She shook her head. "No. I'm not moving into your house. It wouldn't be fair to Ellery and Annie to uproot them again to a strange house. Levi wouldn't care, but the girls? No. Not happening."

"Then adding on is the way to go."

She sighed. "Where would I get the money for that? And don't even suggest I use Meredith's estate."

"Speaking of the estate, that's another thing we need to discuss."

Lydia whirled around, putting her back to him. "I don't want to talk about it."

Jason laid his hands on her shoulders and turned her to face him. "I know you don't. And I'm sorry but we have to."

"Can't you just handle it for me?"

He nodded. "Yes, I can. Some of it, anyway. But we have to deal with the house and all the furnishings, their cars, checking accounts, retirement accounts, a bank lockbox, and a multitude of other small things."

She put her hands over her ears. "I can't handle it." For the first time in weeks, she began to cry. "I just can't put one more thing on my plate. I can't."

He pulled her to him and pressed her head against his chest. "I know, babe. I know. I'll figure out what has to be done immediately and what can wait. Okay?"

She sniffed. "I am such a baby." She pushed away and wiped her face on her shirttail.

"No, you're not. This would overwhelm anybody. I think you're incredible."

The smile she gave him didn't light up her eyes. It kind of stretched her mouth, but that was about it.

"Come on in the dining room while I fold up the clothes I have piled up there. We can talk while everyone is napping. You want something to drink?"

"Lydia. You don't have to ask like I'm a guest. If I want something to eat or drink, I can do it myself."

She sighed and sank into a chair. "Great. Can you bring me a water, please?"

He went into the kitchen and grabbed a couple of

waters from the refrigerator. He sat one at her elbow and took the chair next to her. She picked up a one-piece baby outfit and folded it into a tiny square. He chuckled.

"Not much material to that," he observed.

"And yet, you'd be appalled at what these cost."

"How was the whatever you went to at Olivia's yesterday?"

"It was a children's trunk show. A store or a manufacturer brings in either a clothing line or sometimes the samples, and people can buy them at a slightly lower price. It's more for convenience and fun than money savings."

"You find anything?"

"Some cute things for the girls that should work great for the fall. A couple of pairs of pants for Levi, but not much. Caroline suggested that I go through all the things Austin has outgrown and see what we can use."

"Great idea."

She folded a couple of pairs of small panties. "Apparently, mothers have been swapping around clothing for years for their kids. Who knew?" She sighed. "There is so much I don't know."

He put his hand over hers. "You're doing a wonderful job with the kids. No one could love them more."

He got that same non-smile she'd given him in the living room.

"Thanks." She picked up a tiny shirt and folded it. "Okay. I'm ready. Hit me with what I need to know."

"I'll be right back."

Jason went out to his car and retrieved the folder that contained all the information the probate lawyer had provided.

"I've put together a folder with all the information in

it. I'm going to go over it with you, but I'm also going to leave it here for you to review."

"Okay."

"First is the children."

Her face whipped toward him. "What about them?"

"Meredith and Jim listed another couple who'd agreed to raise them in the event you couldn't or didn't want to."

All color drained from her face. "They asked someone else? They didn't want me to raise their kids?" Suddenly, all the white in her face was replaced by a blazing red. "I am not giving *my* children to someone else. You can just forget it."

He wondered if she'd noticed she'd referred to the children as hers.

"Calm down. Take a breath."

"I'm not calming down. Only over my dead body are they going to some couple I don't know. Forget it."

"Lydia. Breathe. You didn't hear me. The will specifically names you as the guardian for Ellery, Annie and Levi. But your sister was smart to have a backup plan. She had no idea that she and Jim would die so young. What if something tragic and unexpected had happened to you before they died? The kids would have probably gone to your parents, and we both know how hard that would have been on them. And without a backup plan and no other family members to call on, the children could have ended up in foster care."

Lydia took a deep breath. "Okay. Sorry. But after a month, I would die if anyone wanted to take them away."

"Nobody is going to do that. I wouldn't let that happen."

She set down the baby blanket she was folding and

took his hand. "Thank you. Every woman needs a lawyer for a lover."

She chuckled. He did too, but inside, caustic acid ate at him. A lover? She considered him her lover? Now that he looked, he noticed she wasn't wearing the engagement ring he'd given her.

"Where's your ring?"

"What?"

"Your ring." He gestured to her left hand. "Your ring."

"Oh. In my jewelry box. It got in the way the other day when I was bathing Levi, so I took it off."

"Oh." He understood the explanation. He just didn't like it.

"Back to the will," she said, picking up the baby blanket again. "I'm keeping the children, so be sure that's clear with everyone."

"I know," he said. "The will also allows you to take whatever you want from the house in Kansas. It gives you ownership of the house should you elect to move to Wichita and raise the children there."

When she hesitated as though thinking about this as a viable option, he held his breath.

"I don't know a soul there," she said finally. "Not interested. So the house will be sold, right?"

He nodded. "Once it's cleared of its contents. That will be our biggest job."

"Just sell everything," she said. "I don't want anything."

"Lydia."

She didn't look at him.

"Lydia," he said again. This time, she looked up and he saw the glittering of tears. "We need to go there and look. You'll want to keep Meredith's jewelry for the girls.

Jim's too, if there is any. You'll want their photo albums and the baby books for the kids. I don't know what we'll find, but we have to go look."

She dropped her gaze to her lap. "I know. I'm just not looking forward to it."

"There are also a couple of cars. Meredith and Jim had three cars. The SUV from the wreck, Meredith's SUV, and Jim had an old restored 1957 Thunderbird."

"I'd forgotten about that Thunderbird." This time her smile went all the way to her eyes. "He loved that car. He and his dad rebuilt it when Jim was a teenager. He told me it was his father's way of keeping him out of trouble. He was too busy working on that car to do much else. I have to keep that for Levi. I just have to. From a father to his son to his son. You know?"

"Yes, and I agree completely. This is why we have to go there. There are things you need to save for the children."

She blew out a long breath. "I don't want to." She looked at him, her grief etched into her brow. "It's going to be hard to see all their things and know I'll never be with my sister again.

He nodded. "I know. It'll be sad and difficult. But you have to do it." He took her hand. "You don't have to do it alone. I'll go with you if you want. What's the good of having a lawyer for your lover if you can't use him?"

He tried to make light of her comment, but the words were like arrows to his soul.

"Okay. We'll have to take the children along." She shook her head. "But I can't see going back into that house as being good for the girls. I'm afraid it'll be too upsetting."

"I can see two options. One, we can take them and maybe your parents can meet us there and keep the kids in a hotel. Or two, we can get my parents to stay with them."

"I couldn't ask your parents. This place is too small for them to stay here. I mean, they'd have to sleep in the same room with Levi, and he roots around all night."

He saw when she recognized what she'd said.

"This house is too small," she said.

He nodded but didn't say anything. Better to let her come around on her own.

"I don't want to move the girls again."

Once more, he nodded.

"Damn you, Jason."

He chuckled.

"You always think you're right."

He chuckled again.

"I hate when you're right."

He arched an eyebrow.

"Fine," she said. "I agree that I have to do something. As it sits today, my house will not work long term. There. Are you happy?"

He smiled. "I love being right."

She rolled her eyes and chuckled. "Okay," she said on a long exhale. "I need to add on to this house."

He noticed that she chose adding on to her house over moving in with him. That set loose a burn in his gut.

"Cash?" she asked and then held up her hand. "Let me guess. You've already talked to Cash about doing this."

"Maybe."

"Maybe, my ass. I should be pissed when you are so overbearing and presumptuous to assume you know what's best for me."

"I didn't schedule anything, honey. Nothing. I simply asked if it was possible."

She narrowed her eyes in a glare and leaned forward. "When will Cash be here to measure and draw up plans?"

Jason gulped down some water. It was as if he were a law student in mock-trial court all over again.

Tapping a fingernail on the table, she arched an eyebrow. "You look so guilty right now. You might as well spill it."

"Tuesday."

"Tuesday, as in tomorrow?"

"Yeah." He gave her his best win-the-jury-over smile. "You going to kill me?"

"Not today. Maybe in a couple of weeks when there is sawing and hammering going on."

He chuckled and then sobered. "But back to the discussion."

"Which one? I feel like my head is spinning."

"Going to Wichita."

"Oh, that one."

"So, take the kids and get your parents up to Wichita to sit with them, or leave the kids here. Heck, maybe your parents could come here and stay."

She shook her head. "The girls would be too much for my folks to handle. Dad's doing great after his stents, but to be honest, Ellery and Annie need a lot of attention. I don't think Mom and Dad are the answer. Plus, Levi is cutting teeth. He's doing great most of the time, but still, he can be a pill at times. I love my folks, but these kids would be more than they could manage."

"So it's my parents then."

"I hate to ask them to do that. They were nice enough to stay for a few hours for us to go out, but to ask them to keep my children for days is just asking too much."

"Okay, how about this? Mom and Dad can keep Ellery and Annie. We take Levi with us. He won't care about being in the house like the girls might. And instead of Mom and Dad staying here, maybe the girls could go to their house, like going to camp. I think Ellery and Annie would love it."

"I don't know. It's another new place and…"

"But not new people. Let's take them to dinner at my parents' place. We can see how they react to all the animals."

"Have you talked to your parents about this? You know, like how you planned the addition to my house without my input?"

This time, he wouldn't let her rattle him. He would do what was best for her and these children.

"I wouldn't have offered them up as an alternative without asking first."

"What did they say?"

"You know what they said. 'Of course. Bring them here. We'd love it.' Mom enjoys spoiling them. Dad, well, he's a softie when it comes to girls. It's the perfect solution."

"To a problem I wish I didn't have."

"Yeah, I know."

"Let me think about it overnight. Okay?"

"Sure. But I'll need to let the probate lawyer know when we are coming so he can set aside some time for us."

It was almost midnight when Lydia finally made up her mind. Levi had woken her up an hour before with his crying. A diaper change and bottle hadn't fixed his problem. But the frozen washcloth that'd been soaked in chamomile tea before she'd frozen it worked wonders.

For years, she'd advised women about their babies and various remedies for childhood issues like the pain of cutting teeth. All she'd ever known was what she'd read. Whether or not some of her suggestions worked hadn't registered. She'd kept on handing out the textbook advice.

Being a mother had changed so many things for her. This frozen washcloth trick had come from a patient, not a medical text. Her first inclination had been to ignore the suggestion, figuring a medical book would have more valid information than a lay person. How wrong could a doctor be?

She had a large learning curve when it came to being a mother and a short time to learn.

Tomorrow, she would call Jason's mother and ask if she could bring the girls out to see the horses. The first step was seeing how Ellery and Annie responded to the animals. How the twins responded to seeing Jackie and Lane would also be key to any decisions.

By the time Cash knocked on her door a few hours later, she'd accepted that Jason had been right about her house being too small for her new family. When he entered, the twins immediately got shy, hiding their faces on Lydia's thighs.

Cash dropped to one knee. "Hello, ladies. I'm Cash. What are your names?"

The girls bore their faces more into Lydia's legs.

"Well, I seem to have some shy girls today," Lydia said.

Cash smiled and his whole face appeared to shine. No wonder he'd been such a hot ladies' man when he was on the rodeo circuit.

"No problem," he said. "It's only a matter of time before they discover that I never travel without gifts for beautiful girls."

Ellery turned her face toward him, keeping the contact between her head and Lydia's leg intact.

Cash held up two wrapped boxes.

"Cash. You didn't have to bring the girls presents."

"You're just jealous because there are only two."

She chuckled. "You've figured me out."

He held out a box toward Ellery. "What's your name?"

"Ellery."

"What a pretty name. What's your sister's name?"

Annie straightened and looked at him. "Annie."

"Ellery and Annie. I really love those names," Cash said. "I'm Cash. I'm Jason's brother."

"Uncle Jason?" Ellery asked.

He nodded. "Yep. He's my big brother, like you're Levi's big sister."

The girls looked at each other and, like she'd seen them do before, a form of nonverbal communication transpired between them. Then they moved as one toward Cash. He handed each of them a box.

"Can we open these now?" Annie asked Lydia.

"Sure."

The girls tore at the paper, squealing at the dolls inside. Each girl had received an American Girl doll that looked amazingly like them. Lydia didn't know much about dolls, but even she had heard of these.

"Cash. Those are too expensive."

He scoffed and waved off her concern.

"Do you like them?" he asked the girls.

"Oh, yes," Ellery said. "She looks just like me."

"And me," said Annie. She hugged the doll to her chest.

Cash smiled. "Good. I'm so glad."

"What do you say, girls?" Lydia prompted.

"Thank you," they said as one.

"Can we go play with them?" Annie asked.

"In your room please.

They started to leave the room and then stopped and ran back to Cash. Each girl gave him a kiss on the cheek, giggled and then ran to their room to play.

Cash rose. "I think I'm in love."

Lydia laughed. "I won't tell Paige that she's been replaced."

"How do you stand all that cuteness?"

"Ha. Try washing Annie's hair and then tell me how cute she is. Come on in."

Cash followed her to the kitchen.

"Something to drink?"

"Naw. I'm fine. How are you doing?"

Lydia pulled a water from the refrigerator. "Some days are good. Some days, not so good."

Cash nodded. "It's been tough, I'm sure. I'm sorry about your sister and her husband. I know I told you that at their funerals, but I wanted you to know that Paige and I talk about you a lot. You know if you need anything from us, you only have to call."

Lydia snorted. "No, apparently I don't. Your brother calls for me."

"Did you kick his ass for talking to me first? Oh please, *please* tell me you kicked his ass."

Laughing, Lydia shook her head. "I should have. Unfortunately, this time he was right."

"Don't you hate that?"

"More than you know. Why don't you make yourself

at home? Look wherever you want to, or whatever you do. I hear Levi crying. I need to get him."

Cash nodded. "I'll start in the backyard then. See what room we have to work with." He opened the door and got smashed by Jasper pushing his way inside.

"Meet Jasper. Ill-mannered, untrained and a drooler, but we love him."

Jasper stopped long enough for Cash to pull a dog bone from the box on the counter and feed him. Then he was off like a shot through the house.

"Where's he going?"

"The girls' room. I'm pretty sure he thinks he's part of a set of triples."

Cash spent the next thirty minutes walking around inside and outside the house, all the while jotting notes and measurements on a notepad. When he finished his inspection, he joined Lydia in the living room where she was rocking Levi and holding another frozen washcloth to his gums.

"I hate to admit it, but Jason was right. You need more room."

"I know. I know. Let's not tell him, okay? He's bossy enough."

"You're telling me. He grew up with that attitude." He cleared this throat. "You know, Lydia, this isn't going to be cheap."

She nodded. "I know."

"Before we head down the road of tearing out walls, what about the obvious suggestion? Why don't you move in with Jason?"

She stopped rocking, shifted Levi around in her lap and shook her head. "Lots of reasons, Cash. But right now, the primary one is that Ellery and Annie are settled in this house. Let me change that. They've just gotten settled here. It's only been about a month. They've gone from their home to this one. I don't want to uproot them again. Not now. Maybe later, but right now my goal is to give them as much stability in their lives as I can, and that includes staying here. So no matter the cost, adding on is what I want to do."

"Okay, then. You have plenty of space to go out through the kitchen. Let me show you."

He put some rough drawings on the coffee table. "We go out through here. Add a laundry room, which you need badly. A master bedroom and bath can go here, and a small sitting room slash office over here."

She lifted the pages off the table to study them closer.

"Would the girls lose a lot of the play area in the backyard?"

"I don't think so. You have a ton of space to the side of the house too, so anything we do would leave more than adequate room for a swing set or playhouse or heck, even both. You did great picking out this house."

Lydia remembered the day she'd bought the house. It'd been one of the smaller ones that was close to work, close to the hospital and close to a grocery store. She hadn't given any thought to space for swing sets or play-houses. Really, she hadn't expected to still be living here this many years later.

"How much is this going to cost?"

Cash quoted her a price that was way too low.

"No way," she said. "The supplies alone will cost that or more. You're not doing this for free."

"I'm not, but you are getting the Montgomery family discount. I'm getting paid for my time. Don't worry."

"Jason?"

"Just call him a generous benefactor."

"I can't do that. I'll pay you for your time."

Cash stood. "I'll let you two fight that out. If you want to do this, I'll need to get started on the appropriate building permits we're going to need."

She nodded. "Yeah. Let's do this."

Chapter Eight

Later that afternoon, Lydia piled the children into her small sedan, only able to fit all of them because she used the trunk to store Levi's diaper bag, bottles, Pack 'n Play and extra clothes for the girls. Each girl carried her new doll and a stuffed animal. The animals had been theirs before the accident, and Lydia figured there was comfort in the known and excitement in the new.

When she turned into the Bar M ranch drive, there were cows in the fields on both sides of the lane. She stopped and rolled down the windows.

"See the cows, girls? Those belong to Mimi and Papa. Have you ever seen a cow before?"

Wide eyes met her gaze in the rearview mirror, and she had to assume this was a first for them. Now that she thought about it, they probably hadn't ever seen a cow except in picture books.

As the car rolled forward, Ellery said, "Baby," and pointed out the window.

A newborn calf stood alongside its mother.

She stopped the car again. "That's right. That's a baby cow."

"Is that his mother?"

Lydia nodded. "Yes."

"Our mother lives in heaven now, right?"

Lydia swallowed against the painful stone forming in her throat. "That's right."

"Are you going to heaven too?" Annie asked.

"Not for a long, *long* time," Lydia said.

Jackie and Lane were standing in the circle drive when Lydia pulled to a stop. Years ago, Lane had installed an alarm system that rang at the house when a vehicle drove through the gates. However, it also worked when someone drove out, meaning the boys had been caught more than once sneaking out when they'd been in high school.

"Hi," called Jackie. "Hi, Ellery. Hi, Annie." She waved enthusiastically.

The girls waved and twisted, trying to get out of their seats. Lydia unlocked the doors as Lane went for Annie and Jackie headed for Ellery.

"Look who's here," Lane said, unbuckling Annie from her seat. "Come here and see me. Did you bring barrettes for me to try on?"

Annie laughed and went into Lane's arms.

Behind her, Jackie had Ellery out of her seat while Ellery told her about the baby cow.

Lydia climbed out and felt such relief at the reception the girls had received from the Montgomerys that she wanted to tear up.

Jason pulled up in his truck and stopped behind her. "Sorry I'm late," he said, hopping from the driver's door.

"Hi, honey," his mom said. "You're not late at all. The girls just got here."

He leaned in and lifted Ellery's shirt to blow a raspberry on her belly. She laughed and squirmed.

"Me next," Annie said.

Jason took Annie from Lane and tossed her into the air and caught her. The child squealed.

Lydia unbuckled Levi and pulled him into her arms. He seemed to understand everyone was laughing and he wanted in on the action. His arms bounced up and down, barely missing Lydia's nose. He pushed with his legs, hiking himself up and down on her hip as he chortled.

"Well, he's in a good mood," Jason said as he settled Annie on his hip. "How are the teeth coming along?"

"Slowly," Lydia said. "Painfully, but we'll get there."

Lane held out his arms to Levi. "Come here, little guy."

"You might want to wait on that, Lane," Lydia said. "I'm pretty sure we have a little repair work to do in his jeans."

Lane nodded. "Sounds like a plan. Can I help get anything out of the car?"

Lydia snorted. "There's an entire bedroom in the trunk."

"Got it."

Lydia popped the trunk and followed Lane to the rear of the car. She put Levi's diaper bag over her shoulder. Lane hoisted the portable bed slash playpen up by its strap and then grabbed the other two totes.

"This everything?"

"I think so."

When she shut the trunk, she discovered that Jackie and Jason had walked over to the closest corral. A couple of horses leaned their heads over the railing, sniffing the girls' heads. She almost called out to warn them not to let the girls get bit, but she held her tongue. If Jackie and Jason didn't know what to do around horses, then the world would be ending soon.

"Let's go on in," Lane suggested. "I know I would rather have dry britches on."

Lydia chuckled. "Lead the way."

She'd been in the Montgomery home more times than she could count. Bar M had been as much a home to her as her own, but this time she felt like a guest, where in the past she'd always felt like family. Even though she tried, she couldn't put her finger on what was causing the change in her perspective.

She followed Lane into the house and down the hall to Jason's old bedroom.

"I thought we'd set up Levi back here. That way, if he wants a nap, he can have some quiet."

"That's very thoughtful of you. Let me change him and I'll set up his playpen."

"Give him to me. I've changed a diaper or two in my time. Now these newfangled gadgets might stump me, but not a diaper."

She shrugged and handed Levi over. "Diapers and wipes are in here." She let the diaper bag slide down her arm to her hand and set it on the bed. "This will be a good room for Levi."

Lane laid Levi down. Levi immediately rolled to his side and tried to get away. Lane chuckled. "Hold on there, cowboy."

Levi laughed and rolled away again.

"I've got it, Lydia. Don't worry."

Knowing how she personally hated to be watched when she was doing something, she turned around and laid the Pack 'n Play on the floor. After she undid the Velcro straps, she began locking the sides open.

Lane laughed and she turned to look. His shirt was wet down the front.

"Sorry about that," she said.

"You'd think I'd remember something like that after three boys of my own and two grandsons, wouldn't you? Not the first time, and knowing little boys, probably not the last time."

She finished setting up the crib slash playpen and stood. Levi had a fresh diaper on, but one look at the boy's crooked pants and Lydia decided Levi had given Jason's dad lots of trouble.

"Need a hand?" she asked.

"Nope. We guys are doing just fine." Lane straightened Levi's pants and got all the snaps up the legs fastened. Then he picked the baby up into his arms. "Okay. We are ready to party now."

They found Jackie and Jason and the girls in the living room. Toys of all kinds were scattered on the rug. Dump trucks. Race cars. A miniature tea set. Four dolls she'd never seen before. A jump rope. And finally, a gun and holster set. Lydia wasn't sure how she felt about her girls playing with a gun and holster. However, in this family, guns were as common as the coffee mugs at her house.

"Wow. Where did all these come from?" Lydia asked.

"Look," Ellery said and ran over to take Lydia's hand to pull her toward a large box in the corner. "A toy store."

Lydia looked inside the box and chuckled. It was stuffed with an assortment of toys for every age. "Well, I think it's a toy box, not a toy store, but I get what you mean."

Lydia picked Ellery up and carried her back to the main part of the room where everyone else was sitting.

"Impressive collection," she said to Jackie, who was pretending to drink from a tea cup.

"Thank you. I raided Lane's closet."

Lane guffawed.

"What happened to your shirt?" Jason asked his dad.

"Yeah, like you don't know."

Jason snickered. "Old faithful strikes again."

"You'd think I'd remember that, wouldn't you? Be right back. I'm going to change."

"If it's okay with Lydia, I thought we could cook hot dogs on the grill for dinner. Is that okay with you girls?"

Ellery and Annie jumped and bounced around the room. "Yes," they both cried.

Lydia shrugged. "Fine with me."

"Well," Jason said. "I thought maybe you'd like a nice steak."

Lydia shot him a questioning look. "Steak?"

"I was thinking the Lone Star for dinner."

"Um, I'm not dressed for the Lone Star. And besides…" She indicated the girls with a tilt of her head. "I love a good hot dog as well as the next girl. Thanks for the offer though."

"Oh, honey," Jackie said. "You don't have to stay here. You two can go have a nice dinner."

Lydia shook her head. "No. Thanks, but no."

"Mimi," Lane said as he rejoined the group. "Did you tell the girls about the new kittens?"

"Kittens?" Annie said. "Where? I want to see the kittens."

"Me too" Ellery said, jumping up and down.

"They're in the barn. Do you mind, Lydia?"

"The walk might help burn off some energy, if you know what I'm saying."

Jackie grinned. "Come on, girls." She stood and stretched her hands down by her legs. "Grab a hand."

The girls latched on and Jackie led them out of the house, followed by Lane carrying Levi. They left Jason and Lydia sitting in the living room.

"I think your parents are leaving us alone on purpose."

He grinned. "Remind me to thank them."

She stood. "This visit isn't about you and me finding alone time. It's about seeing how comfortable my children are with your parents."

"Are you kidding? Have you been watching? They're fine."

"Still…"

Lane stuck his head through the front door. "Um, Lydia. The girls are a little scared of the barn."

"I'm on my way." She shot Jason a look. "See? They are still fragile and nervous without me." She sighed. "Annie cried for hours last night for her mommy. It almost killed me. Luckily, Ellery had already gone to sleep and Annie was crying in the living room and didn't wake up Elle or Levi." She pressed her hands to her chest. "It hurt, Jason. Really, *really* hurt."

She hurried to the door and turned back. "Well, come on. We need to see the new kittens."

The rest of the visit went very well, as well as Lydia could have hoped. The girls loved the kittens. They were a little upset when Lydia said they couldn't take one home. But she reminded them that Jasper might not like a new kitten right now.

Dinner went fine. Hot dogs were one of her never-fail meals for the girls. After dinner, Annie helped Jackie put the dishes in the dishwasher and get out the supplies for ice cream sundaes while Ellery and Jason went with

Lane to feed a goat that'd wandered up a couple of weeks ago. So far, no one had claimed him. Never one to turn away an animal, Lane had provided the goat a home while he continued to look for the owner.

Lydia fed Levi and put on his sleeper. Fifteen minutes of rocking him and he was gone. She put him in the portable crib and joined Annie and Jackie. Annie's eyes were wide as she studied all the toppings Jackie had set out. Chocolate. Caramel. Nuts. Chocolate chips. Whipped cream.

The sundaes were a hit and a huge mess. Hand washing was not going to be sufficient. The girls didn't want to take baths, but when Jackie put bubble bath into the tub, they quickly changed their minds. When Lydia started to help, Jackie stopped her.

"Let me," Jackie said. "I want to do this."

Lydia shrugged. "Okay." She stayed in the room but remained out of the way. She'd never admit it to anyone, but she wanted to watch Jackie's interactions with her girls. Were the girls comfortable with her? Did they fight with each other while under Jackie's care? Was Jackie keeping a close eye on them so they didn't drown?

She was fully aware that her concerns about Jackie's abilities were silly, but Lydia hadn't ever been a mother before. These girls were hers to protect. They'd already been through so much. Anything she could do to make their lives whole again, she would. It was that simple.

Of course, the bath went fine. The girls—with Jackie's encouragement—blew the bubbles around in the tub. They gave themselves bubble beards and bubble earrings and necklaces and even bubble hats. The girls were laughing, a sound that Lydia doubted she'd ever get tired of hearing.

Ellery and Annie actually used the washcloths to

clean their faces, something Lydia had yet to accomplish. Water was splashed everywhere, not that anyone but Lydia seemed to mind.

"I brought some other things for them to put on," Lydia said. "I'll go get their bag."

"Okay, honey," Jackie said. "We'll be right here until you get back."

She'd packed clean underwear, shorts and shirts for the twins, but she'd also thrown in pajamas as a last minute thought. Since it was close to the twins' bedtime, she pulled out the pjs and fresh underwear.

Jackie had Annie out of the tub and was drying her when Lydia came back.

"First one's been buffed and fluffed," Jackie said.

Lydia chuckled. "Pass her over."

Annie skipped to Lydia and they began putting on her nightwear.

Ellery climbed out of the tub. "I'll do it," she said and reached for the towel.

Lydia almost said no but then backed off. Let Ellery see what she could do. In the end, Jackie helped Ellery get dry, but in such a way that Ellery was sure she'd done it all by herself. Lydia passed down Ellery's clothing and waited as Jackie helped the second twin into her fresh clothes.

When the girls were done, the bathroom looked like a tornado had gone through. Rugs were out of place. Small puddles of water dotted the floor and the wall behind the tub. Lydia didn't even want to think about the ring around the tub the girls had probably left after the numerous trips to see the kittens in the dusty barn and the sticky ice cream.

"Thanks, Jackie," Lydia said. "Let me help you get this cleaned up."

"Absolutely not. The cleaning lady comes tomorrow. Let her do it."

Lydia snorted. Jackie had no cleaning lady.

"Come on, girls. Let's go see what Jason and Papa are doing."

After another thirty minutes, the girls were winding down. Jason and Lane loaded all the kid necessities back into Lydia's sedan while Jackie and Lydia got three sleepy children buckled into their car seats.

"They won't make it to the end of the drive," Jackie whispered over the roof of the sedan with a smile.

"Probably not. Thanks for everything this evening. I know the girls had fun."

Jackie walked around the hood of the car to stand next to Lydia. "Lane and I will be happy to take care of the girls so you can make a run to Wichita."

"I know. It's not that I don't trust you with them, because I do. But I worry about the girls' reaction to me leaving them here. They still have some separation anxiety and they may be too fragile emotionally." She sighed. "I just don't know what to do."

"Do you want me to go with you to Wichita? I could keep them in a hotel while you take care of what you need to. That way, you can come and go as you need without feeling guilty or rushing to get home."

Lydia's eyes teared up. "That is so sweet of you. I don't know what to say."

"Make it easy. Say yes and tell me when we leave."

Lydia hugged the older woman. "Thank you. I'll talk to Jason and call you tomorrow, okay?"

"Of course. I'm not going anywhere."

For the rest of the week, Lydia made plans to be gone to Wichita for a few days. She didn't know how long it would take to deal with everything. Jackie dropped by every day for a couple of hours and Lydia took advantage of the babysitting to run errands or do grocery shopping to help the girls adjust to her being gone. Initially, the girls cried when she left, and the sound pierced her soul like a dagger. It took every ounce of her strength to walk away. She wasn't gone long the first time, a little longer the second, and by the time she'd come in and out for the fifth time, the girls had calmed down and didn't pay as much attention to her leaving.

On Sunday, they left for Wichita. Lane had decided he wanted to come along, so he and Jackie followed in their SUV with Levi in the back seat. Jason and Lydia took the two girls with them in his SUV.

On their first day there, Jason and Lydia met with Sam Wood, her sister and brother-in-law's probate lawyer. He gave her house keys and a safety deposit box key along with the necessary paperwork to allow her to open it.

They pulled into the drive at the large, two-story colonial house. Lydia sat unable to make herself move. After she did this, her sister would really be gone. Rationally, she knew Meredith was gone, but since they'd lived apart for years, she had been able to ignore reality. Once the house was sold, the cars gone and whatever was in the lockbox removed, all traces of her sister's former life would be erased from this world.

This was much harder than she had anticipated.

Meredith and Jim had been gone for almost six weeks and, even though the children were a daily reminder of that fact, her emotional mind did not want to accept that she would never see her baby sister again.

Through a watery perspective, she studied the freshly mowed yard, the spring growth of new leaves on the trees, the flowers that were blooming in the bed that lined the walk to the front door. Meredith had always had a green thumb. She could throw a peach pit in the yard and the next year have a tree growing.

"The house looks good," she said, stalling for time to collect herself. "You had someone mow the yard." It wasn't a question. She was sure Jason had taken care of things she'd never thought of, such as keeping the house looking presentable.

"It's a nice neighborhood. I didn't want things to get overgrown."

"I wouldn't have thought of the grass needing to be mowed." She finally turned to look at him. "You have done so much for the children and me, probably more than I even know. Thank you." She leaned over and kissed him. A flutter tickled her gut. Like it always did when she tasted him, her heart flipped over like a fish.

When this trip was over, she had to find a way to let him go. He needed to find his happily-ever-after with a woman who shared his vision for life, and that woman could no longer be her, not with three children. He'd done the honorable thing by standing by her, but he had to be looking for a way out before he got too enmeshed in a lifestyle he never wanted.

"I haven't done that much. Wood did an outstanding job representing your sister and Jim. They chose well when they chose him. Ready?" He nodded toward the house.

She sighed. "If I have to."

When they unlocked the door and stepped in, Lydia was overcome by the scent of her sister. Maybe it was her perfume still lingering in the air. Or maybe it was the laundry soap she used and the smell had infiltrated the air ducts. Or, knowing her sister, there were probably automatic air fresheners that continued to scent the air.

Whatever it was, the aroma stopped Lydia just inside the door.

"You okay?" he asked.

She nodded. "Give me a minute."

He returned her nod and walked on into the house. Jason was her tower of strength, constantly there for her. She could never repay his kindness, nor his helpfulness. With great sadness, she became even more positive that letting him find happiness with another woman would be the best thing she could do for him.

They spent the first hour roaming the house, looking in closets and drawers, setting aside items they believed would be important to the children. Although the will stipulated that Lydia could take anything from the house she wanted, there wasn't anything here she needed now. Down the road, she would need bigger beds for the girls, but she elected to focus on the here and now.

At noon, they took a lunch break and headed back to the hotel. The children were at the kiddie pool with Jackie. Levi and Lane had stayed in the room. Both guys were asleep when Lydia opened the door, Lane on the bed snoring and Levi in his Pack 'n Play. She quietly shut the door and went back to the pool.

"Both of them are dead to the world," she reported to Jackie.

"Yeah, I was a little suspicious when Lane said that he and Levi were going to watch *Days of Our Lives*."

Lydia laughed. "Yeah, I can't see Lane getting involved with the daily soaps."

The girls were splashing and generally having a good time in the pool, so when she left, they waved and went back to playing.

Before heading back to the house, Lydia and Jason stopped at the bank. The paperwork was in order for

Lydia to access the safety deposit box as well as all the accounts, but jumping through the bank's hoops took some time.

Once they had access to the box and Lydia opened it, she found an envelope addressed to her lying on top. She picked it up, recognizing her sister's handwriting. She wanted to hear from Meredith one last time, and yet, she didn't because it would be the last time. She opened the envelope slowly, bracing herself for whatever was inside.

Dear Lydia,

It's possible that you will never read this, and if so, yay. I made it to old age, which means you're still older than me.

Lydia paused to cry and chuckle at her baby sister's joke. No matter how old Meredith got, Lydia would always be older. Because Meredith had stopped aging.

"You okay?" Jason asked. He handed her a fresh handkerchief for her tears.

"Thanks. I'm okay. My damn sister is making me cry."

He put his arm around her and pulled her in for a hug. "Damn her," he joked.

"I know."

She wiped her tears and continued reading.

If you are reading this, then I am so sorry. It means I'm gone and you have my children to raise. Know that I have given you my life's prize. Nothing I ever did could surpass them. I know you're probably freaked out right now, and probably doubting that you can take over for me, but there is no one I'd trust more. By now, you know we picked an alternative option if for some reason you can't, or won't, take Ellery, Annie and Levi, but I only did that at the insistence of our lawyer. Sam is one of the good guys, Lydia, like your Jason. You can trust Sam with anything.

Jim has given me some nice jewelry over the years we've been together. Some of it too nice, if you know what I mean. Most of it will be here in the box or at home in the safe in Jim's office.

Lydia looked at Jason. "Did we find a safe at the house this morning? I don't remember one."

He shook his head. "I didn't. Maybe their lawyer knows."

If you've been in the house and not found the safe, you're probably wondering where it is. Go to Jim's office. Look in the closet. On the floor to the left side. You'll see a box of Jim's business files. Take those out. There is a release button for the door to the safe. It's on the right side in the corner near the floor. Push it, and a door will open. The safe is installed in the concrete under that floor. The combination is 12-20-74-84. No one, not even our lawyer, knows about the safe. There some cash in there. Take it. Heck, take everything out of there. And don't argue with me about this.

I'd like you to keep my jewelry for the kids, particularly the pieces Jim gave me when each of them were born. Diamond earrings and a diamond bracelet when Ellery and Annie were born and a platinum and canary-yellow diamond ring when Levi arrived. As far as the rest of my stuff, make good use of it. Wear it. In fact, when you marry Jason, wear my earrings for good luck. Of course, since you're reading this, maybe my luck wasn't all that good. (Laugh. That was a joke.) I was lucky in love. Jim is my soul mate and know that he was everything to me.

Lydia paused to wipe a few tears.

The letter went on to tell her that the cars were hers to do with as she liked, but could she please save the Thunderbird for Levi? She smiled. She'd been right on that one.

Meredith had a mink coat that she wanted Lydia to give to her best friend as long as Lydia didn't want it. Lydia didn't and would make sure the lawyer was aware of the gift. There were a couple of other items, such as Jim's golf clubs, that her sister had requested be given to certain people, again provided Lydia didn't have a use for them. All the items were things Lydia had no problem giving away.

In closing, know that I loved you so much. Growing up, I wanted to be just like you. As a big sister, you set the bar high. Take care of my babies as I know you will. I hope you'll tell them about us. Make sure Mom and Dad know that I loved them too.

Don't be sad that I'm gone. I had a wonderful life, no matter how long or short it was.

Raising kids is expensive, but I'm pretty sure Jim and I have set aside enough for their colleges. There are two large life-insurance policies. Make those bastards pay out! They will try to find a reason not to, but I trust between our lawyer and your Jason, you'll get the money. Those policies are in this box also.

I love you, sis. Thank you for loving me and my kids.
Meredith.

"Damn her," Lydia muttered. "I was through crying."

Jason put his arm around her. "Is there anything in the letter I need to know?"

She handed the sheet of paper to him. "Yeah. Take a look while I get the things from here into the tote bag."

She found everything Meredith had described, plus about ten thousand dollars in cash.

After they finished with the box, she closed the checking and money market accounts and sent the money to a special account that Jason had set up.

By the time they pulled back into the hotel lot, it was close to eight p.m. She was emotionally drained and physically exhausted. Jason hadn't complained about anything she'd asked him to do today, but his face was drawn and the creases around his eyes appeared more pronounced, so she assumed he was as exhausted as she.

The girls were tucked in bed and fast asleep. Levi and Lane were watching some drama cop show, Levi with a bottle and Lane with a beer. Jason went over to speak with his father.

Lydia chuckled and pointed toward Lane and Levi. "Good thing they didn't get their bottles mixed up," she told Jackie, who snorted a laugh.

"I'm pretty sure Lane would have noticed after the first few sips."

"How's the teeth cutting coming along?"

"He was a little cranky earlier, but the cold washcloth helped. Have you and Jason had dinner?"

Lydia shook her head. "We were gone today longer than I thought we'd be, so I felt like I needed to get back."

"Everything's fine here. You should eat," Jackie said. "You look a little pale."

"I probably do. I knew handling all the estate details would be draining, and it was, but I'm more exhausted than I expected."

"Go get a nice dinner and then get some sleep." Jackie tilted her head toward the open adjoining door. "I'll keep an eye on the girls. They'll be fine. I can't get

Levi out of Lane's arms, so I'm not too concerned about him."

Lydia smiled. "They do seem taken with each other. Maybe Jason and I can just do room service. I'm too tired to go anywhere."

"Use his room," Jackie suggested. "It'll be quieter."

Lydia suspected this was another effort on Jason's mother's part to throw them together and give them private time. It wasn't that she didn't want time alone with him. She loved spending time with Jason. However, she knew she had to learn how to live without him.

"Ready for dinner?" she asked Jason.

"More than. My stomach is resting on my spine."

Lydia rolled her eyes with a chuckle. "Exaggerate much, Counselor?"

"Never."

"Since the twins are asleep in *my* room, what would you say to ordering room service in *your* room?"

Something hot flashed through his eyes and a smile made its way onto his lips. "That sounds like a winning plan."

The hotel had been very accommodating giving them three rooms that adjoined. She closed the door that connected her room to his and leaned against it.

"So…what are you hungry for?" Lydia asked with a slight lift of an eyebrow.

Chapter Nine

Jason studied Lydia standing there against the door, one leg bent, her hand trapped behind her ass on the door.

"Darlin', nothing looks better to me right now than you."

She smiled and a zing of lust rattled through him.

"I meant food."

He shook his head. "No, you didn't. You knew exactly what you were asking."

"Maybe," she said and tilted her head to one side. Then her posture changed and she stood straight. "Probably not a good idea. I don't know what I was thinking." She strode across the room, picked up the in-room menu and began flipping through the pages. "What sounds good? Steak? Burger? Club sandwich?" She glanced up and their gazes locked.

"What's going on, Lydia?"

"I don't know what you mean?"

"Yeah, you do. Ever since you got Meredith's children, you've kept me at arm's length...well, except for one night. I've been there for you every step of the way. I haven't asked you to choose between me and the children. So what's wrong?"

She sighed and sat on the foot of his bed. "We're both tired tonight. I know I am. I'm physically and emotionally beyond exhausted. Let's not have a serious talk tonight. It won't go well."

Shoving his fists on his hips, he asked, "What does that mean? 'It won't go well'?"

Dropping flat on her back, she stared at the ceiling. "I don't know. I really don't. My plate is full, overflowing. I feel like someone's handed me chainsaws and expects me to juggle them even though I don't know the first thing about juggling or chainsaws. For tonight, can we just eat and worry about *tomorrow* tomorrow?"

Unease gnawed at him. She was slipping away. He could feel her growing more distant each day. If he pushed her, fought for her, he was sure what her reaction would be. She would drop him from her juggling act, as she envisioned her life. Dealing with a pushy boyfriend could be easily solved by erasing that stressor from her life. That's not what he wanted, so he'd back off. She'd come back to him when things settled down.

"You're right," he said, dropping on his back beside her on the bed. "It was a long day. I'm tired and a little punchy."

She rolled to her side and grinned. "You? Punchy? No, surely not?"

She poked his ribs. He caught her finger in his hand and rolled on top of her. "I'll give you punchy," he joked and began to tickle her. She laughed and pushed at his shoulders, trying to get away, but he was too heavy, too strong for her to throw off.

Remembering his vow to ease up on the pressure to

get their relationship back on track, he rolled off her and sat up with a sigh. "Okay, let's eat. Did they have prime rib on that menu?"

They stayed two more days in Wichita filling Jason's SUV with the children's toys and clothes. The valuable jewelry was packed away to be put into a lockbox until the kids came of age. Everything else would be sold at an estate auction, one she didn't have to attend, something she was thankful for. Anything not sold would be donated to the local charity run by Meredith and Jim's church. A realtor was lined up to list the house once it was empty. The agent assured them it would sell quickly and at a desirable price high enough to pay off the outstanding mortgage.

Claims were filed against the life-insurance policies, but that was a waiting game. Jason and Lydia agreed that the company would not be happy about paying off two million-dollar policies. He promised to stay on top of it.

Meredith's SUV turned out to be a new, fully loaded Cadillac Escalade. Lydia had liked her small sedan when she'd purchased it three years ago. However, she needed something larger for her family. She decided the Escalade would come home with her.

Jim's restored Thunderbird was stunning. When Lydia told Jason how many hours of labor had gone into the car, he had to admit it showed. While the car could make the drive back to Texas, he convinced Lydia to let him pull it on a trailer back to Whispering Springs. Where the car would be stored was a problem that would have to be resolved later.

Their now three-car caravan started home on Thursday morning. The three children rode with her in the Escalade. After spending so much time with her over the past week, Jason's car felt empty and was way too quiet.

At the end of a long drive, Lane and Jackie left the caravan and turned toward their ranch with a toot of their horn and a wave.

Lydia pulled into her drive, the huge SUV taking up every inch of parking space. Jason parked across the street, jumped out and hurried over to meet her. In front of her house sat Cash's old truck.

She exited the SUV with a nod toward the trucks. "I see Cash has gotten started."

"I called him when we were about thirty minutes out to give him a heads up. I figure that's the only reason you had an open driveway."

"Thanks. Let's get everybody out and see what's happening. I'll take care of the girls if you'll get Levi. I don't want them getting into nails or whatever might be lying around."

The living room looked normal until her gaze hit the plastic sheeting that sealed the kitchen off from the rest of the house.

"Yikes. Cash, you here?"

"Coming," was the muffled reply.

The girls crowded her, pushing against her legs.

"What's that?" Ellery asked, pointing to the plastic popping in and out with the change in air pressure.

"We're getting a new laundry room and that plastic is keeping all the mess in there and not out here."

"Oh," Ellery said.

"I'm here," Cash said, coming through the front door. "I was out back and had to come around the house. Nice new ride."

"Thanks."

"Hey, girls," he said, squatting down to their level. "Remember me? Jason's brother?"

They nodded.

"You have a good trip?"

They nodded again.

"Still a tad bashful," Lydia said. "Safe to turn them loose to their room?"

"Yep. Just as you left it."

"I'll take them," Jason said. "That'll give you and Cash time to chat."

"So, where are we?" Lydia asked after Jason and the kids were gone. "Making progress?"

"Slow, but yes. Come on. Let me show you the new laundry room area."

The concrete slab for the new laundry slash mud room had been poured and the room was framed in, so Lydia got an idea of how large a room it was going to be...

"It's going to be huge," she said.

Cash chuckled. "It'll look a lot smaller when the washer and dryer get in there."

"Still, it beats what I have now."

Cash pointed to a couple of concrete blocks. "Step through the doorway that leads to the backyard and let's walk around to your new master suite."

"Oh. Master suite. I like the sound of that."

Cash had knocked out the end of the hall leading down to the bedrooms where a large closet had been. He'd made a door that would be the entrance to her new room.

"Here's what I decided. Instead of using more of the backyard, I found that I could go out through the closet and add on to the side of the house and extend into the back. That way, the kids keep most of the yardage for play."

She nodded. "Sounds reasonable."

"I built the extension over a crawlspace instead of a slab since it will be easier for all the new plumbing that'll be required for the master bath."

Laughing, she said, "Cash. I don't know anything about slab versus crawlspace, but I trust you. Whatever you think is best probably is."

She had known Cash for years, had watched him mature from a cocky bull rider, to a broken man on the edge of self-destruction, to a mature man confident in his abilities in construction. His marriage to Paige Ryan had been a weekend surprise to all the guests at the Montgomery family camping week last fall. In the eight months since then, she couldn't remember a happier Cash.

"How much time are we talking about to get this done?"

"At least another month."

"But your vacation," she protested.

He held up his hand. "Don't even start. My wife promised me a vacation to remember if I did this for you, regardless of how long it took."

Lydia laughed. "I'll have to thank Paige."

"I've got to get home. Okay if I go in and say bye to the girls?"

"Of course."

Later that night, after all the kids were in bed and she and Jason had collapsed on the sofa, he looked at her. "Living in all this construction is going to be noisy and dusty."

She shrugged. "I know."

"So while it's going on, why don't you and the kids

come stay at my place? Just temporarily," he added.

She gave the idea serious consideration, but given how strongly Jason didn't want children in his life, she couldn't make it okay in her mind to dump three small and potentially destructive children in his refurbished Victorian mansion.

"Thank you, I mean that, but I'll try it here. If it gets to be more than we can take, I'll think about it."

"The door's always open."

She kissed him. "Thanks."

FOR THE NEXT COUPLE OF WEEKS, LYDIA FOUND activities away from the house to keep the girls busy during the daytime. Swimming lessons at the Y. Beginning ballet classes at the dance academy. Gymnastics at the youth gym. She filled their days with activities. At night, all of them fell into bed in exhausted heaps. But she couldn't keep out of the house all day and then start cleaning it after everyone was asleep.

By the second week of construction, Cash moved the plastic off the kitchen entrance to cover the new laundry room door. That gave her the ability to cook, but she had to admit the housecleaning was sorely lacking.

Thanks to Jason's sister, Lydia found the ideal housekeeper and babysitter for the children, which would allow her to return to work by the end of May. Polly Henry began working for Lydia about halfway through the construction, keeping as much of the sawdust and mess out of Lydia's house as possible.

Luckily, the girls seemed to like her and she them. Levi was beginning to develop an awareness of strangers and new situations, so it took a little longer to win him over, but Mrs. Henry had the patience to wait him out.

With all the activities, the construction and the continued dealings with Meredith and Jim's estate, May flew by, and suddenly it was Memorial Day weekend. Whispering Springs loved any holiday, and Memorial Day was an excellent one, judging by the excitement in the city.

On the eve of Memorial Day, the biggest event in the county was the party thrown at Bar M Ranch. Lane and Jackie invited all the surrounding ranchers and most of the town out for a barbeque in the afternoon, followed by an extravagant fireworks show over the lake on the original homestead. Lydia had gone to this party for years as Jason's date, but taking the girls to see the fireworks gave her a renewed anticipation for the evening.

Memorial Day signaled the end of her sabbatical, and she faced that with mixed emotions. She loved being a doctor, the compilation of years of hard work, and she was proud of her accomplishments. Helping the sick and keeping the healthy from getting sick brought her a lot of satisfaction.

On the other hand, her sister had given her something she'd never thought she would experience...motherhood. Sure, motherhood had its good days and its not-so-good days, but caring for those three precious children had given her pride and satisfaction she'd never experienced from anything in her life thus far.

Sometimes at night, she would stand in the twins' bedroom and watch them sleep. The love she felt for them was powerful enough to bring her to her knees. She'd experienced love, she knew she had. She loved Jason, but what she felt when she looked at the children defied words.

At close to ten that morning, her phone rang.

"Hello?"

"Morning," Jason said. "How are things at Casa De Destruction?"

She got that familiar tug behind her belly button she always did when she heard his voice. "Messy."

"I wish you would have taken me up on my offer. The kids and you are still more than welcome at Chez Montgomery."

She shook her head, not that he could see her reaction. "And I appreciate the offer. I really do, but we're fine. Mrs. Henry is keeping most of the dirt and disorder under control. Cash and the guys he hired are doing their best to help, so we're fine. Plus, it gets me out of the house. The girls are loving the new classes. All their energy is burned by the time we get home. Did I tell you that Levi is crawling?"

He laughed. "No. Well, your days of freedom are over."

"Yeah, like I had any of those days anyway. So that's another reason it's probably good we didn't come to your place. All those beautiful knick-knacks the decorator sat around your place would be at high risk from little hands."

"Who cares? It's just stuff."

"Hold on a second. The timer is going off on the stove."

She set her cell on the counter and pulled an apple pie and a cherry cobbler from the oven and set them on the back of her stovetop to cool.

"I'm back. My pies are ready for this afternoon."

"What'd you bake this year? Tell me you made a cherry cobbler."

"A cherry what?" she teased. "Never heard of it."

"Not funny," he said. "I've got my mouth all set for your cobbler."

"Well, I'll see what I can do."

He chuckled. "Thought maybe you and the kids would go with me to Mom and Dad's this afternoon."

"You don't have to come get us. Since I got Meredith's SUV, I have loads of room."

"Well, how about I ride with you then?"

Her belly tug became a hard jerk. She hadn't seen him this whole week. He'd been in court representing a client on a complicated mail fraud case while she'd been hauling the children all over town. They'd talked on the phone in the evenings after the twins' fell asleep, but her brain was pretty much dead by that time, making intelligent, adult conversation difficult.

"Do you want to?"

"Sure. No sense in taking two cars. You know how tight the parking gets. Going together frees up a parking spot for someone else."

Ah. So he was being considerate more than really wanting to be around her and the children.

"If you want to, then fine. We'd love to have you. Do you need to be there early to help your dad with anything?"

"Not this year. With Cash and Travis living so close, they pulled the set-up job."

"Great. What time do you need to be there?"

"Dad is ringing the dinner bell at four, so maybe by three or so."

"That works for me. That's about the time I'd decided anyway."

"See you about two."

She'd already picked out her outfit for the barbeque,

but maybe she'd do a little more with her make-up before he arrived.

For some reason, the twins were irritable and had been arguing and fighting all morning. By noon, she was giving serious consideration to throwing in the towel and staying home, and she would have if she didn't think the girls would really love the fireworks. She put both girls in their beds and told them to stay there. She hoped maybe they would fall asleep and wake up in better moods. They didn't, of course. Why should fate make it easy on her?

Levi was a terror on knees. She spent most of the day finding items Levi shouldn't have, such as Jasper's dog biscuits, and putting them out of his tiny reach. Jasper loved having Levi on his level and barked and jumped over him as he crawled around the room. After lunch, she found Levi sucking on an ink pen, his lips and tongue a lovely shade of green.

Great. Her baby would go to the Montgomery party with kelly-green gums and everybody would talk about how she was out of her league trying to raise these children. She scrubbed his mouth and hands, successfully getting most of the color off. However, if she looked carefully, she could still see shades of green.

This mother thing was tough.

JASON PARKED IN FRONT OF LYDIA'S HOUSE. THE BIG, white Escalade filled her one-car driveway. The back of the SUV was open and he could see she had already begun to load the myriad of necessities required for three children.

He'd always been somewhat aware that his siblings

traveled with stuff for his nieces and nephews, but he'd never really given that much thought. Since he'd accepted the idea he'd never father children—which had taken him years to accept—he'd simply not mentally catalogued the various bits and pieces. Now, as he exited from his car, he realized how much stuff it took to move a child from one place to another. It gave him a new appreciation for his siblings. They made childrearing look so effortless when, in reality, it was far from it.

He hurried from the street in time to help Lydia store Levi's portable sleep pen.

"Thanks," she said.

"That everything?"

She laughed. "You are so funny."

He hadn't meant to be. "What can I do?" he asked.

"There are a couple of small suitcases by the front door. Can you bring those out? I want to do a little rear-ranging back here before we leave."

He found a pink suitcase and a purple one just inside the door. Good Lord. They were only going to his parents' house for a few hours. Did she really need to pack suitcases?

"These?" he called, holding them up.

She replied with a thumbs up, so he carried them to the Caddy.

"You do realize we aren't moving in at Bar M, right?" he joked.

"Honest to God, I had no idea all the stuff and junk required for kids. I really didn't."

"Why two suitcases?"

"Two changes of clothes, swimsuits, arm floaties, pajamas and an extra pair of shoes for each girl."

"You have got to be kidding."

"I wish. But you know they are going to want to get

into your parents' pool. And you know as well as I do that dinner will be on their shirts and shorts, requiring clean clothes. And the fireworks are so late that if I have them already in pajamas when we go to watch them, I won't have to wake the kids up when they get home to undress them. The extra set of clothes are just-in-case. " She grinned and pointed to her head. "Lessons learned over the last two months."

He loved when she smiled. A flock of butterflies always took off in his gut when he saw it.

He nodded. "You've come a long way, baby."

She laughed. "I guess I'd better warn you that Ellery and Annie are spatting today."

"About what?"

"Who knows. Neither of them would take a nap, so I'm hoping they'll fall asleep riding to your folks' place."

"Okay, no loud radio in the car. I've got it."

She grinned. "No singing either."

As the saying goes, he couldn't carry a tune in a bucket. "But," he protested, "my voice is so calming."

"Only to a barn screech owl, who thinks you're a relative."

Jason laughed. "Point taken." He rubbed his hands together. "Let's get this show on the road."

The girls greeted Jason with squeals, immediately hogtying him with arms around his knees. He walked across the room, lifting Annie on his left leg and Ellery on his right. They laughed with each step.

Lydia came down the hall with Levi perched on her hip. He chortled when he saw Jason and put his arms out. Jason took him and stood there…a girl on each leg and a baby on his hip. It was if he were swaddled in kiddie love. His heart swelled so large he could barely expand his lungs to take a breath.

Lydia picked up her car keys. "Okay then. Let's go." She headed for the front door, stopped and turned back. "You're mighty slow today, Counselor."

Jason laughed. "I've got kid moss growing on me."

"Okay, girls, let Jason go so we can get in the car."

Once they climbed off his feet and unwrapped their arms from his legs, he missed them immediately.

"Take my hands," Lydia said.

Each girl grabbed a hand and Jason, carrying Levi on his hip, followed them to the porch.

"Lydia?" Ellery said.

"Yes?"

"Are we going to ballet?"

"No, honey. Remember Mimi and Papa? We are going to their house."

"Oh, goodie," Ellery said.

"I love them," Annie said.

And Jason's heart split into a million pieces.

The drive took place during Ellery and Annie's nap time, so the girls nodded off about ten minutes into the forty-five-minute drive. The traffic along the narrow back road that led to the Bar M was heavy. Cars lined the drive all the way to the front door of his parents' place. Lydia pulled the SUV around the house to the parking area that been reserved for family. From all the other cars parked there, it looked as if he was the last Montgomery to arrive, but not by much. Mitch was just unloading his daughter from her car seat when Lydia turned off the engine.

"Hey, bro-in-law," Jason said as he stepped from the car.

Mitch nodded. "Nice new ride, Lydia."

"Thanks," Lydia said. "The extra room is such a luxury."

"More a necessity for us," Mitch said.

"For Lydia too," Jason said. "Don't let her kid you. That old car of hers was just too tiny for three kids and all the crap they require."

Mitch chuckled. "Crap is about right. Let me pass Eliza Grace off to Olivia and I'll come back and help you guys."

"Appreciate it."

Once Mitch was out of hearing range, he looked at Lydia. "He's a good guy. I'm so glad that he and Olivia got back together."

Lydia set the cooler from the rear seat on the roof. "I agree."

Ellery and Annie were stirring as Mitch came back with Jackie and Paige.

"We're here to help," Jackie announced. "Where are my precious girls?"

"Back here," Ellery cried from the rear seat.

"Get those girls out of there immediately," Jackie said to Jason. "I need some hugs."

"Yes, ma'am."

Jason got Annie from the car and set her on the ground. She ran over to his mother and threw her arms around Jackie's legs. Ellery followed her sister straight to Jackie. Lydia had taken Levi from his seat and he was straddling her hip. Paige held out her hands, but the little boy turned his head and wouldn't go to her.

"Sorry," Lydia said. "He's a little clingy these days."

"That's okay. I've got years for him to decide Aunt Paige is the best."

Jackie took both girls into the house while Mitch and Paige helped Jason haul in the bags, beds and food from the cargo space. For as far back as Jason could remember, his parents' house was always packed with people for this barbeque. Today was no exception. Most he knew. Some he recognized by sight, but the town was growing. New people were moving in every month. There were some strangers, and he made a point of keeping an eye on the children because of that.

He found Lydia in the yard, still holding Levi, and the girls sitting on his father's lap.

"Found you," he said.

Lydia smiled at him. "Thanks for getting everything unloaded."

"No problem. The girls not too freaked out by all the people?"

"Oh, yeah. They're pretty quiet. They're clinging to your mom and dad or me."

"I'm here. They're okay with me."

"Yes, but I don't want to stop you from having a good time. Go on. Find your friends. We'll be fine."

Okay, that hurt. She was sending him off like they weren't together, like she'd given him a ride to the party but having him beside her all evening would be an imposition.

"I'll just grab a beer. I'll be right back."

"No problem." She waved at Caroline and walked to where her partner stood.

He snatched a beer from one of the iced tubs, twisted off the top and flipped it into a trash barrel.

"Who pissed in your corn flakes?" Travis asked.

"Nobody," Jason said. He took a long draw off the beer, sucking down about half of it in one gulp.

"Yeah, it's as plain as the honking nose on your face that nothing's wrong."

Jason's gaze went to Lydia standing by Travis's wife. Levi's chubby legs hung down Lydia's body. He held a bottle to his mouth and rested his head on Lydia's shoulder. The image was too perfect, too sweet. Jason's heart sagged under all the emotional weight.

"Ah. Lydia. You're not jealous of the kids, are you?" Travis asked. "I mean, I realize you're not father material, but surely you don't begrudge them for halting your wedding. That's sick, bro."

"What? No, of course I don't hold anything against those kids. And what do you mean I'm not father material? Just what makes *you* father material and me not?" His tone heated with resentment. "Who are you to decide who would make a good father and who wouldn't?"

"Whoa. Slow down. I only meant that you never wanted all the responsibilities that go with raising kids. I've heard, heck, we've all heard you say for years that you love being an uncle but no thanks to fatherhood."

Jason poured the rest of the beer down his throat, which did nothing to extinguish the fire raging in his gut. But before he could respond, Annie pulled on the hem of his shorts.

"Jason?"

Annie had stopped using the term uncle. He wasn't sure if that was progress or regression in his relationship with her.

He picked her up and she clung to him like a monkey.

"Whatcha need, pumpkin?"

She whispered in his ear. "Potty."

He looked at Lydia in conversation with Caroline and decided he could handle this.

"Okay. Come on."

"Ellery too," Annie said.

He nodded.

"Be right back," he told his brother. "Nature calls."

Travis grinned but didn't say anything.

Ellery was at the back door, her hand between her legs with her legs crossed. Crap. He needed to hurry. The closest bathroom was the half-bath in his mother's laundry. He sure wasn't taking them to one of the many port-a-potties brought in for the event.

He grabbed Ellery's free hand and took her with them into the house, across the kitchen teaming with women—who surely knew more than he did about these things—and into the laundry room. Since Ellery appeared to be the one with the pressing problem, he got her on the toilet first, and not a moment too soon. He helped Ellery wash her hands when she was done while he kept an eye on Annie. Once both girls were done and hands washed, they went back through the kitchen.

"Everything all right, honey?" his mother asked.

"Everything's fine. Just a pit stop for my girls."

His mother's eyes widened and she smiled. "You should have said something. I would have taken them."

"We did fine. Come on, girls. Let's see what's going on outside."

"There you are," Lydia said the minute they were back outside. "Travis said you took them to the bathroom."

"Yeah. So?" He let go of the girls' hands and they wandered a few feet away to pet Tiger, the large barn cat who was stretched out on the patio.

"You should have come gotten me. I could have taken them."

"Yeah, you could have." He frowned. "But why does everyone seem to think that taking two little girls to potty is beyond my skill set?"

She scoffed. "I didn't say you couldn't do it. I said you didn't have to." She glanced toward the girls squatting down beside Tiger and lowered her voice. "I feel like I'm putting you in an impossible situation."

He reached over and played with Levi's dangling foot. "You're not. Want me to take him? He's got to be getting heavy."

"Actually, I thought I might take him inside and feed him dinner. That way I can actually eat later."

"Want me to do it?"

Her eyes warmed with her smile. "No, but can you keep an eye on the girls?"

"Sure."

Caroline joined them. "I thought I'd let Austin and Britney swim a little before dinner. Eliza Grace and Adam are coming along. Want me to take your girls?"

Ellery and Annie had gotten close enough to hear Caroline's offer.

"Yes, yes," the both cried.

"Please, Lydia," Ellery said.

"Yeah, please," Annie said.

Jason looked at her. "If you want to gossip with the women, Levi and I can find some manly things to do."

"We don't gossip," Caroline said with a huff. "We inform."

Jason chuckled. He adored his sister-in-law. In his opinion, she was the best thing that'd happen to Travis since his first wife had died so young.

"I stand corrected," he said, grinning. He held out his hands to Levi. "Come on, big guy." Levi fell into Jason's arms. "I'm thinking beer and steaks. What are you thinking?" he said to Levi.

"He's thinking strained peaches and turkey," Lydia said.

"Same thing," Jason said. "Where'd you put his bag?"

"Your old bedroom."

"I think I remember where that is." He settled the growing boy on his hip and headed back into the forest of women in his mother's kitchen.

LYDIA WATCHED JASON WALK OFF WITH LEVI CLINGING to him.

"For a man who was so adamant about not having children, he seems to be doing okay," Caroline observed.

"Yeah, but it's only been a couple of months. I can't see Jason changing his mind about fatherhood for the long haul. He was pretty adamant about that." Lydia shrugged. "He'll get tired of the whining, the crankiness, the dirty diapers, the constant vigil to make sure they are all right."

"Like you?" Caroline asked.

"Never. I love my kids." She glanced over at Annie and Ellery with Britney, all three girls sitting on the ground with the cat. "Come on, girls. We have to get you in your swimsuits if you want to get in the pool."

"You too, Britney," Caroline said.

Caroline's brother, Noah, a mature seventeen-year-old high school senior, was already in the pool when they returned with the children. Noah had lived with Caroline and Travis since he was a troubled fourteen-year-old runaway. Lydia remembered Noah as sort of a scrawny kid but work on the ranch had given him well-developed, muscular chest, broad shoulders and a well-defined six-pack abdomen.

"Lifeguard Noah reporting for duty," he said. "Hi, Lydia. Good to see you."

"You too, Noah." The girls stood in front of her,

their eyes glued to the boy, or really, young man, in the pool. "This is Ellery," she said putting her hand on Ellery's head, "and this is Annie. Girls, this is Noah. He's Ms. Caroline's brother." She wasn't really sure if they would get the familiar relationship but maybe if they linked him to Caroline in their minds, they'd probably think he was okay.

She didn't have to worry. Her girls were going to have fine taste in men as she saw their first boy crushes flare on Noah, not that she blamed them.

"Hello, ladies," Noah said, walking to the shallow end. "Want to come in with me?"

Britney and Austin wasted no time joining their uncle. Ellery and Annie were a little bashful as they walked down the steps.

Soon all the Montgomery kids were in the pool. Olivia dragged a chair over to where Lydia and Caroline were sitting watching their children in the water.

"God," Olivia said as she sat. "I feel like such a dirty old woman."

Lydia snorted. "Me too."

Caroline frowned, "What are you two talking about?"

"Your brother," Olivia said. "Don't tell me you haven't noticed the change in him since he arrived."

"Yeah," Lydia agreed. "Those high school girls aren't going to know what hit them."

Noah had been homeschooled up until his senior year. He'd asked to go to the local high school this fall for his final year.

Caroline sighed. "I thought if I ignored it, no one would notice all the changes."

"Again, dirty old women here—" Olivia pointed to herself and then to Lydia, "—and here."

"Yeah, sorry, Caroline, but he's a rockin' stud."

Caroline laughed. "Great. I have to keep all the high school girls away *and* fight off middle-age women."

"We are not middle-aged," Olivia huffed. "We are in our prime, right, Lydia?"

"Damn straight."

The three ladies chuckled.

Lydia indicated the pool with the tilt of her head. "My problem is that my girls have already fallen for him, an older man."

All three gazes shifted to the pool as they watched Ellery and Annie hanging on Noah.

"They are cute kids," Olivia said. "How are they doing? This has to be rough."

Lydia blew out a breath and took a sip of iced tea. "It has been so hard. They still cry some at night and ask for their mommy and daddy, but it's getting a little better. It's going to take time, I know that." She paused for a minute. "There are nights when I am so mad at Meredith and Jim for dying. Horrible, huh?"

"You know, that's normal," Caroline said.

"Yeah, but still, I feel terrible when I do. I wish we were a year down the road already. I think they will be adjusted better then."

"Are you kidding?" Olivia asked. "You're doing an incredible job. Look at them, Lydia. Just look. They are laughing right now. Their faces are bright and they are having fun. Sure, nights might be a little rough right now, but they are so tired at night. That allows all that sorrow to push through. But don't marginalize what a great job you've done stepping into your sister's shoes. There aren't many women who could jump in like you did."

"Sure there are. I mean, I didn't have a choice."

"Yeah, you did," Caroline said. "You could have sent them to your parents."

"No. That would never have worked. My folks are too old to start raising kids again."

"Doesn't matter. Grandparents get stuck raising their grandkids all the time, whether they want to or not. Like Olivia said, you're doing great. I'm impressed with my partner." Caroline held up her iced-tea glass, condensation dripping down the side from the day's warmth. "To the best new mom I know."

"I'll drink to that," Olivia said and clinked her wine glass to Caroline's iced tea.

"And thank God, I'll have my practice partner back on Tuesday," Caroline said with a laugh.

Lydia lifted her glass slowly. It made her feel good to hear two women she respected say such nice things about her. She might have blushed a little as her cheeks heated under their compliments.

"Thank you," she said, and meant it from the bottom of her heart.

Chapter Ten

Lydia got the girls through dinner with only a few barbeque stains on their white T-shirts, not to mention the strawberry ice cream drips. She left them in their dirty clothes to play since all the other children were sporting similar stains. She had to admit that having Jason help Ellery with dinner and leaving her free to deal with Annie had been heavenly. Levi had played in his portable playpen nearby and it had seemed easy to help one child eat while keeping an eye on another.

After dinner, the girls played with Britney and Eliza Grace and some kittens Lane brought up from the barn while the adults sat at picnic tables nearby.

Beside her, Jason's thigh was pressed tightly against hers. He'd rested his hand on the bench, letting his wrist rest casually on her ass. How, after all the years they'd been together, could the simple brush of his leg against hers or the heat from his hand on her butt bump her heart rate into overdrive and constrict her lungs?

She knew that right now, he was enjoying playing the role of pretend father, but he only got the good stuff. He didn't have to get up in the middle of the night to feed Levi, or stroke a crying child's back. He didn't know what it was like to be so exhausted in the morning that you couldn't remember whether you'd brushed your teeth or the girls'.

Jason came by after work, played, helped get them ready for bed and then sat with Lydia while she folded clothes or finally ate dinner at nine o'clock. Letting him stay the night was out of the question. She slept in the same room with a baby…a baby who farted, sniffed, shuffled around on his mattress, pooped, and did a lot of other activities that produced smells and sounds all night long.

From across the table, Jason's cousin-in-law, Porchia asked, "So, when are you two going to get your wedding going again? I froze your cake, but I figure you deserve a fresh one. I'd like to get you back on my baking calendar."

Porchia owned the local bakery and had recently started a small baking academy for students.

Beside her, Jason stopped talking to Cash. Lydia swallowed, although that was tough when all the moisture was gone from her mouth. She coughed, choking a little.

"Um, I don't know," Lydia replied. "Things are a little discombobulated in my life."

Porchia nodded, obviously not realizing how stressed the question made Lydia. "I get it. Well, give me at least a couple of weeks' notice, if you can. Otherwise, I'll have to defrost the original cake."

Lydia pushed a smile on her face. "You got it."

WHEN PORCHIA HAD ASKED HER QUESTION, JASON'S gaze had fallen to Lydia's hand. The engagement ring still hadn't been put back on. Sure, he believed her when she said it got in the way during bath time with Levi, but he was beginning to wonder if there was more to it than that. He frowned. Were they even still engaged? He hadn't a clue. He could ask her, but one of the tenets of cross-examination was to never ask a question that you didn't know the answer to. Lawyers did not like surprises. Surprises meant you hadn't done your homework.

Not that he would admit it to anyone, but he was afraid of her answer should he ask the question. If she said no, they were no longer engaged, then what were they? And if she said yes, they were still engaged, then why wasn't she wearing her ring and why wouldn't she set a date?

Had he done such a good job selling the idea that he didn't want children, rather than that he couldn't father children, that she believed him incapable of loving her nieces and nephew? Was it possible that she was choosing motherhood over marriage to him, and if so, did she think he'd make her choose?

"Want to take a walk? Exercise some of these calories off?" he whispered in Lydia's ear. The Montgomery brothers had a history of using the babysitting support to sneak off with their dates—or wives now for Travis and Cash—for a little reconnecting, as his mother liked to call it. Over the years, Lydia and he had found some interesting places to reconnect.

She shook her head. "I don't feel right leaving the children."

"My parents are right here. So are all my siblings and their spouses. They'll keep an eye on them."

She shifted on the bench until their gazes met.

"Those children are my responsibility. I am not going to ask other people to watch while we run off somewhere for some touch and tickle." Crossing her arms over her chest in a defensive poise, she added, "I'm a little astonished that you would even suggest it."

The repulsion in her eyes was like a slap. His head jerked back as though she'd struck him physically.

"Sorry," he said. "Excuse me. I'll be back."

He stood and stalked away. Damn. Maybe it was over with Lydia and he was too clueless to see it. Now that he thought about it, they'd had sex exactly one time since the night of her sister's accident.

He wasn't a total idiot. Of course he realized how hard she'd been hit by her sister's death and how different her life was now with the three children. But it wasn't as if they hadn't had opportunities to get naked and reconnect. They had. But she'd either been too tired or too stressed. Maybe she just wasn't interested.

The barn doors were open, so he paced down the aisle, stopping to stroke and talk with various horses who greeted him. He came to the ladder leading to the hayloft and chuckled. Growing up, he and Travis each had complicated signals involving a shovel, a bucket and a pitchfork to show when the hayloft was in use. They'd had to develop the signals or risk climbing in on something the other didn't want to see.

Tonight, the wooden rungs were unobstructed. The hayloft was available for trysts...not that Lydia appeared the least bit interested.

"Whatcha doing out here?"

Jason turned toward the voice. "Oh, hi, Lisa. Where's Joe Ray?"

Lisa Billings was the town librarian. Rumor had it, or rather his receptionist had told him, that Lisa had taken up with Joe Ray Arnold, the local bad boy who ran the best damn automotive repair shop in a four county region. At twenty-nine, Lisa was a little younger than him, but they certainly ran in the same circles.

Lisa was the furthest thing from the stereotype people pictured when librarian was mentioned. She was tall with long blond hair and a rockin' body that had every teenage boy in town taking up reading.

Lisa frown at his question. "I don't know where he is and I don't care."

"Oops. Did I put my foot in my mouth?"

"No." She sauntered to where he stood. "Not at all." Flipping her hair over her shoulder, she leaned against the loft ladder. "I saw you walk in here and you looked pissed."

"Did I?" He arched a brow. "I'm surprised you noticed."

"I've noticed you for a long time, Jason."

That took him aback. It had been a while, years even, since a woman had flirted so openly with him. He wasn't sure whether to be flattered and flirt back, or be cool and reserved since he was engaged.

Hell, he didn't even know if he *was* still engaged.

"Well, hell, Lisa. That's flattering."

She moved a little closer, very much into his personal space. "Sorry to hear your wedding got canceled."

He smiled. "Postponed."

Arching an eyebrow, she said, "Really? I heard that Lydia wasn't wearing an engagement ring any longer."

Jason loved living in a small, tight community. Liked knowing his neighbors. Liked them knowing him. But sometimes, Whispering Springs should be named Whispering Rumors.

"Just temporary," he assured her.

"Hmm." She leaned in a little more. If she moved much closer, her lips would brush his when she spoke. As it was, her breath brushed his mouth with each word. "Well, if that change becomes more, let's say, permanent, I hope you'll let me know. I love ranches, horses, living in Whispering Springs and—" her lips were millimeters from his, "—no children."

Her breath was minty and warm. As much as he didn't want to notice, his cock did. But it was damn near impossible for a guy not to notice an attractive woman, especially one who was expressing her interest so, um, interestingly.

"There you are, Jason," Lydia said.

Lisa jumped back, but she still gave him a sexy, whatever-you'd-like smile. "Nice talking to you. I'll be waiting to hear your suggestions on that permanent loan situation." She whirled around toward Lydia. "Hi, Lydia. I sent a card when you lost your sister, but I wanted to tell you in person how tragic the whole thing was. I'm so sorry for your loss."

"Thank you. I appreciate it. I don't mean to interrupt you and my guy's cozy little chat."

"Oh, no," Lisa said with a flip of her hand. "We're done. Better scoot." She waved over her head as she sauntered back down the barn aisle. "Later."

Lydia was carrying Levi on her hip and she adjusted her hold. "You left so abruptly."

"I was done. I told you I wanted to walk off dinner with a little exercise. As I remember, you turned me down flat." He held out his arms. "Here. Give him to me. You've been hauling him around for hours. Your back has to be getting tired."

Levi moved from her arms to his, the ever-present baby bottle conking the side of Jason's head as he got the baby settled. Levi rested his head on Jason's shoulder and something deep inside his soul mourned his inability to father children.

"You're upset," Lydia said, stating the obvious.

The muscles in his jaw tightened.

"Hell, yes, I'm pissed," he snapped.

"You're mad about the children. I know, I know," she hurried to say before he could correct her. "You don't want kids and here is your fiancée with three of them. Well, I'm sorry, but this situation isn't going to change for at least the next eighteen years. If you want to wait eighteen more years, I'm pretty sure we'd be safe from the childrearing dilemma."

He stared at her, so spitting mad he couldn't speak.

"Well, say something," she said.

"Fine. I'll say something. You're not wearing your ring."

She looked at her hands and then back at him. "I told you why I took it off."

"Yeah, it scratched Levi during his bath, but you never put it back on."

"So?"

"So I have to wonder why."

"What are you trying to say, Jason? Spit it out."

"It's quite simple. I'm trying to figure out if we are still engaged or not. There. Is that plain enough for you?"

Levi began to cry, probably because of their angry voices and the swirling tension in the air.

"Are you happy? Now you've gone and made him cry?" Lydia said, reaching for the baby.

He twisted so she couldn't take Levi. "Me?" he said in a whisper. He rubbed Levi's back as he pressed the baby more snuggly against him. He began to rock his body to soothe the child.

"It's okay, little guy," he said in a cooing voice. "Don't be upset. Everything's fine." He might have changed to a soft, calming voice, but he shot glares at Lydia. "Maybe we can discuss this later, like after little ears go to sleep."

"I'll look forward to it," she said, a sneer wrinkling her upper lip.

Lord knew he wasn't.

THE DRIVE BACK TO LYDIA'S HOUSE WAS MIGHTY quiet. All three children were asleep. Jason wasn't speaking. She, personally, didn't know what to say. Well, actually she did, but it might be cutting off her nose to spite her face, as her mother used to say.

"You and the new librarian sure were getting friendly."

Jason looked at her. "Innocent party here."

"Honey, I'm pretty sure I couldn't have slipped my business card between your two mouths if I'd tried."

"Again, innocent party. Minding my own business when Lisa followed me to the barn."

"Hmm."

"Don't give me that, Lydia. I am totally in the right here.

She sighed. "Maybe you're right. Maybe I'm not being fair to you."

"What do you mean?"

"I appreciate all you do for us, the kids and me. I know this isn't really what you bargained for when you asked me to marry you."

"Maybe not, but marriage means taking whatever life throws at you."

"But we're not married."

"We would be by now," he said. He reached over and stroked her cheek. "I love you, Lydia. I've loved you for a long time. Hell, maybe since I first laid eyes on you."

She smiled. "You were determined that night, weren't you?"

"All I knew was that I had to get to know you."

Glancing toward him, she said, "That was a long time ago."

"Seems like yesterday."

"How did the years pass so fast?"

He sighed. "I don't know. I should not have let you talk me into waiting to get married. I should have driven you straight to Vegas."

She laughed. "You mean instead of taking me to breakfast after we met, you should have hustled me straight to the Elvis Presley wedding chapel?"

"Would you have gone?"

Smiling, she shook her head. "Who knows? I was coming off a thirty-six-hour shift. You probably could have talked me into anything."

"So I'm forgiven that I'm such a hunk that a beautiful woman followed me into the barn and tried to have her way with me?"

Chuckling, she said, "You are, but I might have to have a talk with the town librarian."

DURING HER LAST FOUR DAYS OFF WORK, LYDIA SPENT time with Mrs. Henry, making sure she and the children were comfortable with each other. The plan, if it worked, was for Mrs. Henry to keep the children at home on Monday through Thursday. On Fridays, she had a standing appointment to get her hair fixed and nails painted for church on Sunday. That worked great for Lydia. She could ease back into the office at four days a week. There was a mothers'-day-out program at the Whispering Springs United Methodist Church on Fridays. She booked Ellery and Annie into the morning sessions, deciding they needed the socialization with other children.

She was ready to head back to the office. She only hoped she didn't use the words pee-pee or poo-poo with any of her patients. After two months with the girls and Levi and Disney theme songs, her brain was turning to mush. She was looking forward to some adult conversation…if she could remember how.

The morning of her first day back at work arrived and, of course, fate thought it a great idea to throw a monkey wrench into her plans. She had the girls up and having breakfast when Mrs. Henry called to say she wasn't feeling well. Taking the children to the office with her was a horrible plan, but she didn't have a backup at the moment and she really needed to get back to work.

Cash was parking his truck at the curb as she was trying to herd everyone into the SUV.

"Morning," he called.

"Morning. When am I going to have my own bath?"

He laughed. "Soon. I promise." He smiled at the twins. "Good morning, ladies."

Now that he'd been around a lot, Ellery and Annie had become quite attached to Cash and his smile, which Lydia could understand. She'd become quite fond of Jason's little brother too. Without him, she and the three kids would still be trying to survive in a two bedroom, one bath house. The girls ran over to him.

"Guess what?" Ellery said.

He squatted. "What?"

"Our babysitter is sick and we get to go to the office today."

He rolled his gaze up to Lydia. "Well, that's going to be quite the adventure."

"I know," Lydia said. "But we'll have to do the best we can. Come on, girls. Climb in your seats."

"What's wrong with Mrs. Henry?"

"She thinks it's food poisoning from something she ate yesterday at a church picnic. She's coming to the office later this morning so I can check her out."

"How are you going to work with the kids running around?"

"I don't know," she said brusquely. "Sorry. I'm a little stressed."

"What can I do to help?"

"Nothing. No, wait. Finish my house."

"Two more weeks. Maybe three, and then I'll be out of your hair."

Lydia bussed a kiss on his cheek. "Thank you. Sorry I snapped at you."

He chuckled. "That's nothing. You should see Paige when I'm really in trouble."

She grinned. "Have a good day."

"You too."

She made a quick stop at the dry cleaners to pick up her white lab coats and then headed to Whispering Springs Medical Clinic. When she pulled into the staff parking area in the rear, she was surprised to find Jason leaning against his SUV.

"Morning," she said, climbing from the driver's seat. "What are you doing here? Are you sick?"

He straightened. "Nope. Just missing my girls and my favorite guy."

"Sorry we didn't make dinner at your folks' house last night, but I had so much to get done before this morning."

"No problem, but you were all greatly missed."

She crossed her arms. "Jason Montgomery. You are not here because you were lonely. What's going on?"

"I came to get the kids. I thought they might like to spend the day at my office."

She laughed. "You're kidding, right?"

He shook his head.

"You're not kidding?" She narrowed her eyes into a squint. "What brought on this sudden urge to babysit? Did your brother call you?"

"My brother? What are you talking about?"

"Lord, I hope you are better in the courtroom in front of a jury than you are right now."

"Look, I might have talked to Cash."

She waved him off. "We'll be fine. Really."

He sighed. "Honey, you can't see patients with a couple of three-year-olds and an eighth-month-old who's mobile."

"I'll figure it out. You don't have to rescue me."

"Rescue you? Never. I was rescuing the girls." He leaned over and looked in the back window. "Right, girls? You want to spend the day playing with me, right?"

"Jason. Stop it. You can't want to do this."

He stood. "Sure I do. I have absolutely nothing on my schedule that can't be changed. Plus, KC's in the office today and so is Margie."

She hesitated.

"It'll be fine. If it's not, I'll call you, okay? Except I'll need to take your Cadillac. No sense to load all that stuff I know you have into my car so I can unload it at my office." He wiggled his fingers. "Hand over the keys and kids."

She sighed. "I'll try to make it a short day."

"Don't worry about it. We'll be fine. I have matches in my office they can play with and when they are done with those, I'm pretty sure I can find some sharp knives around."

"Ha. Ha."

He kissed her. "Go play doctor."

"If you're sure…"

"I'm sure. Go."

He lifted the car keys off her finger. "Go," he said again. Then he climbed into the Cadillac and pulled out of the parking lot.

———

ONCE JASON GOT TO HIS OFFICE AND PARKED, HE WAS at a loss of how to proceed. He couldn't leave the children in the car while he unloaded all of the bags and crib that were essential for the day. On the other hand, he couldn't turn them loose in the office while he ran back and forth. Other parents made this look so easy.

Think. He was a smart guy. He could do this.

Since the office parking area was behind the building, there was no traffic to be concerned about. So his first step was to release the Krakens, er, the twins.

"Okay, ladies," he said as he lifted Ellery out of the car and set her on her feet next to her sister. "You stand right here while I get Levi out."

He turned back to the car to unfasten Levi from the

more confusing tangle of straps. Finally, he lifted him out and turned back only to find the girls roaming around the lot.

"Annie. Ellery. Get back over here."

As one, their heads snapped up at the sound of his voice. Bright smiles popped onto their faces…smiles so sweet that there was no way he could scold them the way he should. Holding hands, they skipped back to where he stood.

"Think you girls could help me with your bags?"

They nodded.

"Great."

With Levi riding on his hip, Jason popped the hatch. In the back, Lydia had stored Levi's portable playpen, a diaper bag, an insulated cooler and two small suitcases. The cases were new, or at least he'd never seen them before. They had rollers on the bottom and an extension handle. He set them on the pavement and then looped the cooler's long strap and the diaper bag over his shoulder. Levi's portable corral would have to wait.

"Do you two think you can pull these?" he asked as he extended one handle and then the other on the roller bags.

They nodded. Each girl grabbed a handle and pulled. Surprisingly, they had no trouble tugging the cases.

He locked the car and started toward the rear employee door.

"Y'all stay with me, okay? Don't go wandering off."

Ellery and Annie did as he asked, following him into the building and walking the short distance to his office.

One of the perks of being the founding partner was his larger office toward the rear of the building. The entire office wasn't comprised of a huge amount of space. It'd been adequate when he'd begun practice with only him and his assistant, Margie. Then he'd added his cousin, KC Gentry.

He hadn't planned to take on another lawyer into the practice, but last fall he'd added Michael Buchannan. Now that KC was weeks, if not days away from delivering her first baby, adding Michael to pick up some of the workload looked like Jason had the gift of prophesy.

Jason had expected only him and Margie to be in the office today. Michael was out of town on an oil contract deal with a company in Denver. KC was hit or miss these days. But that was fine. Even on days when she stayed home, the woman could produce an impressive volume of work.

"Hey, Margie," he called. "Can you come here for a minute?" He opened the door to his office and shepherded the girls inside. "This is where we'll be playing today."

His office was comprised of two distinct areas, although there was no physical separation between them. His work area contained his desk, visitor chairs, a credenza and files. He used the other half of the room, the space closer to the office reception area and the entrance for clients, as an informal living room. It contained a sofa, wingback chairs, end tables with lamps and an office phone. A large, brightly patterned rug pulled it all together.

Sometimes, his clients needed the informality of this area. And sometimes his office space worked best.

"You bellowed, Master?" Margie said as she stepped into his office. Her eyes widened, followed by a smile. "We have visitors." She dropped to one knee. "Hello. I'm Margie."

The girls wrapped their arms around his legs.

"Isn't it great? Ellery, Annie and Levi are going to be here all day."

"Well," she said on a long exhale. "How fun."

"I need to get Levi's portable crib from the car. I was going to ask you to stay here while I did but…" He looked down at the girls adhered to him. "That idea might not work."

"Is it something I can carry?"

"It's not that heavy. Lydia can carry it easy enough." He passed her the keys. "It's in the back of the white Cadillac."

She arched an eyebrow. "New car?"

He chuckled. "Not mine. Hers."

"Be right back."

While she was gone, he got the twins plucked from his legs and settled in the living room area with paper and crayons. He set a ream of used paper on the floor. Printed on only one side, the paper would be put to good use for their drawing.

It didn't take Margie long to haul the portable pen in. "Where do you want it?"

He looked at the girls with their toys, crayons and paper spread out on the rug and then to the space on the other side of his desk.

"I think over here," he said, lifting his chin toward the space beside his desk. "In the long run, it might work better."

"Want me to help set it up?"

He shook his head. "It's a little tricky the first time, so how about you take Levi?"

Margie smiled and lifted the infant from his arms and then groaned. "Wow. He's a, um, solid one, isn't he?"

Jason chuckled as he started setting up the portable

playpen. "He's a little over twenty pounds, I think. Got an appetite like a defensive linebacker."

"Hey, sweet boy," Margie said with a soft voice. "You are quite a looker."

Levi gave her a hard stare and must have decided she was okay because he settled against her chest.

"It's been a while since I've held a baby," Margie said. "I've forgotten how much a strain they are on the back, not to mention hot to hold."

Jason looked at her. "Do you think he has a fever?"

"Calm down. I didn't say that," she said. "He's fine. I meant that holding a little person so closely against me makes me hot…and not like that either."

He chuckled as he locked the side in place, followed by the padded bottom. "There." He turned and held his arms out. "I'll take him or you can set him down on the floor, but watch out. He's crawling."

Margie swung away from him. "I'm not ready to give him up yet."

"You will be. I'd be willing to bet there's a diaper that needs a little work."

She shrugged. "I have grandchildren, although they're all past the diaper age. I know what to do." She checked the back of Levi's pants. "We're fine."

"Surprising."

The office phone rang. "That's my cue. Gotta go." Margie handed over Levi and lifted the receiver on Jason's desk. "Good day. Montgomery and Montgomery. How can we help you?"

Jason pushed a piece of paper and pen toward her. While she was on the phone, he and Levi went over to where the girls were coloring. Sheets and sheets of paper littered the floor. He sat in one of the chairs and put Levi on the floor. Levi immediately went to his hands and knees and began crawling away.

"Come back here," he said with a laugh.

Margie hung up the phone.

"For me?" Jason asked.

"Nope. For Michael."

"He turning into a rainmaker?"

She laughed. "Only if by rainmaker you mean drawing all the single women to the office." Waving the paper she'd written on, she added, "This one was the librarian."

"Lisa?"

That brought a surprised expression to Margie's face. "You actually know the name of the new town librarian?"

Heat crawled up his neck. "She and I crossed paths over the weekend. Anyway, what did she need? Since Mike's away, is there something I can do for her?"

"Only if you're free for dinner on Friday."

"Probably not a good idea."

"Nope, probably not. Your fiancée might object."

Hearing his assistant call Lydia his fiancée sent a quiver into his gut. Was she? Or had she decided to permanently postpone their wedding? He was saved from replying when the office phone began to trill again.

"First day back after a holiday. It's going to be a wild one," Margie said and hurried from his office to her desk to grab the phone.

He glanced around for Levi and found him pulling on the electrical cord of a lamp. "Oops." A couple of giant steps put him beside the baby. "Not a good thing to be playing with." He unwound Levi's fingers from the cord, trying to decide if he should unplug the lamp or secure the cord.

"Jason?"

"Hmm?" he replied.

"I'm hungry."

Annie stood looking up at him.

"Did you have breakfast?"

She shrugged. "I don't know."

Knowing Lydia as well as he did, he was positive the girls had eaten, but if they were hungry, they were hungry. He checked the cooler he'd sat by his desk and found juice, milk, bottles of formula, cheese and crackers. After putting Levi in his playpen, he got the girls settled with juice and cheese and crackers.

Finally, ninety minutes after they'd arrived, he sat at his desk and pulled up the estate will he was preparing. It wasn't long before he felt a tug on his pants leg.

"Yes?" he asked, looking down into Ellery's green eyes.

"I'm bored."

"Me too," Annie said.

How did Lydia, or any parent, do this all day, every day? Levi was easy compared to the attention span of three-year-olds.

"Well," he said. "Would you like to watch some television?"

"Yes," Ellery shouted. "SpongeBob."

Since he had no earthly idea who or what SpongeBob was, he flipped on the flat screen TV and found a cartoon network showing the old cartoons like Bugs Bunny, so he left it there. The idea showed merit when the girls dropped to the floor, cross-legged, and became engrossed in the action.

Levi was getting restless. A quick sniff at Levi's bottom had Jason's head snapping back.

"Good Lord, little man. What did you eat?"

Levi's face screwed up for a cry.

"Now, now. No reason to be doing that. Come on," he said, lifting the baby out and laying him on a blanket. "Let's see what we've got."

He'd just gotten Levi's pants unsnapped when his door opened.

"You in here?" KC asked.

"Down here," he answered. "Shut the door."

"What smells? Oh, I see," she added as she stepped around his desk. "You know, this is a side of you I bet no one has ever seen. In fact, you could have won a lot of money off me."

"What are you blabbering about?" He ripped the tape off the sides of the diaper and pulled it down.

"You. A diaper change? Who are you and what have you done with my cousin?"

"Ha. Ha. Oops," he said, putting the diaper back over Levi as he let loose with a stream of pee.

"Nice catch."

Jason looked up with a grin. "I learned that one the hard way." He turned back to the baby. "Okay, now that we've gotten that out of the way, let's get the rest of your mess cleaned up."

Once the diaper was off, Jason reached for baby wipes, his other hand holding Levi in one place. "Scoot the trash can over closer, will ya?"

KC pushed the can over with her foot. "You can't leave that diaper in here all day."

"Like I don't know that."

She giggled. "What kind of blackmail pictures does Lydia have of you? Must be something powerful for you to be here alone with three children."

"I can take care of three children. Why does everyone think I'm inept when it comes to kids?"

"Maybe because you've always been so outspoken about not wanting any."

He shrugged. "It's not that hard."

Laughing, KC took a seat in his big, leather desk chair. "You say that now, but I'll check back after lunch. I bet you're singing a different tune."

"When are you going out on maternity leave?"

"God, I hope soon. My feet are swollen. I'm the size of a whale. I'm completely miserable."

Jason stood, lifting Levi to his hip. "How much longer?"

"A couple of weeks." She stood. "I'm going home so I can sit around in something more comfortable."

He checked his watch. "Well, it is almost ten-thirty. Another full day at the office."

Laughing as she struggled to her feet, she said, "Bite me." She pulled the liner from his trash and tied the top into a knot. "I'll do you a solid and take this with me."

"Thanks."

Levi drank a bottle of formula after KC left and was happy to play in his pen with the toys Lydia had packed. Jason had gotten a whole two paragraphs reviewed when Annie tugged at his pant leg.

"Whatcha need, honey?"

"Potty."

After both girls hit the bathroom and he got them back into his office, a loud game of screaming while weaving in and around all the furniture in his office ensued.

And that's pretty much how his entire morning went, meaning he didn't get through one page of review.

Finally, at noon, when his hearing and his nerves had had all they could take, he suggested lunch, which was met with jumping enthusiasm. Margie kept Levi while he took the twins out to lunch for chicken strips and fries, thinking—or maybe hoping—that maybe the carbo load would give them heavy eyelids after lunch. He made a mental note to do something extremely nice for Margie after today was over. A massage maybe?

He took the twins to a well-known local cafe with outside seating that catered to the youngest customers, which he decided was a brilliant decision on his part after numerous spills of honey mustard, catsup and one glass of milk.

It was close to two by the time he and the twins parked back at his office. He exited Lydia's new SUV and removed them from the back seat.

"I wanna ride in," Annie said, her arms lifted toward him.

"Sure." He swung her up and onto his shoulders for the ride. That action was met with squeals of giggles.

Ellery stepped on top of his once-polished loafers and wrapped her arms around his waist. "Walk," she demanded.

He chuckled and shuffled forward. The twins' giggles were loud and echoed into his lobby as he walked to his office door with stiff legs.

"Duck," he said to Annie as he opened his door. The sight that met him sent an eddy loose in his gut.

Lydia sat in his desk chair holding Levi. Long strands of hair curled over her shoulders and down her arms. The minute her head lifted and she saw him and the girls, a bright smile broke across her face.

"Got yourself quite the load, Counselor."

He laughed, set Ellery off his feet and then lifted Annie off his shoulders and set her on her feet.

"Lydia," both girls shouted and ran to where she was sitting.

"We went to lunch," Ellery announced.

"You did? What did you eat?"

"Ice cream," Annie answered.

Lydia rolled her gaze up to him. He held up his hands.

"For dessert. They had chicken strips and fries for lunch, right girls?"

They nodded.

Lydia lifted the tale of Ellery's shirt and studied the stain here. "I'd say you had chocolate ice cream and—" she studied Annie's shirt, "—strawberry."

The twins nodded.

"Can you two go pick up all your papers so I can talk to Jason?"

Ellery and Annie ran to the seating area and began stacking the sheets of paper that littered his office.

Jason went over to her, leaned down and kissed her. "Good to see you, but what are you doing here so early?"

Levi held up his arms to Jason and he picked the baby up from Lydia's lap.

"Mom and Dad are in town. They called a little while ago."

Jason stroked Levi's back. "Is something wrong? Why are they here?"

She shrugged. "I have no idea. They're coming over for dinner and to see the kids this evening. I thought I'd better get them home and cleaned up before my folks arrive. I don't want them to think I'm doing a crappy job."

He leaned over for another kiss. "Nobody would ever suggest that. You are doing a fantastic job with the kids."

"Maybe, but I need to get something going for dinner too."

"Just call Di Roma's and get a family lasagna to go. Want me to pick one up and bring it over tonight?"

"Thanks, but no. It's a good suggestion though. I think I'll do that, but I think it might be better if we have just the family at dinner tonight."

Just the family? Her words stung.

"What? I'm not family?" he asked, trying to keep a teasing tone to his voice.

She chuckled. "You know what I mean."

No, no, he didn't, but he let it go.

"We're done," Annie stated, setting all the collected paper on Jason's desk.

"Good," he said. "Very good."

Lydia stood. "We need to get going, girls. Grandma and Grandpa are coming over tonight."

That statement caused more shrieks and jumping.

Jason passed Levi to Lydia and then squatted. "Come here and give me a kiss bye." He held out his arms and both girls flew into them and he gave each of them a kiss. "I sure had fun with you two today. Did you have fun?"

Both blond tikes nodded.

"Good. We'll do it again sometime, okay?"

He stood. "See ya, big guy," he said to Levi. "Don't let the dirty diapers get you down."

Lydia chuckled. "Okay, gang. Let's move it."

Once the foursome was gone, taking all their kid necessities with them, his office was too quiet and too neat.

Chapter Eleven

J ason's suggestion to pick up Di Roma's was a time-saving, brilliant idea. Lydia had time to give all the children quick baths before her parents were scheduled to arrive. The lasagna was warming in the oven with the garlic bread sticks and there was a salad in the refrigerator awaiting dressing. The table was set and she'd had time to run a fast vacuum around to suck up as much Jasper shedding as possible. She was ready.

Her parents were scheduled to arrive at six, so a little before that she headed to the laundry room to fold a load of clothes. She'd just finished folding up a sheet when the doorbell rang.

"I'll get it," Ellery yelled.

"Wait," she called. "Don't open that door until I get there."

The next thing she heard was her mother's voice. "Ellery! Annie! I can't believe how much you've grown in only a couple of months."

"Tomorrow, I'm buying a deadlock," Lydia muttered to herself. "I'm coming," she called.

By the time she reached the living room, which was really only a few steps, her parents had their arms around the twins—Annie with her dad and Ellery with her mom.

"Hi, Mom. Dad," Lydia said.

Her mom straightened. "Hi, honey." She hurried over and embraced Lydia in a tight hug. "How are you? You're looking great. The kids look great. Where's Levi?"

Lydia laughed. "Slow down, Mom. Levi is in the kitchen, probably making a mess with the cracker I gave him."

Her mom chuckled. "Sorry. I'm just so glad to see everybody."

Lydia kissed her mom's cheek. "And we are glad to see you two also."

"Smells good in here," her father said.

"Thanks. We're having your favorite tonight."

"Lasagna?" Larry asked.

"Yep."

"We're hungry," Ellery said.

Annie nodded. "Me too."

Lydia looked at her parents. "Dinner's ready if you are."

Her father rubbed his stomach. "Starved."

"I could eat," Ida said.

"Come on then," Lydia said. "We can eat and you two can tell me why the surprise visit."

As soon as Levi saw his grandparents, he began banging his cracker on the edge of his playpen. "Babababababababa," he shouted.

"Hey, sweetheart," her mother said and lifted the nine-month baby into her arms. "He's grown so much," she said. "Hi, Levi. Hi." She jiggled him in her arms.

Levi laughed and cooed.

Larry grinned. "Watch your back, Ida. Looks like the boy has gained a few pounds."

Ida shook her head and continued talking to her grandson in a playful voice. "Don't pay any attention to your grandpa. You are perfect."

Lydia held out her arms. "Let me have him. I'll feed him while we are all eating.

Lydia plated up the piping-hot lasagna onto plates and set them on the table. Finally, she took her seat at the head of the table by Levi.

"This is delicious," her mother said after her first bite. "I really had no idea you could cook like this."

Lydia laughed. "I wish. Picked this up at Di Roma's on the way home."

Larry pointed his fork at Lydia. "You can serve this to me anytime."

Lydia spooned a bite of pureed peaches into Levi's mouth. "Not that I'm not thrilled to have you guys here, but other than seeing your grandbabies, is there another reason you're in town?" Her gaze went to her dad. "Are you having trouble with the stent you had done in Dallas?"

"Nope," he said. "I'm doing great. Feel better than I have in a while."

She nodded. "Your color's better too."

Ida set her fork on the side of her plate. "We do have some news." She smiled as she looked to her husband and then to Lydia. "We're moving to Whispering Springs."

An electrical jolt hit Lydia. "What? When? What?"

Her mother chuckled. "Surprised you, huh? Glad we can still do that."

"Surprised? Yes, but thrilled. What brought on this decision?"

Larry took a swallow of his iced tea and said, "We have all evening to talk about the whys." He rolled his gaze down to Annie and back up. "For now, let's just be happy we'll all be together."

Lydia nodded, getting his nonverbal message that he didn't want to explain their move in front of the children, but she worried there was more to their relocation. Dallas had some of the world's best cardiac doctors, and the concern that there was more wrong with her father's heart than she knew sprouted in her mind.

"Love your new laundry room," her mother said, pointing toward the open door in the kitchen. "You needed that."

"With these three, more than ever," Lydia agreed. "But wait until you see the new bedroom and bath I'm adding. Poor Levi will finally have a bedroom to himself."

"Poor Levi or poor Lydia?" her mother asked with a chuckle.

Grinning, Lydia said, "A little of both."

When dinner was over, Ida and Larry took the twins to their bedroom to get ready for bed. Since they'd had a bath this afternoon, albeit a quick one, getting them into pajamas would be simple. Meantime, she cleaned up Levi and got him into a sleep shirt for the night. It took another hour and a gallon of little girl tears before Ellery and Annie would part from their grandparents and go to bed.

At close to nine, Lydia dropped onto the sofa beside her mother. "I am so glad to see you guys."

Her mother put her arm around Lydia and hugged. "Us too, honey."

"Now, what's going on?" Lydia looked at her father. "Is it your heart?"

"What?" her dad said. "No, no. I'm fine. But your mother and I have been talking."

Her mother turned on the sofa to face Lydia. "Your father and I always talked about how we needed to get up to Kansas more often to see Meredith and the children. And we did go, but not enough. It always felt like something we could do tomorrow. And then…" She drew in a stuttering breath. "And then our baby died."

Lydia placed her hand on her mother's arm. "No parent should have to bury their child."

A tear trickled down her mother's face. "We can't control life." Ida wiped the tear with the back of her hand. "But we can control where we live. We want to be near you and near our grandchildren. We want to watch them grow up, be a part of their lives."

Lydia understood what her parents were saying, but there was one thing she had to be clear on. "Okay. I can see that but tell me the truth. Are you wanting to move here because you don't think I can do this? Raise Meredith's children as well as she could?"

Ida's mouth dropped open. "What? No! Of course not."

"Absolutely not," Larry said. "The children look great. Happy. Growing like weeds."

"And then there's your father's heart," Ida said. "That scared the poop out of both of us. We got home to Florida, looked at each other and asked what we were doing there when we wanted to be up here? But we also knew that we had to deal with your dad's heart issues before we could begin to think about moving."

Lydia looked at her dad. "And you swear your cardiologist gave you walking papers?"

Larry held up the three-finger Boy Scout salute. "Scout's honor."

Lydia grinned. "In that case, this is great." She hugged her mother and then went over to where her father sat to give him a tight squeeze. "I know Ellery and Annie will be thrilled to have you close. I am so happy that Levi will get to know his grandparents." She retook her seat. "Have you given any thought to the type of house you want to look for?"

Her parents exchanged a glance.

"Okay, I saw that," Lydia said. "What's up with the house? Why are you two acting so squirrely?"

"Well—" her mother shrugged, "—we have already found a house to rent."

"Really?" Lydia's tone betrayed her surprise. "Already? When did you get to Whispering Springs?"

"Today."

"And you've already found a house? Where?"

Her mother chuckled. "We haven't actually seen it yet, but it's only two houses down."

"You rented a house on this street? How? Whose?"

"I was chatting with Jackie Montgomery the other day—"

"Somehow I should have known Jason's mother was involved in this."

"Not really," her mother said. "Jackie and I talk on the phone often. Anyway, I mentioned to her that Larry and I had been thinking about moving here, and she said that her nephew had recently married a girl who lived here and that the girl had a house close to you."

Lydia nodded. "Darren. Right. He married Porchia Summers."

"Jackie called Porchia, who was happy to rent to us for a while until she decides what she wants to do with her house." Her mother leaned in. "I was thinking that we could rent for a while, and then after you and Jason marry and you move into his house, your father and I could buy this place from you."

Lydia's heart sank. No matter what happened in her life, everything seemed to circle back around to her not-going-to-happen marriage. She sighed.

"I don't think there is going to be a marriage."

Ida's eyes opened wide. "What? Why in the world not? You and Jason are perfect together." Her face turned harsh. "Did he do something?"

Lydia shook her head. "No. I did. I took in three children."

"Jason resents Meredith's children?"

"No, no. Nothing like that, but he never wanted children. Ever. He's been dead set against having a family since I met him. He's done great with the kids, but for the long term? I don't think it's right to tie him down with them." She leaned against the back of the couch and looked up at the ceiling. "I don't see that I have much of a choice but to break it off with him permanently."

"Have you asked him?" her father said. "Sounds like something he should have a say in."

Lydia looked toward her dad. "No, and I'm not going to. Jason is a wonderful man. He's honest and dependable. But I know him. He would stay with me out of loyalty, because in his mind, he made a commitment to marry me. He's the type of guy who stands by his word. But it wouldn't be fair for me to tie him into a situation he made no bones about not wanting."

"Are you sure, honey?" her mother asked.

Lydia shrugged. "Who can be sure about anything, Mom? This just seems like the right thing to do. I need to give Jason his walking papers so he can find someone else who can give him the life he wants." As the reality of her words settled in her heart, she rubbed at the pain in her chest.

LYDIA'S CONVERSATION WITH HER PARENTS REPLAYED over and over in her mind as she saw patients the next couple of days. She'd meant what she'd told them. She loved Jason more than she could put into words. However, she also realized she loved him enough to let him go, to push him to find the kind of life he wanted even though it meant seeing him with someone else.

It was long past time that she was honest with him and give him back the engagement ring. But actually ending it, giving his ring back to him, was too painful to think about, so she kept shoving reality to the back of her mind.

"Dr. Henson?"

Lydia looked up at her office door at the front desk receptionist.

"You have a call on line four."

"Thanks." She lifted the receiver. "Dr. Henson."

"Good afternoon," Jason said. "Your first full week back at work is half over. How's it been?"

His deep voice scattered the butterflies in her belly. Her heart rate picked up. An involuntary smile pulled at her lips.

"Pretty good. I haven't yet asked for a pee-pee sample, so I think I'm ahead of the game. How's your case going?"

"Rough. I didn't get home until midnight last night and was in court at nine this morning." He sighed. "I have really missed you, missed talking to you."

The boulder in her throat prevented her from replying, it didn't stop the tears that built in her eyes. How would she ever learn to live without him?

"How did Monday night go with your folks? Why are they here?"

"They surprised me with the news that they are moving to Whispering Springs."

"Really? That's great news, right?"

"Yes, it is. I want the kids to know their grandparents, and honestly, I like having them closer to me. Dad scared me with his heart. Made me realize they aren't as young as they used to be."

"None of us are, babe."

His comment elbowed the guilt inside her. He wasn't getting any younger. She'd made him wait while she got her professional life going. First, through her residency and then while she got her practice up and going. It wasn't fair to ask him to wait again while she got her personal life back on track.

"I'm glad they're coming here, but…"

"But?"

"Nothing. Think you could run by this evening after work?"

"Wish I could, but I'll be stuck at the office until midnight again, and I've got court first thing in the morning. How about I come by tomorrow night? That work for you?"

"Let's do Friday night instead. That okay?"

"Sure. Probably better anyway. Depending on how my case goes on Thursday, I could end up working late again."

"Okay. Friday night then."

"Friday night," he repeated. "I can't wait to see you. I've been missing you like crazy. And the kids too," he added as though an afterthought.

"Great. I'll see you at my house. We need to talk."

FRIDAY NIGHT, JASON PARKED IN FRONT OF LYDIA'S house, pleased to see that Cash was almost done with the addition. Once he and Lydia married and moved everyone into his house, these additions would add quite a bit of value to the property. She should make a nice, tidy profit when she sold it. Whispering Springs's population was exploding and housing was getting tight. Buying instead of renting had been an excellent financial decision on Lydia's part.

He knocked on the door.

"I'll get it," a young voice yelled seconds before the door was flung open.

"Jason," Ellery yelled. "Lydia. It's Jason."

Lydia came from the kitchen drying her hands on a kitchen towel. "So I see. I thought we'd talked about your opening the door without me."

"But it's Jason," Ellery protested.

"Why don't you keep the door locked?" Jason asked, stepping in and setting his messenger bag by the door.

"It was locked," Lydia said. "They know how to unlock it. Deadbolt is my next option."

He chuckled. "Got yourself a couple of smart ones."

"That I do. Come on in the kitchen. I'm making meatloaf and I want to get it in the oven."

He followed her in, stopping to pick up Levi from his pen for a wet, sloppy baby kiss. "How's the big man today?" he said as Levi banged a plastic teething ring against Jason's head.

"He's good," Lydia said. "The teething is much better, so my happy baby is back."

"You've always been a happy baby. Isn't that right?" Jason said in a sing-song voice to Levi.

"Want a beer?" Lydia asked.

"Sure." Jason set Levi back into his pen. "I'll get it since you're up to your elbows in raw hamburger meat."

He cracked off the top, tossed it in the trash and took a draw off the longneck. It was sweet and cold as it rolled down his throat. Once he had the dryness in his throat quenched, he kissed Lydia behind her ear. She shivered and he grinned. Yeah, he knew all her hot spots.

"Have a good day?" he asked.

She looked over her shoulder. "Pretty good. You?"

Actually, it'd been a bitch of a day—three days actually—but he wasn't going to unload on Lydia. She had enough on her plate.

"Spent the day in Judge Worthy's court. Never has a name been such a misnomer."

She laughed. "Ass, is he?"

Jason slipped off his jacket, hung it on the back of a kitchen chair and loosened his tie.

"He's an ass on his good days. Today wasn't one of his good days."

Tiny, but loud, footsteps pounded on the hardwood flooring as Ellery and Annie ran into the kitchen.

"Can we draw pictures?"

Lydia looked at the girls and smiled. "Sure. Do you have paper?"

Annie nodded.

"Okay."

The girls raced from the room.

"Do they ever walk anywhere?" Jason asked with a laugh.

"Only to bed at night."

Jason polished off the beer and tossed the bottle in the trash. "Can I help with dinner?"

"Nope." Lydia slid the meatloaf into the oven. "We need to talk."

"Yeah, you mentioned that. What's up?"

Lydia washed her hands and then walked to a chair as she was drying them. She sat and folded her arms on the table in front of her.

"This is tough," she said.

A niggling fear tickled Jason's spine. "Just spit it out."

"It's about our wedding, well, marriage actually."

"Okay. You ready to set a date?"

Lydia's face was a window into her every thought. He could see where she was headed written all over her face.

"No. I'm not." She reached out and laid her hand on his forearm. "I'm not going to either." She sighed. "You've been my rock over the past two months. Always being there when I, or the children, needed you, but I can't expect you to take on all this." She pulled her hand back. "My life is a total mess right now. I'm glad my folks are moving here, but that's just another issue on my already crowded plate."

"So you want to postpone our wedding until next year?"

She shut her eyes and slowly shook her head. "Permanently." She dug into the pocket of her shorts and set her engagement ring on the table. "It's not right to keep you hanging on when I don't know where my life is going to take me next. You deserve more than I can give right now."

He stared at her, not believing what he was hearing. "You are breaking our engagement."

She sighed. "I am. Look, Jason, when you asked me

to marry you, I didn't have three children to raise. And now my aging parents are moving here to be with us. It's too much to ask of you."

"Don't you think that should be my decision?"

Even though she gave him a smile, the sadness etched on her face drove a sharp dagger into his soul. "You are the type of guy who stands by his word. I know you." She swept an arm around the room. "You didn't bargain for this. You didn't want this life. You made that crystal clear, and I appreciated that. I knew marrying you meant that I would never have children and, while giving up that option was painful, I loved you enough to do that. But now?" She shrugged. "Now I have three children that I love with every ounce of my being."

"And you believe me such a shallow man that I can't accept and love these children?"

"Not at all. I'm saying I'm not asking you to. My life is a wreck, and I love you too much to suck you into my whirlpool of problems."

He clenched his teeth, furious at her and her placating words. She pushed the twenty-thousand-dollar ring toward him.

"I can't keep this."

"This isn't you, Lydia." He raked his fingers through his hair. "You're not thinking right. I won't accept this."

"Jason," Ellery yelled as she raced into the kitchen. "Look what I drew." The blond-headed girl waved a piece of paper at him.

"Beautiful," he said. His vision swam, making it impossible for him to focus on anything but Lydia's face, the face he'd loved for so many years. Lightheaded and totally thrown by her words, he'd answered without looking at the crayon drawing or the paper.

"Ellery. Where did you get that paper?" Lydia asked.

Now he did look at the drawing he was holding. The paper was thick and yellow with age. Slashes of orange, blue and pink crayon bisected the sheet. His heart fell to his gut.

The girls had used his great-great-parents' original land grant from eighteen-eighty-five for their coloring project. He'd lifted the valuable papers from his parents' house a couple of weeks ago. The plan had been to have the papers framed as a wedding anniversary present to his parents from their children. Now, an orange crayon drawing of something—a dog, maybe—took up residence in the top left corner. On the back of the paper, streaks of orange, purple and pink filled the page.

"What is that?" Lydia asked.

"The original land grant giving my great-great-grandparents one-hundred and sixty acres to start a farm." He swallowed against the knot in his throat. "The originals," he repeated. "Not a copy."

"I am so sorry, Jason," Lydia said. "Ellery, you had no right to go into Jason's papers."

"But he said we could."

"He most certainly did not," Lydia replied.

Ellery nodded vigorously. "At his office. Said we could write on the backs."

Jason's heart was a sledgehammer on his chest. "What else did you write on?" His voice was much calmer than he felt.

"Show him," Lydia said.

Ellery ran back to the living room, Lydia and Jason close on her heels. He missed a step as he took in the array of scattered papers.

"All of this came from that bag?" he asked, pointing to his leather messenger bag.

Ellery nodded. "Just like at the office. We only wrote

on the backs." She smiled as though she'd been so smart to remember.

He picked up the pages nearest the toe to his shoe. The first one was page seventy-four of a 200 page corporate filing. The second sheet was page five of a divorce settlement for the Jernigans—the *signed* divorce agreement that'd taken him more than a month to get Wanda Jernigan to finally sign under protest.

"I don't know what to say," Lydia said. "I am so sorry."

Jason's jaw cramped from grinding his teeth. "Don't say anything. I think you've said enough." He looked at Ellery and Annie, who were watching him with wide eyes. "Girls, please pick up all the pages and bring them to me."

As they raced to do as he'd asked, he looked at Lydia. "Once I have my papers, I'll be gone, from here and from your life." She opened her mouth to reply, but he held up a hand. "I'll make this easy for you. I'll respect your wishes. Have a good life."

Chapter Twelve

The hollowness that'd formed in Jason's chest when he'd slipped Lydia's engagement ring into his pocket consumed him, growing deeper and darker as the days passed. He continued to go to work every day. With all his legal work stored on his computer, replacing the Ellery and Annie colored documents simply required a reprinting. Mrs. Jernigan signed the divorce papers a little more quickly this time. Thanks to Leo's Bar and Grill, it seemed that she'd discovered the nightlife of a newly single lady and was ready to embrace it, new cowboy boots and all.

Nights were the worst. His house was too quiet, although it was no more silent than it'd been before. However, now there was an emptiness there, a sense of a house too big for its occupant. Maybe his imagination had always filled the rooms with memories to be made with his wife. Now, each room echoed the loneliness he felt.

Two weeks had passed since the night Lydia had shoved the engagement ring back to him. There'd been no communication between them. No texts. No emails. No phone calls.

Sure, over the years they'd had their fights and break-ups, but never had it felt so final, so irreversible. Never had he felt so hopeless.

Another week went by, not that Jason could remember a damn thing about it. He went to work. He ate a cold sandwich and drank a beer for dinner when he got home. He went to bed. Up the next morning and repeat.

On Friday of the fourth week, his receptionist Margie stuck her head through his office door.

"Jason," she said. "You've got a visitor."

"Who is it and do they have an appointment?" He glanced at the clock. "It's after five on a Friday. Tell whoever it is to make an appointment for Monday."

He was exhausted. KC had had her baby—a son— the previous week. Michael had been in Dallas on a case this week, which meant he'd been in the office solo for over ten days.

"In fact," he said. "I'm not sure why you're still here."

"I'm leaving now," she said. "But you're going to want to see this person."

He sighed. "Fine. Send them in. Lock the front door so no other person who just has to have legal advice after hours sneaks in."

She nodded. "Will do, boss. Good luck."

Good luck? What the heck had she meant by that?

He heard Margie speaking and then an answering voice. She might have been whispering but that voice had murmured love vows and promises in his ear for so long, he'd know it anywhere.

The back door slammed, he assumed by Margie.

And then Lydia walked into his office.

Against his wishes, his heart leapt at seeing her. His mind sent out warning alarms that the rest of his body ignored. He stood, wanting to go to her, hold her. Instead, he grasped the edge of his desk, forcing himself to remain motionless.

She looked exhausted. Her brunette hair, usually shiny and full with waves, hung limply down her back. Her face was wan, making the blush on her cheeks stand out. The light creases around her mouth that intensified when she smiled were deep grooves. She chewed on her bottom lip.

"Hi, Jason."

He shook his head, his heart continuing to throw itself against his chest. "Really? A month of no communication and you waltz in here like you expect me to be glad to see you?"

She momentarily shut her eyes and sighed. "I don't blame you for being upset with me."

"Upset? Upset is a word that describes how I feel when the Dallas Cowboys lose a home game. Furious is the word I'd use for the woman who used me and kicked me to the curb."

Her lips parted in a gasp. "Used you? I…I never used you. I loved you."

He scoffed. "Right. Love. Whatever." He retook his seat. "You called this meeting, so what's up?"

"May I sit?"

He waved to the chair in front of his desk. "Sure. Make yourself at home. Say your piece. I have a cold beer waiting for me at home."

She sighed. "What did you do about the land-grant deed? I still feel terrible about that."

"Framed it. Gave it to my parents, who thought it

was so cute that Ellery had drawn on it." He stood. "If that's why you're here, we're done. Deed framed. Present delivered. Parents loved it."

She shook her head. "No, it's something else."

"Fine." He sat. "This isn't the only law firm in town. If this is a legal matter, I would strongly suggest using another firm."

His heart jackhammered against his chest. Drawing in a depth breath was damned near impossible. Below his ribcage, a sharp, intense pain radiated to his gut. The sooner he could get her out of his office, the sooner he could get home and get drunk.

"Spit it out, Lydia. What do you want?"

"I'm pregnant."

Of all the things she might have told him, this would have been dead last on his list.

He dropped his head heavily against the headrest. "Well, it all makes sense now."

She frowned. "What makes sense?"

"Why you took off your engagement ring but kept me hanging around. What happened? Did your lover dump you when you told him you were pregnant? Or did you find a new lover during the past month?"

"What are you talking about? You're the father."

His laugh was harsh. "Not hardly, my little two-timing ex."

If her face had been pale when she walked in, it was positively bloodless now.

"I never two-timed you. Ever. We made this baby back in May. At your house. After the massages."

He leaned on his desk. "Well, I did have a mighty fine massage that night, but I doubt that would have cured my lifelong infertility."

"What?" She sagged against the back of her chair. "Infertility? What are you talking about?"

"Me." He pointed to his chest. "Infertile, as in no fathering babies. You're a doctor. You understand what that means."

"But…but until I went on the pill, we always used condoms Why didn't you tell me?"

He snorted. "The condoms started as protection from disease, not pregnancy, but now? Damned wish I'd kept on using them. I have no idea who you've been fucking behind my back. Do I need to get checked for some horrible STD?"

His words were mean and cruel, and he didn't care. How dare she come in here and try to pass off some other man's baby as his.

"Jason. You aren't infertile." She swept her hand across her abdomen. "I'm walking proof of that. You can't be. I haven't been with anyone but you."

"Sorry. Not buying the crap you're selling, Lydia. I suggest you head back to the poor sap you're sleeping with and tell him your sob story." He narrowed his eyes in a glare. "I am not the father of any child. I will never be the father of any children. Do. You. Understand?" He rose. "I loved you. I love those three children you're raising, and I might have even been able to accept another man's child if you'd been honest with me. Instead, you come in here and try to pass off another man's child as mine. No, darling. That I cannot accept. Now leave and don't come back."

Tears rolled down her cheeks. "Jason. You *have* to believe me. This is your child."

"Leave, Lydia." He pointed toward his door. "I believe you know the way out."

As she left, she slammed his office door hard enough

to bounce his undergraduate diploma off the wall. It fell to the floor with a crash. Tiny shards of glass scattered in all directions around the floor, along with his heart.

———————

JASON HAD NO MEMORY OF HIS DRIVE HOME. HE barely remembered locking up the office and getting in his SUV.

Grown men do not cry, he told himself over and over as he sped through town. If that were true, why was the view through his windshield so blurry?

Once home, he went directly to the kitchen for a beer. He twisted off the top, flipped it toward the trash, watched it land on the floor, decided he didn't give a shit and tipped the bottle to his mouth. The cold, yeasty liquid rolled down his throat and did nothing to ease the burn in his chest. The bottle emptied after two long swallows. He pulled the carton holding the five remaining beers from the fridge and headed out onto his back deck.

The next two beers slid into his gut as easily as the first one had, but the fire of anger continued to rage.

Lydia with another man. His mind refused to accept the fact, but what other explanation could there be? As much as he would have loved to have children with her, his crappy physiology prevented that.

"Damn it."

With every molecule of strength in his body, he hurled an empty bottle at the oak tree at the end of his deck. The green glass exploded into jagged fragments, the shards scattering on the deck and ground below.

The woman he'd believed to be his soul mate, the woman he'd trusted with his heart had destroyed him with two words. He'd been serious when he'd told her that if she'd come in and told him the truth about another man, he might have been able to accept raising the child. That's how much he loved her. That's how much he'd already come to love three children who weren't his biologically. He'd been ready to adopt them, raise them with Lydia.

After being told in his twenties that he would be infertile, he'd given up on ever having a family. He made sure everyone knew he'd never have a family because he didn't *want* one.

But he did want a family. He wanted the family he'd been a part of with Lydia and her children. He'd fallen in love with Ellery, Annie and Levi. Even after the twins had colored on important documents, the love he felt for them had never wavered. Sure, he'd been upset, but that hadn't put a dent in what he felt for them.

Then Lydia had jerked the rug from under him by dumping him and taking the children out of his life.

As he tipped the fourth bottle of beer to his mouth, he heard a car door slam. He didn't move, other than to lower the bottle after he'd sucked it dry. Whoever was at his front door could leave. He didn't want company.

The doorbell chimed. He stayed where he was.

There was a loud rap of knuckles on the door. He sent his rocker into motion, but only to lean over and grab another beer.

Boot heels clomping on the stairs leading up his deck penetrated his beer haze. Damn it. Had to be family. They were the only ones who would come to his back door if he didn't answer the front.

"Jason?"

He should have known. Travis, the nosiest older brother ever born.

"Jason?"

Oh goodie. Travis had brought his wife.

The gate at the top of the stairs creaked as it swung open.

"There you are," Travis said. "You didn't answer your door."

"And yet you couldn't take that as a hint," Jason answered.

"What are you doing? How many of these have you had?"

Jason rolled his eyes—which he suspected were bloodshot—up toward his brother, who was hulking over him like a vulture.

"Don't know. Don't care." Jason lifted the last of the six-pack to his mouth.

"Jason." Caroline squatted beside his chair. "Lydia called. We've been worried about you."

Jason looked at his sister-in-law and sighed. "I'm fine. Thank you for worrying about me."

When he lifted the bottle to his mouth, Caroline reached over and rested her soft hand on his arm. "I love you as much as I love my own brother. It hurts me to see you like this."

Her words ripped a hole in the secret place he stashed grief. His next couple of breaths came in shuddering gasps.

"Lydia's pregnant," he said, the words acid to his soul. "And it's not mine."

She didn't appear surprised at his revelation.

"Come on," she said, taking his arm. "Let's go inside and talk where we'll be more comfortable."

Jason allowed her to lead him inside his own house. He dropped into a leather chair in the living room as Caroline and Travis found seats on the matching sofa.

"I know you never wanted children," she began, "but accidents happen."

He shook his head. "Not mine," he stated flatly.

"How can you be so sure?"

He glanced at his brother. He'd almost rather cut off his balls than admit in front of Travis that he was less than a real man.

He shook his head. "I know, okay?" He started to rise, but Caroline set her hand on his knee.

"You can trust me, Jason. There's nothing I haven't heard and nothing you could tell me that would change how I feel." She looked at Travis. "Maybe you could give Jason and me a little privacy."

Travis stood.

"Wait," Jason said. "He might as well stay. You'll just tell him everything later anyway."

"No, I wouldn't," Caroline said. "I don't discuss patients with him. *Ever.* Whatever you tell me stays between you and me."

"Sit down, Travis. You might as well know the truth." Jason rubbed his eyes, stalling for time, not that time would change anything about his reality. "Okay," he said on a long exhale. "I know that the baby Lydia is carrying isn't mine because—" he gulped in a breath and blurted, "—I'm sterile. Okay? You happy now?" He dropped his gaze to the floor.

"Oh, bro," Travis said.

"Wait a minute," Caroline replied, her skepticism obvious in her tone. "Sterile? Are you sure?"

"Yeah," Jason snapped. "Sterile, as in shooting blanks. No swimmers. Sterile."

"Who told you that?" Caroline asked.

"I didn't make this up." Jason met Caroline's gaze.

"I've known for almost ten years that I couldn't have children."

Caroline patted Jason's thigh. "Start at the beginning. Who told you that you were sterile?"

He sighed. "Dr. Franks in Austin. When I was in law school, I saw him for fatigue. I was so exhausted my brain was fuzzy. My hair was falling out. My skin itched like crazy. I thought it was all due to the lack of sleep and long hours of studying. He ran some tests and told me I had hypothyroidism."

She nodded. "Right. We talked about that last year when I refilled your prescription for levothyroxine."

Jason threw up his hands. "There you have it."

Caroline frowned. "There I have what?"

"You're the doctor, Caroline. Do I have to paint you a picture? The hypothyroidism made me infertile."

She shook her head. "Um, Jason. I think you may have misunderstood Dr. Franks. *Untreated* hypothyroidism may lead to infertility, but you've been taking your levothyroxine, right?"

"Yeah. Every morning."

"Let me ask you something else. Have you had a semen analysis done?"

"Jeez, Caroline." Heat soared up Travis's neck to his face.

Caroline looked at her husband. "Shoo. I think your brother and I need some alone time."

Travis leapt to his feet, the relief to be leaving evident on his face. "Yeah. I'll, um, go on the back deck and, um, do something." He charged for the door as if being chased by a bull.

As soon as the deck door clicked shut, Caroline turned back to Jason. "Okay. It's just me and you. Semen analysis?" She arched an eyebrow.

"Yes. Of course I did. I'm not an idiot, Caroline." He wiped his hands down his face. "This is embarrassing."

"Not for me," she stated matter-of-factly.

"Fine, then. For me."

"Jason, didn't your doctor explain that the infertility can often be reversed over time if your thyroid problem is treated? We need to get another semen analysis and find out."

"Can you stop saying semen?"

She chuckled. "Fine. Not sure what I'll call it instead. How about your man juice?"

Jason snorted. "Not much better."

"Here's what's going to happen. I'm going to call a doctor I know in Dallas. You are going to go see him and we are going to get a definitive answer."

"Okay, I guess."

She stood and he rose. "I'll call Dr. Sherman first thing Monday morning. Be ready to go see him." She kissed his cheek. "And you might want to think about how you are going to apologize to Lydia."

"We'll see."

"Jason. Do you honestly believe for one second that Lydia has been with another man?" She waved her hand when he opened his mouth. "And exactly when would she have had time to have an affair with another man? On her lunch break? Hard to do since we almost never leave the office, and when we do, it's lunch together." She tapped the side of his head. "You've got a brain. Use it. From what I could gather through her crying is that you were pretty harsh with her today."

"I know, I know. She caught me off-guard with that pregnancy bomb. I was so jealous at the idea that she'd been with another man, I lost it."

"We'll get to the bottom of this. I promise."

The next two days comprised the weekend from hell. On Sunday, after a million false starts, he called Lydia. After ten rings, her answering service picked up, but he didn't leave a message. After all, he wasn't exactly sure what he wanted to say.

After a couple of beers, and a few more false starts, he rang her cell. There was a click and then he heard, "The number dialed has call restrictions in place that prevent the completion of this call." After that, the phone disconnected. Stunned, he held out the phone and stared at it. Lydia had blocked his cell phone number. Calls from his house phone resulted in the same message. All his personal phone numbers had been blocked.

He stretched out on the couch, pissed at her for cutting him off and angry at himself for being such an ass. Thanks to his sister-in-law, he'd know this week one way or the other if he was shooting blanks or firing live ammo.

If blanks, then there was no way for him to be the father of Lydia's baby. Oh, he hadn't bothered to question if she was sure she was pregnant. If Lydia said she was, then she was. But if it wasn't his baby, then who was the sonofabitch he was going to kill with his bare hands?

If he found out he'd been wrong all these years and wasn't sterile and the baby was his...then what? He'd done a damn fine job destroying any chance he might have had to get Lydia back.

He draped his forearm over his eyes. What he should have done two days ago was throw his arms around the woman he loved when she said she was pregnant and shout, "Thank you, Jesus."

Instead, he'd kicked her out of his office, his boot firmly planted in her ass.

Yeah, he was the ass in this story.

As he drifted off to sleep, he knew exactly what he needed to do. It wasn't going to be easy, but he refused to spend the rest of his life without Lydia no matter what the sperm test revealed.

Chapter Thirteen

✤✤✤

I da and Larry Henson wasted no time in getting set
up in their rental house down the street from Lydia.
Since they had decided to keep their Florida house as a
second home, relocating to Texas basically involved
moving clothing. Lydia was trying to give them space
while also giving them all the time they wanted with their
grandchildren. And they wanted a lot of time. On Friday
afternoon, they took Ellery and Annie to their house for
the weekend. The plan was for Lydia to come on Sunday
for lunch.

Sunday morning, Lydia woke with a dull throb in her
chest. She rubbed at the pain, but no amount of finger
massaging could reach the sting she still felt from Jason's
rebuke. Of course she'd known he would probably be
surprised—and maybe a little upset—at the unplanned
pregnancy. However, never in her wildest fantasies had
she imagined that he would accuse her of being with
another man.

And the "I'm sterile" had been a bombshell she
hadn't seen coming. All those years together and he

hadn't trusted her enough to mention he might be sterile. She was a doctor, damnit. Not only would she have understood, but there were tests she could have done to figure out the extent of his problem. He obviously wasn't sterile. She bore the evidence of that in her uterus.

Her hand dropped to her abdomen and she pressed. In the hustle and confusion of her sister and brother-in-law's deaths, their funerals and dealing with all the details of the estate, she'd missed some birth control pills. Many birth control pills. But she hadn't given the skipped pills much thought. She had so many other things to worry about. Even after their night together at his house in May, she hadn't been concerned about getting pregnant. There'd been no other man for her since Jason had entered her life. She'd never wanted anyone else.

When she'd first missed a period, she'd shrugged it off as stress. Lord knew, she'd been carrying her load of it. When she'd missed her second period, she'd almost blown it off too. Instead, she'd done a pregnancy test, almost fainting when it came back positive.

The only person she'd confided in was Caroline. Pregnancies could be unpredictable in the first trimester. Miscarriages early in pregnancies were not uncommon. She wouldn't have told Jason, but Caroline had insisted—and Lydia agreed—that he had a right to know.

She heard cooing and babbling coming from her old bedroom. She smiled. Levi was awake. Man, she loved that kid. He made her laugh every day with his attempts at talking and his natural curiosity. Keeping him safe, as in tiny fingers out of electrical outlets, was a daily challenge.

But there was a definite lack of noise in the house without Ellery and Annie. She glanced at the clock.

Almost eight. If the girls had been home, they'd have been up by seven. She missed those two.

It was impossible for her to imagine her life now without children. She would have missed so much. Sure, raising kids was as hard—no, harder—then she'd ever imagined. But the rewards outweighed the stress tenfold. How could Jason have not wanted children?

Was it that he didn't want children, or had he only said that because he believed himself sterile? A million dollar question that she'd never have the answer to.

Pushing her arms over her head, she stretched and yawned. Having her own bedroom and bathroom was a blessing. She climbed out of bed and headed to her old room. Levi must have heard her coming. He was standing and bouncing when she walked in.

"Morning, big guy."

Drool ran down his chin as he laughed.

Her heart swelled with love as she lifted Levi into her arms. The depth of love she felt for these three kids was like nothing she'd ever experienced before.

And before long, she'd be having her own baby.

Four children. All under the age of five. She had no idea how she would cope, but they'd make it.

Levi rubbed his face on her nightshirt, leaving a glob of mucus. She hugged him tight. Yeah, she would have missed a lot without having children.

MONDAY BROUGHT HEAVY RAIN AND AN EVEN HEAVIER patient schedule.

"You'd think some of these people would have canceled because of the weather," she grumbled to Caroline as they passed in the hall.

"Nah. They all want to see your smiling face and sparkling personality."

Lydia snorted. "I'm hiding in my office for five minutes to put my feet up."

"No problem. Enjoy."

Lydia dropped into her desk chair moments before their receptionist knocked on her office door. "Look what came for you." She set a bouquet of two dozen red roses with baby's breath and fresh greenery on Lydia's desk. "They are beautiful."

Lydia pulled the card from the holder.

Love, Jason

She tore the small white card into tiny pieces and dropped them into her waste basket. Screw him.

"Care you take these with you?" Lydia gestured to the floral arrangement. "Maybe put them at the front desk so our patients can enjoy them."

The receptionist nodded. "Sure," She swept up the vase and left, wise enough to leave her questions unasked.

Caroline took the chair in front of Lydia's desk. "Pretty roses."

"Hmm."

"Did he call this weekend?"

"I don't know. I blocked his phone numbers."

Caroline scoffed. "Serves him right. But on the other hand, it's going to be hard for him to grovel his way back into your good graces if you block his calls."

Lydia leaned back in her chair with a long exhale. "I don't know what to do."

"I can't tell you. I wish I could, but Travis and I blundered our way along until we figured it out."

"Did Travis talk to Jason this weekend?"

Caroline shrugged. "Travis worked all day Saturday

and Sunday. They might have talked, but if they did, he didn't share the conversation. Look, Lydia, Jason screwed up. I know that. You know that. Hell, I'm sure Jason knows that. But jealousy can produce some very strong reactions."

"What do you mean?"

"Remember Memorial Day when you walked into the barn and found Lisa Billings millimeters from kissing Jason?"

Lydia scoffed. "I wanted to snatch every strand of hair from her head."

"Exactly. Now, think of how Jason must have felt on Friday. He believes he's sterile. You walk in and announce that not only are you pregnant, but he's the father. He can't see how that's possible. You must have been with another man. You don't think he wouldn't be crazy with jealousy?"

Lydia chewed on her nail. "Maybe." She winced. "Okay. I grant you that it's possible that he was jealous, but you didn't hear all the horrible things he said."

Caroline nodded. "Yeah. Men can be asses."

"No argument from me."

"The only advice I have is give him some time."

"And then?"

"And then make him grovel."

"What if I don't want him back?"

Caroline arched an eyebrow. "Really? Have you thought about how it's going to feel when you see him with another woman? Lisa Billings maybe?"

Lydia's stomach tumbled like a dryer. "I... It will kill me."

"So don't do anything drastic."

"Unblock his number?"

"Oh, hell no. Not yet. Let him suffer."

"You do realize that I was the one who called off our engagement, right?"

Caroline shrugged. "Things change."

Lydia sighed. "Exactly why I called off our wedding."

"I bit my tongue when you told me about that." Caroline leaned forward. "You did to him basically what he did to you. You each made rash decisions without talking. You decided for him that he wouldn't be happy with your kids. Did you even ask him?"

"But he'd always had been so adamant about not wanting children."

"Let me plant this idea. What if his hard stance about children was based on his belief that he was sterile more than his lack of desire for a family? What if he said all that to protect his ego? He's a man. It'd be easier to say he didn't want kids than to tell the world he couldn't have them, don't you think?"

"You can deny it, but you've talked to him. I know it. One of the things I admire about you is your ability to keep confidential conversations confidential. But right now, I hate that about you. And, yes, I've thought about what you just suggested."

Caroline chuckled and stood. "I'd better get back to it. I've got a new patient with a toenail fungus. And they say medicine isn't glamorous."

JASON KNEW HIS FACE HAD TO BE THE COLOR OF A fresh summer tomato as he exited the exam room at Dr. Sherman's office. His sister-in-law had come through as promised and gotten him in for a semen analysis on Monday afternoon. The staff could not have been more professional. No odd stares or grins. For them, this was another day at the office, but for him? The most embarrassing thing he'd done in a long time.

One of his concerns had been an inability to perform in Dr. Sherman's office. But that hadn't been an issue. The exam room had just about anything a man could want to get in the mood from porn magazines to dirty movies.

His second concern had been about walking out of the room carrying his cup-o-sperm. No worry there. The room backed up to the lab. There was a small door in the wall where he could simply place the specimen cup and leave. Simple.

Except that everyone outside the room knew he'd been playing the slide trombone, so to speak.

Lydia was worth it. A future with her was worth anything he had to go through, even the most embarrassing day of his life.

He wondered if Lydia had gotten his roses yet. Since he had a long drive back from Dallas, he hit the call button on his cell. The blue-tooth connection rang over the car speakers.

"The number dialed has call restrictions in place that prevent the completion of this call."

He hit disconnect. Still blocked, but maybe she just hasn't had time to unblock him.

He rang her office.

"Whispering Springs Medical Clinic. This is Jessica."

"Hi, Jessica. This is Jason Montgomery. Is Dr. Henson available?"

"Hold on, Mr. Montgomery. I'll check."

On-hold music filtered out of the speakers, music that went much longer than he'd expected.

"Sorry for the hold, Mr. Montgomery," Lydia's

receptionist said. "I'm sorry, but Dr. Henson isn't available and...um...she asked that I...um..."

"Spit it out, Jessica. What did she say?"

"Something about hell and freezing over."

"Got it. Thanks. Hey, before you hang up, did a vase of roses for Dr. Henson arrive today?"

There was a slight pause and then, "Yeah. Red ones. Very pretty."

"Great. Do you know if she saw them?"

"Um, yeah. Hold on."

He waited.

"She got the roses," Jessica said in a whisper. "But she tore up the note and dropped it in the garbage."

He snorted. "She's a little upset at me."

"Don't tell her I told you, okay? But ever since y'all broke up, she's been cranky."

"Really?" He chuckled to himself. "I won't say a word. And thanks, Jessica."

He disconnected. Cranky since the breakup. Yeah, he liked hearing that since he wasn't the one who'd done the original dumping. That would be her. He needed to find a way to get a message to her that she couldn't rip up and toss.

DR. SHERMAN'S OFFICE HAD TOLD HIM IT WOULD BE A few days before they had the results of his test, but that didn't stop his heart from sputtering every time he got a phone call. By the end of Tuesday, concentrating on the will he was preparing was impossible. He'd actually typed sperm once and semen twice. After saving what little work he'd done, he shut down his computer and packed up.

"I'm going home," he told Margie, who immediately looked at her watch.

"At four?"

"Yep. At four."

"Got a date?"

"Not hardly."

"Oh. Too bad. I had hoped that Lydia had decided to take your grumpy ass back."

"Grumpy ass?"

Margie shrugged, not nervous about losing her job. She knew she was as vital to the office as he was, and frankly, he knew it too.

"I call 'em like I see 'em," she said.

He scoffed. "That you do. See you tomorrow."

"Get some rest," she shouted at his back. "You look awful."

He glanced over his shoulder. "Yes, Mom."

Instead of heading straight home, he turned into Leo's Bar and Grill lot and grabbed a parking spot at the front door. He chuckled. Old people dinner time. He wondered if Leo had a senior menu with discount prices he could take advantage of.

"Good evening, Mr. Montgomery," the hostess in the restaurant said. "Would you like a table?"

"Thanks, Holly. I think I'll eat at the bar."

She nodded and went back to rolling silverware into cloth napkins for the evening.

He slid into a booth and a waitress came over almost immediately.

"Hi," she drawled in a true Texas accent. "I'm Shelly. What can I get cha?"

"Bring me a draft and a menu."

"Sure thang, honey."

As there were only two other patrons in the bar, she was back with his beer and a menu almost immediately.

"There ya go," she said, setting down the beer. "Need some time with the menu?"

He glanced at the steaks. "Rib eye. Rare. Baked potato."

"Sure thang. Be up in a jiffy."

'Sure thang' must be her standard answer to any request. He chuckled. God, he loved Texas folk.

He leaned back in the booth. The test results hung over his head like a boulder ready to drop. What-ifs rang through his brain. What if he wasn't sterile? What if he was? What if the baby Lydia was carrying was his? What if it wasn't?

And the answer hit him so hard he would have staggered if he hadn't been sitting down. None of that mattered. The test results were no longer of any significance. All that mattered was being with Lydia and loving the family she'd given him.

Had he not fallen totally in love with Ellery, Annie and Levi? Was that not evidence that he had the ability to love and care for children who were not from him? If Lydia's baby was his, wonderful. If not, he didn't care. It was part of Lydia, and there was nothing about her he didn't love.

He would welcome this new child into his life as its father, parentage be damned.

"Need some company?" a female voice inquired.

Jason's head snapped up. "Hello, Lisa. What are you doing here at this time of the day?"

Lisa Billings slid into the booth across from him. "Same as you, I reckon. Was at the library at six this morning and missed lunch. Thought I'd grab a quick bite on the way home."

He nodded as Shelly stepped up to the table.

"What can I get ya?" she said to Lisa.

"Mind if I join you?" Lisa asked Jason.

He shrugged. "Sure."

Lisa ordered a white wine and a grilled chicken salad. Shelly left with her standard, "Sure thang, hon," and walked away.

"So, how's the world treating you?" Lisa asked.

He grinned. "Kicking my ass every day."

She laughed. "Know what you mean."

Shelly set Lisa's wine on the table. "Your meals should be out shortly."

"You and Lydia are…what? Done? On a break? Back together?"

Jason took a long drink of his beer, draining about half of the glass. "Not done if I have anything to say about it."

She put her hand over his. "Good luck. She was a fool to let you go."

"I'm the fool for letting her."

She gave his hand a quick squeeze. "I hope she knows how much you love her."

"She will tomorrow. Hell, everyone will."

Chapter Fourteen

I t was close to lunchtime, if the growling in Lydia's tummy was any indication. And she had to pee. She'd gone from patient to patient to patient without a break since eight. She needed food, the bathroom and a nap...and not necessarily in that order.

"Want to escape for lunch?" Caroline asked. "For some odd reason, we have no patients scheduled until two this afternoon."

"Are you kidding?" Lydia threw up her hands in relief. "Thank the Lord. And, hell yeah. Let's blow this pop stand."

Caroline laughed. "I have one more patient and I'll be ready."

"Great. I'm hitting the restroom, grabbing my purse and will be tapping my foot at the back door waiting on you."

Fifteen minutes later, Caroline joined Lydia at the door.

"Where to?" Lydia asked.

"How about that new place? Rick's On the River? I

hear that Porchia's Heavenly Delights is supplying all the bread products."

"Good idea. I haven't been there, and I love anything that comes from Porchia's bakery. If Rick's lunches are as good as her bakery stuff, we'll come back fat and happy." Lydia patted her gut. "And I'm already working on the fat part."

For mid-July, Texas was having freaky cool weather, or at least cool for Texas. The day's high was forecast at eighty-five. Apparently, every other Whispering Spring resident had the same need to get outside today as Rick's On the River was packed.

Caroline wiggled through the throng of people waiting and somehow scored them a small riverside table.

"How did you pull this off?" Lydia asked as a hostess led them to their table.

"Family connections," Caroline replied with a grin.

"Right."

They sat and took the menus.

"And I bribed the hostess," Caroline said.

"You did not."

"Did too."

"Being a Montgomery must have its advantages," Lydia said with a laugh.

"And don't you forget it."

Before Lydia could ask what that meant, a young waitress approached their table. "Hi. I'm Ruth Ann. I'll be taking care of you today. You're lucky to get a table. I guess that ad in the paper today really brought out people wanting to watch."

Lydia frowned. "Watch what?" She looked at Caroline. "Did you read the paper this morning? I never had time."

Caroline shook her head. "Nope. No idea what Ruthie here is talking about." She looked at the waitress with wide eyes. "How about some water with lemon?"

"Me too, please," Lydia said.

The young girl hurried away.

"Wonder what's happening today?"

"No clue, but we are on the river. Boat race? Yellow duck race?"

"Wouldn't that be fun? Not the boats, but the yellow duck race. We should talk about doing something like that as a hospital money raiser. I've seen that done."

Caroline took a sip of the water that'd been set on their table. "Don't know what you're talking about. Explain."

"The hospital ladies' guild would sell the ducks for some nominal fee, say five bucks. Each duck has a number on it. That number would be assigned to the person who bought it. The day of the race, all the ducks are released at the same time upriver. There's a finish line somewhere downriver. The first duck that crosses the line wins."

"And what does the winner get?"

"No clue." Lydia laughed. "Maybe the guild gets businesses to donate prizes so all the money goes toward the children's unit the hospital needs so badly."

Caroline nodded. "Love this idea."

Around them, a buzz of excited conversation filled the air. Café diners stood and pointed toward the sky.

"What in the world?" Lydia asked.

Caroline shrugged and took another sip of her water. Her normally curious friend was abnormally disinterested, and that made Lydia a tad suspicious.

The *grrr* of a plane engine could be heard over the

din in the restaurant. A red plane circled overhead towing a banner that read *Jason Loves Lydia.*

Lydia stood, her hands over her mouth. *Ohmigod.* Her heart did a roller coaster dip and spin. Her knees weakened, making her grab the edge of the table for support.

The plane circled the café about seven times before it flew away.

Lydia looked down at her friend, who'd remained seated through the whole show. She squinted her eyes in a glare. "You knew about this, didn't you?"

Caroline carefully selected a slice of fresh bread from the basket on their table, slathered it with butter and took a bite. "Wasn't there a presidential candidate who said women couldn't be leaders because they couldn't keep a secret?" She took another bite and grinned. "Proved him wrong, didn't I?"

Lydia dropped back into her seat with a long-suffering sigh.

Around them, their fellow customers were clapping and laughing. At the table next to them, one woman said, "I don't care what he did. If my boyfriend did something like that, he'd get so lucky tonight." The women at that table laughed and nodded in agreement.

Maybe the woman had a point.

"You want to fill me in?" she asked Caroline, who pulled off a corner from her bread slice and popped it in her mouth.

"Nope," she said. "Not yet."

Lydia stood. "I'm going to go get a newspaper."

Caroline grabbed her arm. "Not yet. Sit. Enjoy the show."

Lydia retook her seat. "There's more?"

Caroline shrugged with a grin. "Maybe."

Lydia hid her face in her hands. "What am I going to do with him?"

Caroline tugged Lydia's hand away from her face. "That's the million dollar question, isn't it?"

Ruth Ann slid their burgers onto the table. "So I just have to ask. You're Lydia, right?"

Lydia groaned. "How did you know?"

"First, we don't have *reserved* tables. It's first come, first served. And second, your face is as red as a Bloody Mary."

Caroline laughed while Lydia groaned again.

"The Montgomery men are hard to shake when they want something," Caroline said.

Lydia picked up a hot french fry and popped it in her mouth. "I'm beginning to see that."

The plane's engine roared again in the sky. Lydia closed her eyes with a head shake. "Do I want to look?"

Caroline laughed. "This time, maybe not."

Lydia cracked open her eyes and looked up and moaned.

The banner this time read: *Unblock my number, Lydia. Love, Jason.*"

"I am going to kill him," she said, but then she laughed.

"I guess that's one way to get a message to someone who's blocking you," Caroline said.

"Is there more?"

"I don't think so, but I doubt this campaign is over. Montgomery men—"

"Yes, I know. Don't give up easily."

When they got back to the office, all the staff was chatting about the banners. Seemed everyone had stood in the street to watch the plane do its work.

Lydia unblocked Jason's numbers as requested, but

he didn't call all afternoon, leaving her a tad confused and mystified. However, she'd been with him long enough to realize that his afternoons could get busy and figured that's probably what had happened.

That evening, she kept her cell phone in her pocket, again expecting it to ring, except it never did. About seven, her house phone rang and she hurried to answer it.

Her heart raced and she tried, unsuccessfully, to answer in as normal a voice she could. "Hello?"

"Hi, honey. It's Mom."

Lydia's heart continued to pound against her chest. "Hi, Mom. What's up?" She took a couple of deep breaths to calm her overreaction to her phone ringing.

"Your father and I are having kiddo withdrawal."

Laughing, she asked, "You want to come down? Dinner's over."

"Actually, we were wondering if maybe we could keep them tomorrow instead of sending them to Mother's Day Out."

"Sure. I know the twins would love it. Levi pretty much loves everything these days."

"Great. What time will you leave for the office? What time do we need to be there?"

"I'll leave about seven-thirty or so."

"Great. We'll be there about seven-twenty."

Once she hung up, she looked around the house. It wasn't too bad, but she could at least run a vacuum to pick up the dog hair. Frankly, she was amazed that Jasper wasn't bald.

The rest of the evening, her damn phone sat as quiet as a dead mouse. By bedtime, her eyes stung from staring at the stupid device and willing it to ring.

She didn't get it. Jason told the whole world he loved

her and asked her to unblock his number, which she'd done, and then he doesn't call? What's up with that?

Sleep that night was elusive. She flopped around for hours trying to find a comfortable position. When her radio alarm clicked on and music filled her bedroom, she was trussed like a mummy in her sheets. For the first time in forever, she was actually glad it was time to get up. At least she could stop pretending to sleep.

As promised, Lydia heard her mother's knock at seven-twenty.

"Coming," Lydia called, which was a total waste of breath. Ellery beat her to the door, unlocked it and was letting Ida through the door. She made another mental note for a deadbolt lock that Ellery couldn't reach.

"Hi, Mom."

Ida hugged Lydia. The scent of her mother's cologne and face powder took Lydia back to how she'd felt as a ten-year-old girl taking comfort in the smell and feel of her mother.

"Good morning. Now, let me at those children. I've got some spoiling to do."

"So do I."

Lydia's gaze snapped back to the door as Jackie Montgomery walked into her house. "Hope you don't mind, but when I was chatting with Ida and she told me that she was spending the day with the kids, I just invited myself along."

"Hi, Jackie. Of course I don't mind. Should I go stand on the porch and look for Dad and Lane?"

The two older women laughed. Ida had Ellery cocked on her hip and Jackie stood with Annie. But before either woman spoke there was a third knock at the door. Since the usual doorman, or rather doorgirl was currently getting attention from her grandma, Lydia went to the door expecting either her father or Jason's father. Instead, a uniformed limo driver stood outside her door.

"Good morning," he said. "I'm here to pick up Dr. Henson."

Lydia frowned. "I'm Dr. Henson, but I didn't call for a limo."

"Her bags are on the porch," Ida said. "She's all ready to go."

Lydia whirled around. "I'm all ready to go where? And what bags are on the porch?"

Her mother grinned, as did Jackie. Obviously, these two were up to something. Lydia assumed an akimbo posture.

"Would someone like to tell me what's going on?"

Ida looked at Jackie, who looked at Ida, then both women turned to Lydia.

"Not really," Ida said. "You know I'd never do anything that would hurt you, right?"

"Yeah, so?"

"Get in the limo."

"Let me get this straight. You want me to get into a car I did not order with a man I've never seen?"

Ida chuckled. "Well, when you put it like that, it does sound a little strange, but you're a smart gal. You'll figure it out. Now, go on before you're late."

Lydia sighed and stopped just short of stomping her foot on the floor. "Late for what?"

Her mother leaned over and kissed Lydia's cheek. "We love you, honey. Now be a good girl and go get into the strange car with the strange man. I packed some nice clothes for you. Don't be afraid to not use them."

Jackie laughed, which made Ellery and Annie laugh, not that the twins understood what was happening.

Lydia had her suspicions, however. Jason was behind what was going on. Probably a limo to a fancy breakfast and an apology. At least the ride over would give her time to think about her response. Should she make him grovel just a little more or forgive him straight away?

"Fine but—" she wagged her finger at both women, "—this isn't over."

She clomped down the stairs to where the driver held the back door open. Sliding onto the leather seats, her nose caught the aroma of fresh coffee.

The driver leaned in. "There's coffee in the carafe, some fresh Danish in the box and today's newspaper. Enjoy the ride." He closed the door.

The ride? It was maybe ten minutes to her office, which wasn't much of a ride, but she was pretty sure that wasn't the destination. Still, she had to make sure Caroline knew something was going on.

"Help," she said to Caroline when she got her on the phone. "I'm being kidnapped."

"Hmm. That's interesting," Caroline replied in a totally bored tone.

"Really? That's how you respond to a kidnapping call? That's interesting?"

Caroline laughed. "Sorry. Let me try again. *Ohmigod.* Should I call the police?"

Lydia chuckled. "That's much better. Seriously, I'm pretty sure I won't be in the office today, especially since the limo driver has just driven out of town toward the interstate."

"I know. Have fun."

"Have fun at what?" Lydia demanded. "No one will tell me anything."

"Neither will I. Drink the coffee. Eat a Danish. Sit back and enjoy the ride."

"How did you know I had coffee and Danish?"

"Oops. Gotta run. Patients and all that." Caroline clicked off.

Lydia shook her head, poured a cup of coffee and dug through the Danish from Porchia's bakery. She moaned with the first bite of sugary goodness.

Only Jason knew her well enough to bribe her with fresh coffee and pick out her favorite Danish from Porchia's bakery. Wherever she was headed, she was fairly sure who would be waiting at the end of the trip.

She settled back and decided to go with the flow, as if she had any other choice, short of being a total ass.

The coffee was strong and hot, just like she liked it. No one had done the crossword puzzle, which thrilled her. Usually one of the clinic staff would do the daily crossword before she got to it. For the next hour, she drank, ate and filled in blank spaces. It might have been the best hour in the past six weeks.

When the limo took the exit for Dallas/Fort Worth airport, she wasn't surprised.

When the limo pulled into the airport's departure lanes, she wasn't surprised.

When the limo came to a stop and Jason flung open the rear door and yelled, "Surprise!" she wasn't.

Not at all.

Chapter Fifteen

❧❦❧

L ydia also wasn't surprised to find their seats in first
class.

"Can I get you something to drink before we take
off?" the attendant asked.

"Orange juice," Lydia said.

Jason nodded. "The same."

"So," Lydia said on a long exhale. "You want to fill
me in?"

When he grinned, a serious tingle charged through
her veins and lit up her heart like a Christmas tree. But
then, he'd always had that effect on her since the first
time she'd seen him all bloody in her emergency department. He'd grinned up at her from where he sat on the
stretcher, blood dripping from a small cut over his eye,
and she'd felt the floor quake.

"Just a short vacation away from our families, the
children, work demands, Whispering Springs and
anything else that keeps us apart." He leaned over and
said in a quiet voice, "Anything that keeps us in clothes."

She rolled her eyes and laughed. "I'm still pretty

pissed at you." And she was. In fact, she wasn't sure going away with him was the best idea. They probably should have had a long talk before this. Depending on a number of factors, this weekend could set the course for their future.

Yeah, good job putting no pressure on whatever Jason has planned.

He took her hand and kissed her knuckles. "I know. I was pretty pissed at you too. But, honey, I love you too much to give up. Give us this weekend. Give me a chance to change your mind about us."

His words wound around her heart and squeezed. A love so powerful it brought tears to her eyes streamed through her.

"Okay. I can do that."

After a change of planes in Miami, their plane landed on Grand Bahama Island. Lydia looked around. "You brought me to the Bahamas?"

"Nope. We're not done yet."

They changed to a small prop plane with eight other people and took off again. This flight was a fast up and then down to land on a short runway on a different island.

"Where are we?"

"Sugar Island," he said.

"Never heard of it."

"Neither had I, until KC took off to here with Derek Gentry about eighteen months ago."

A smile spread across her lips. "We're at the Sand Castle."

Returning his smile, he asked, "So you have heard of it?"

"Sure, from KC. Their trip sounded incredible."

"Then hold on, darlin'. Ours is going to be even better."

Lydia remembered KC's description of the miniature cars, which were actually customized golf carts. A Mercedes-themed cart that'd been stretched to accommodate six guests waited on the tarmac. Attached was a small wagon. There was a second stretch cart that would carry an additional six passengers.

Her heart raced with excitement. If this place was as nice as KC had described, this would be the vacation of a lifetime for her. With three children at home and a fourth on the way, time away might be hard to come by in the foreseeable future.

When she stepped from the plane, hot, humid air blew her hair away from her face. The breeze was a scent combination of ocean salt and sweet florals. She drew in a deep breath and felt the tense muscles in her neck release a tiny bit of their hold. Of course, the humidity would blow her hair up to triple its regular volume, but she really didn't care. Her plan was to spend the entire weekend in the water with all her strands slicked to her head.

She bounded down the stairs with a bounce in her step that'd been missing since April. She knew the kids were fine, although she worried about undoing all the spoiling her mother and Jason's mother would be providing this weekend.

But the thought of the children with four adults who adored them made her smile.

Jason clanged down the stairs after her and then grabbed her around her waist from behind. The kiss he planted behind her ear kicked a bolt of lust through her veins.

"I have no idea what your mom packed in your suitcase, but if I have my say about it, you won't need one article of clothing in there."

Desire and arousal engulfed almost every cell in her body.

But there remained those few cells that held out, worried this weekend wouldn't provide the answer to all her questions. She loved Jason and realized he held the power to crush her emotionally. If she let herself get too comfortable with the idea of a future with him and this weekend didn't go that way, it would take a long time for her to recover. She had to protect her heart.

KC HAD SHOWN JASON PICTURES OF THE RESORT, BUT sometimes exaggeration was the modus operandi for a lawyer. Except, for once in his cousin's life, she hadn't been embellishing. As their transportation stopped at a plaza, he caught Lydia's arm as she stumbled getting out of the cart.

"Sorry," she said. "I wasn't paying attention." She whirled around to look at him. "This place is incredible." She pointed across the plaza to the resort's lodge. "That looks exactly as though it's been constructed out of the sand we are standing on."

Jason nodded. "I know. KC showed me pictures, but they don't begin to do the place justice. You have to see it to believe it. Come on. I want to take a look at the moat."

"Moat?"

He pointed to the open space between the plaza and the castle. "KC told me that the moat is part of the water attractions here. You can swim or float on tubes around the castle and end up back in the main outdoor pool."

Her responding smile made all the thousands he'd paid for this weekend worth every penny. Frankly, the money meant nothing. Without her, his life had been a hollow shell of its prior self. If it took every dime he had to get her back, he would consider it a good investment.

She looped her arm through his. "Let's go."

As they reached the center of the plaza, they were met by a fine mist from an enormous three-tiered fountain. Water shot into the air before it fell back into the upper basin and flowed over the lip to a second and then third basin. Around the fountain, an assortment of red, yellow and white floral blossoms nodded in the breeze.

"Wait," she said, pulling him to a stop. "Stop here." She pulled him up to the fountain and stopped the first person walking by. "Can you take a picture?"

"Of course," the woman said.

"There. That will make a wonderful memory for you," she said, handing Lydia's cellphone back to her.

Lydia crossed her fingers that it would be a wonderful memory and not a painful one later.

They followed the woman to the bridge over the moat. She went into the castle as casually as he walked into his office. Conversely, he and Lydia stopped on the bridge and watched three couples float by.

"We will be able to do that, right?" Lydia asked, her eyes wide with anticipation.

"We'll do whatever you want." He took her hand. "You name it, and it's yours."

At check-in, Jason was handed the keys to their own cart. The receptionist explained that they could opt for bicycles instead, but Lydia snapped the cart keys out of his hand before he could reply.

"No way," she said. "I'm dying to drive one of those cars."

The car assigned to their cabin, and thus to them, was a fire-engine-red cart that'd been transformed to resemble a 1957 Chevy truck. Their luggage had been stacked in the open rear bed.

"Ohmigod," Lydia said. "This is just too cool." She hopped behind the wheel and patted the seat beside her. "Come on."

Jason laughed and slid in beside her.

"Hold on," she warned before stomping on the power pedal. They shot out of the paved parking lot and onto crushed-shell roads. "You navigate. I have no idea where I'm going."

Chuckling, he asked, "Have you always been this bossy and I've just never noticed?"

She glanced toward him. Her mouth was spread wide with a smile. The twinkle in her eyes matched the happiness etched on her face.

"Probably. Is that a problem?"

"Nope." He grabbed a hold of the roof to stabilize himself. "Take a left at the next intersection."

She wheeled to the left and sped down the unpaved path. Flowering bushes and trees flashed by.

He smiled at the way her hair had thickened in the damp air and was now dancing around her face.

"Why are you grinning?" she asked after a quick glance his way.

"I'm just so damn glad to have you with me." And as far as he was concerned, this would be how he spent the rest of his life...beside Lydia, her mere presence bringing calm to his restless soul.

They parked at Cabana Sixteen and climbed out. Elevated off the sand, they had to climb a short flight to stairs to the door. Walking in to the living room was akin

to entering another world full of tropical colors and
bright sun.

"Holy shit," Lydia said, turning in a full circle before
pointing toward the curved wall of windows. "Look at
that ocean."

Just beyond their stone terrace with its private pool
lay the turquoise water of the Caribbean. Sugar-white
sand lined the water's edge. White-capped waves
produced constant crashes on the shore. White birds
squawked and flew above the waves.

"Incredible," she said in an almost reverent tone.

"What's incredible is you," he said, pulling her
against him to kiss her. "In case you haven't heard, I love
you, Lydia Henson."

Turning in his arms until they were face-to-face, she
returned his kiss. "I might have read that somewhere."

He grinned. "You saw that, huh?"

With a playful swat, she laughed. "My poor partner. I
can't believe you got Caroline involved in your
crazy-ass plans."

"She's a good sister-in-law," he said.

A knock at the door stopped her reply. "Without
Ellery to do the honors, who will answer my door?"

"I will," Jason said. "Whatever it takes to get you
back into my life, I'll do it."

There was a mature man dressed in khaki shorts, a
Sand Castle polo and canvas boat shoes standing on the
other side.

"Hello," he said. "I'm Jeffery, your concierge for
your stay."

"Excellent." Jason stepped back to allow the man to
enter. KC had told him about her butler, but he hadn't
been sure if one came with this unit. His reservation for
the weekend had been not only a last-minute deal, but a

fortunate one as the resort usually booked out months, if not years, in advance.

"I have brought your luggage from your car. May I bring it in and unpack for you?"

Lydia wore a look of surprise.

"Sure," Jason said.

The man retrieved the bags he'd left outside the door and carried them through the living room and into the adjacent bedroom.

Lydia arched an eyebrow. "If this is your idea of groveling, we will need to do it on a regular basis."

Jason pulled her to him and kissed her. Her lips parted and he swept his tongue into the warmth of her mouth. Their tongues met and touched and twisted together.

The past month had been one of the worst of his life. He needed this woman. He'd missed the way she tasted, the way she felt in his arms.

No, he wasn't giving Lydia up without a damn hard fight.

"Excuse me," Jeffery said. "Ma'am. This envelope was on top of your clothing."

Lydia stepped out of Jason's embrace, took the white envelope and slit it open. Two one-hundred dollar bills flittered to the floor.

"What the...?"

She pulled the notebook paper out, read and laughed.

"What?"

"My mother didn't like my bathing suit. Said it wasn't sexy enough, so she didn't pack it. She gave me the money to buy something small and sexy to keep you interested."

Jason laughed. "Honey, you don't need anything but yourself to keep me interested."

After Jeffery left and they'd explored the bedroom with its king-size bed and the master bath with its shower made for two, Lydia said, "Come on out on the patio. Let's talk."

His heart beat a little faster at her words. It hadn't occurred to him until this moment that it was possible that Lydia would use this trip as her goodbye to him. He hadn't exactly given her much of a choice in coming. He'd pretty much boxed her in with their mothers and his sister-in-law.

"Mind if I get us something to drink first? There is a great breeze, but it's still hot out there."

"Yeah, I'd like that."

He grabbed a cold beer for him and a bottle of sparkling water for her. She was stretched out on a lounge chair. A quick debate ping-ponged in his head. In the past, he would have made her lean up, and would have slipped behind her and pulled her against his chest to cradle her between his thighs. Now he was unsure of what her response would be. Maybe more importantly, he wanted to see her face while they talked. Would her expressions match her words?

He pulled a chair from the patio table up beside her and handed her the water. "Here ya go."

"Thanks. Sparkling? Oh yay. My favorite." She took a long drink and sighed. "Okay. We need to talk."

"So you said." He settled back in the chair and tried to assume an air of nonchalance. "Fire away."

"We were together a long time."

He nodded.

"And we talked about children a lot. You never varied in your stance. Not once. You were adamant.

When I accepted your proposal, I didn't have children. Now I have three with a fourth on the way." She patted her abdomen.

"We have."

"Excuse me?"

"We have three children and one on the way."

She shook her head. "The situation has changed, Jason. I'm on a totally different path than I was six months ago."

"Let me ask you this. If we had been married when Meredith and Jim died, would you have divorced me?"

Drawing back, her face wore a mask of offense. "Of course not, but that would have been different."

He shrugged. "I don't see the difference."

"The difference is we *aren't* married. You can make a new life with someone who wants the same things you do."

He leaned forward and put his hand on her abdomen. "First, this is *my* baby. Do you believe for one minute that I'd walk away from my child? And second, I love your kids. Every day I don't see them feels incomplete. And third, I don't want a life with someone else."

"It was only a week ago that you accused me of sleeping with another man, trying to pass off another man's child as yours." She pushed his hand away. "How are you suddenly so sure that I haven't been screwing around?" She snapped her fingers. "Semen analysis. You had one done and got the results back and found out you're not as sterile as you thought, huh?"

"Yes and no."

"Spoken like a true lawyer."

"I am so sorry about last Friday. I was just so shocked when you told me that you were pregnant. I may have overreacted."

She arched an eyebrow.

"Okay," he admitted. "I overreacted. I never expected to hear a woman say that the baby she was carrying was mine. I didn't," he added when she looked skeptical. "And, I guess I went nuts at the mere idea that you might be with another man." He held up a hand when she started to speak. "Look, we'd been apart for a month, a timeout, if you will. I don't for one minute think you would ever be unfaithful, but we were broken up. You'd booted me out of your house and your life. It terrified me that you might find someone else."

She crossed her arms. "So I ask again…why the sudden about-face? Semen analysis?"

Holding up one finger, he said, "Hold on. Be right back."

He went back into their suite, opened the zipper inside his suitcase and pulled out the test results. Never would he have admitted it but his heart pounded in nervous fear. Back on the patio, he handed her the white envelope with the lab's name and return address in the corner.

"There. You were right. I did have a semen analysis run."

Lydia studied the envelope and then looked at him. "It's not open."

He shook his head. "Nope. I don't need lab results to tell me what I already know." He dropped to his knees beside her chair. "We—you and I—made this baby. Maybe it'll be the only one we ever have or maybe it's the start of our own basketball team."

Her eyes shimmered with tears. "Oh Lord, no. No basketball team."

He smiled and leaned in. "I love you, Lydia. I love Ellery and Annie and Levi. And I love this munchkin inside you. I want to be your husband. I want to be the father to these children. Our lives together won't be what we expected when we agreed to marry. It'll be so much more."

He took her hand and pressed it to his heart. "I gave you my heart years ago. I don't want it back. I want you to hold it for the rest of your life."

Fat, heavy tears rolled down her cheeks. "Are you sure, Jason? Being a parent is so hard. I had no idea."

"Hey, any kid with us as parents is going to turn out awesome." He laid his head on her abdomen. For a minute, he basked in the knowledge that his baby grew beneath his head. Then he pressed a kiss there and stood.

He joined her on the lounger, wedging in near her hip. "For the past five weeks, my life has been too quiet. I need to see you, touch you, kiss you. I need to hear Ellery and Annie playing dolls. I need Levi giving me wet kisses. I want to spend the rest of my life loving you. I want to get double massages and make love until we can't move. And babies. I want to have babies with you. I know I've made some mistakes. I'll make more, but I promise that no matter what the future brings, I will never leave. Marry me. I'll be the best husband to you and the most awesome father to our kids."

She leaned forward, caught his face between the palms of her hands. "I think I fell in love with you when I walked off a horrible thirty-hour shift and found you waiting in the lobby for me." Smiling, she rubbed her thumbs over his cheeks. "You waited six hours to get a cup of coffee with me. No person in their right mind would do that."

"I wasn't in my right mind. I was in love."

As he leaned in to kiss her, the envelope holding his

test results caught wind and landed in the middle of their small, private pool.

"Your results," she said and started to move.

He stopped her with the kiss he'd been waiting to give her since she'd exited the limo that morning. Deep and wet and full of all the love and promises he could give her. When they finally came up for air, he glanced toward the water and back to her. "I don't need those. Everything I need is in my arms."

"I'm having a Montgomery maverick baby," she whispered.

He chuckled and hugged her. "And I wouldn't have it any other way."

Epilogue

"No. Absolutely not. I forbid it."

Lydia pulled the pies she'd made for the annual Montgomery Memorial Day bash from the oven and set them on the stove to cool.

"Mom, tell Dad everyone else will be wearing bikinis."

Lydia turned from the stove, and as it always did when she saw her husband, her heart flopped over like a fish. "What's the problem?"

Thirteen-year-old Ellery posed in her pink and black bikini. Beside her, Annie struck a similar pose in her yellow and green suit.

"Lydia. They barely have anything on," Jason sputtered. "Those suits are indecent."

"They're bikinis, honey. They're supposed to be skimpy." She circled her finger in the air to indicate the girls should turn around. They did. Their butts were covered, just barely, but covered. And the suits weren't as skimpy as some of the others she'd rejected. These were downright modest compared to the original ones the twins had picked out. "They look great, girls. Do me a favor please. I don't want to be late to your grandparents' house. Can you see what Grayson is doing? He's supposed to be dressed, but he's probably playing."

"Do we have to?" Ellery whined. "I've got to do my hair."

"And I haven't finished my makeup," Annie said.

"Makeup?" Jason whirled back to the girls. "No makeup. You're too young."

"*Mom*," Annie drew out.

"Honey, you don't need makeup. You're already pretty enough without it."

Annie sighed. "But Aunt Caroline lets Britney wear eye shadow and lipstick."

"Aren't you going swimming at Mimi's when we get there?"

Annie shrugged. "I don't know. Maybe."

Noah Graham was due home from law school. Lydia figured the bikinis and new interest in makeup was probably all about showing Noah that she was all grown up, not that she was, nor would twenty-seven-year-old Noah notice a couple of teen girls. But she remembered trying to get the attention of a few older guys back in the day.

"Okay, eye shadow and lip gloss only."

"Thanks, Mom," Annie said and turned to leave.

"Don't forget to check on Grayson. And if he's got another rope, let me know."

Five-year-old Grayson had recently decided he wanted to be a cowboy. On more than one occasion, she or Jason had found him trying to lasso various targets in his room. Where he kept getting the ropes was the question, although her money was on her brother-in-law Cash.

"Lydia."

"Jason."

He grinned as she did a perfect imitation of his voice. He wrapped his arms around her waist. "Those girls are going to be the death of me."

She chuckled. "Spoken like every father I know."

He kissed her. "You know those suits are just asking for problems."

"The other girls will be wearing similar suits. And I suspect the menfolk in your family will be having the same conversation with their wives."

Dropping his head on her shoulder, he asked, "When did I get so old and stuffy?"

"Hey, five kids will do that to you." She laughed. "For a man who didn't want kids, you ended up with the most of any of your siblings."

"Speaking of which, I haven't seen Levi or George."

At ten and nine, the boys were only sixteen months apart and almost inseparable. "They're already gone. Porchia came by and picked them up early to take them on out to the ranch. I think all the boys went early to help your parents set up."

"How is it possible that you are as beautiful today as you were the day I married you?"

"You're old and your eyesight is failing?"

He laughed. "Never." After a long and rather passionate kiss, he held her away from him. "If we start that now, we're going to be late."

Snuggling back in his arms, she said, "Want to send the kids out to the ranch without us? We could practice giving each other massages?"

"Would you two stop it?" Ellery said. "It's gross and you're too old."

Lydia lifted an eyebrow at her husband. "Too old?" she whispered.

"Never," he answered. "I'll never stop wanting you."

"Mom! Annie took my rope."

She sighed. "Think your parents will mind when we drive off and leave the kids there tonight?"

"Us and everyone else."

"Twelve grandchildren." She shook her head.

"They'll be in heaven." He nuzzled the spot behind her ear that he knew drove her nuts. "As we'll be later tonight."

"Would you two knock it off?" Annie said. "Here's the latest rope I found in Grayson's room. What time are we leaving?"

Lydia gave her husband a quick kiss and stepped back. "Forty-five minutes."

Annie wheeled around and left the kitchen.

"Not the life we envisioned, is it?" Lydia said.

"Not even close," Jason agreed. "It's so much better."

And it was.

About the Author

Photo by Tom Smarch

New York Times and USA Today Bestselling author Cynthia D'Alba started writing on a challenge from her husband in 2006 and discovered having imaginary sex with lots of hunky men was fun. She was born and raised in a small Arkansas town. After being gone for a number of years, she's thrilled to be making her home back in Arkansas living on the banks of an eight-thousand acre lake. When she's not reading or writing or plotting, she's doorman for very spoiled Border Collie, cook, house-keeper and chief bottle washer for her husband and slave to a noisy, messy parrot. She loves to chat online with friends and fans.

Find her online or send snail mail to:

Cynthia D'Alba PO Box 2116 Hot Springs, AR 71914

You can find her most days at one of the following online homes:

www.cynthiadalba.com
cynthiadalba@gmail.com

Read on for more
Whispering Springs, Texas books
by
Cynthia D'Alba

TEXAS TWO STEP

WHISPERING SPRINGS, TEXAS BOOK 1 ©2012
CYNTHIA D'ALBA

**Secrets are little time-bombs
just waiting to explode.**

After six years and too much self-
recrimination, rancher Mitch
Landry admits he was wrong. He left
Olivia Montgomery. Now he'll do
whatever it take to convince Olivia
to give him a second chance.

Olivia Montgomery survived the
break-up with the love of her life.
She's rebuilt her life around her business and the son she
loves more than life itself. She's not proud of the
mistakes she's made—particularly the secret she's kept—
but when life serves up manure, you use it to mold yourself into something better.

At a hot, muggy Dallas wedding, they reconnect, and
now she's left trying to protect the secret she's held on to
for all these years.

Read on for an excerpt:

The woman stood on tiptoe in the baggage-claim
area of the Dallas/Fort Worth airport looking for all the
world like someone who'd been sent to collect the devil.
Mitch Landry had expected Wes or one of the other
groomsmen to come for him. Instead, his gaze found a
statuesque blonde arching up on her toes, a white T-shirt

with Jim's Gym in black script stretched across her lushly curved breasts and long tanned legs extending from tight denim shorts. His heart stumbled then roared into a gallop.

Blood rushed from his brain to below his waist. His nostrils flared in a deep breath, as though he could smell her unique fragrance across the crowded lobby.

She hadn't looked in his direction yet, which gave him an unfettered opportunity to study her without having to camouflage his reactions.

No make-up covered her creamy rose complexion, not that she needed any. Not then and not now. No eye shadow was required to bring out the deep blue of her eyes. Nor did her mouth need any enhancement. Her lips radiated a natural pink, although the bottom one grew redder as her upper teeth gnawed on it.

Six years had passed since he'd seen Olivia Montgomery, but he'd swear she was more beautiful today. She had an appeal that came only with age and maturity. A smile edged onto his mouth. He was surprised—pleasantly surprised—to admit how glad he was to see her.

He watched as her glare bounced around the room, searching faces until it fell on him. As a look of resignation flashed across her face, she frowned.

His smile faded. Not exactly the reaction he'd hoped for.

TEXAS TANGO

WHISPERING SPRINGS, TEXAS, BOOK 2 © 2013
CYNTHIA D'ALBA

Sex in a faux marriage can make things oh so real.

Dr. Caroline Graham is happy with her nomadic lifestyle fulfilling short-term medical contracts. No emotional commitments, no disappointments. She's always the one to walk away, never the one left behind. But now her grandmother is on her deathbed, more concerned about Caroline's lack of a husband than her own demise. What's the harm in a little white lie? If a wedding will give her grandmother peace, then a wedding she shall have.

Widower Travis Montgomery devotes his days to building the ranch he and his late wife planned before he lost her to breast cancer. The last piece of acreage he needs is controlled by a lady with a pesky need of her own. Do her a favor and he can have the land. She needs a quick, temporary, faux marriage in exchange for the acreage.

It's a total win-win situation until events begin to snowball and they find, instead of playacting, they've put their hearts at risk.

Read on for an excerpt:

Friday afternoon, Travis Montgomery pulled his truck under the only shade tree in the Montgomery and Montgomery Law Offices parking lot. He hoped his brother had some news for him about Fitzgerald's place. After ten years of unsuccessfully trying to get Old Man Fitzgerald to sell, Singing Springs Ranch would finally be his. He could feel it in his bones.

He hadn't known Fitzgerald had family, so finding out Caroline Graham was his great-niece was a tad of a surprise, but no big deal. Other than Caroline, no other Fitzgerald family members mentioned in the obit lived here. He couldn't imagine that old tightwad leaving his ranch to any of them. And even if he did, there was no way anyone would up and move to Texas just because they inherited a rundown ranch, especially if that person knew nothing about ranching. Yup. Whoever ended up with Singing Springs would be thrilled to unload it, and Travis wanted to make sure that person unloaded it right into his hands.

He let himself in the back door of his brother's office, stopping long enough to grab a bottle of cold water from the kitchen, then headed for the reception area.

After removing his beige straw cowboy hat, he leaned over the reception desk to give Jason's secretary a wink. "Hi, Mags. Is little brother available?"

"Hey, handsome," Margaret said then sighed. "If only I were twenty years younger and not married…"

Travis slapped his hat across his heart. "My bachelor days would be over."

She smiled and nodded toward the closed door down the hall. "He's on the phone. I'll let him know you're here. I'd offer you something to drink, but you seemed to have helped yourself."

He rolled the dewy bottle on the back of his neck. "Can't decide if I want to drink this or pour it over my head. Man, it's a killer out there. What about KC? Is my lovely cousin around?"

Before Margaret could respond, Jason's door opened. "I thought I heard a reprobate out here. Stop flirting with my secretary and c'mon back. I've got a date with Lydia tonight and you know she hates when I'm late." He ducked back into his office, leaving the door ajar.

Travis groaned. "I'm coming." He looked at Margaret and hitched his thumb toward the door where his brother had just been standing. "He been in this bad mood all day?"

She shook her head. "Nope. He was quite pleasant when KC headed out about thirty minutes ago. Your cousin's got perfect timing. She always knows to clear out and avoid the Montgomery brothers when something's brewing."

"Lucky me. Wish I knew her magic."

Travis entered his brother's office and closed the door behind him. He dropped onto the thick leather sofa running along the office wall then set his hat crown-side down on the cushion beside him. He draped his arm along the back of the sofa. "I hope you've got some good news for me. I've had a bitch of a day."

"What happened?"

"One of the Webster kids spooked a new stallion I'd just unloaded. The bastard almost trampled me, John and a couple of hands before we could get him under control."

Jason frowned. "I'd think your foreman's kids would know better than to get near a stallion, especially one I suspect was antsy to begin with. Which kid?"

Travis's mouth cocked up on one side in a grimace.

"Rocky. He had a classmate visiting, and I think he was trying to impress him. But after John and Nadine get done with him, I suspect his ears will be ringing for the next week." He gave a small chuckle. "And I'm getting my stalls mucked out for free for at least a month, maybe two."

"I hated mucking stalls."

"So I remember. What's the good news?"

Jason took a seat closer to the sofa. "Well, I've got good news and bad news."

"Great. Bad news first then."

"Fitzgerald had KC prepare his will about a year ago, so his estate won't be going to the state to resolve."

Travis scowled. "I was afraid of that," he growled. "So what can you tell me now?"

"All the beneficiaries have been notified and the will duly probated. It was fairly straight forward. I don't foresee anyone challenging it."

"So don't keep me waiting. Who do I need to talk to about buying Singing Springs?"

"Dr. Caroline Graham."

TEXAS FANDANGO

WHISPERING SPRINGS, TEXAS BOOK 3 © 2014
CYNTHIA D'ALBA

Two-weeks on the beach can deepened more than tans.

Attorney KC Montgomery has loved family friend Drake Gentry ever since they were kids, but she never seemed to be on his radar. Fate puts in the same bar when Drake's girlfriend dumps him, leaving him with two all-expenses paid tickets to the Sand Castle Resort in the Caribbean. KC seizes the chance and makes him an offer impossible to refuse: two weeks of food, fun, sand, and sex with no strings attached.

University Professor Drake Gentry has noticed his best friend's cousin for years, but KC has always been hands-off, until today. Unable to resist, he agrees to her two-week, no-strings affair.

The vacation more than fulfills both their fantasies. The sun is hot but the sex hotter. Once home, KC finds it harder than she had expected to go back to her regular life. For Drake, their short two-week fling leaves him wanting more, but what's he to do when KC makes it clear she wants nothing more?

TEXAS TWIST

WHISPERING SPRINGS, TEXAS BOOK 4 © 2014
CYNTHIA D'ALBA

Real bad boys can grow up to be real good men.

Paige Ryan lost everything important in her life. She moves to Whispering Springs, Texas to be near her step-brother. But just as her life is starting to get back on track, it's derailed again when the last man in the world she wants to see again moves into her house.

Cash Montgomery is on the cusp of having it all. But a bad bull ride leaves him injured and angry. His only comfort is found at the bottom of a bottle. His family drags him home to Whispering Springs, Texas, the last place he wants to be. With nowhere to go, he moves temporarily into an old ranch house on his brother's property surprised the place is occupied.

The best idea is to move on but sometimes taking the first step out the door is the hardest one.

Loving a bull rider is dangerous, so is falling for him a second time is crazy?

TEXAS BOSSA NOVA

WHISPERING SPRINGS, TEXAS BOOK 5 ©2014
CYNTHIA D'ALBA

A heavy snowstorm can produce a lot of heat

Magda Hobbs loves being a ranch housekeeper. The job keeps her close to her recently discovered father, foreman at the same ranch. She is immune to all the cowboy charms, except for one certain cowboy, who is wreaking havoc on her libido.

Reno Montgomery is determined to make his fledging cattle ranch a success. He's content with the occasional date until Magda Hobbs. She is rocking his world and then she's gone, leaving him confused and more than a little angry. He's shocked when he learns the new live-in housekeeper is Magda Hobbs.

When a freak snowstorm cuts off the outside world, the isolation rekindles their desire. But when the weather and the roads clear, Reno has to work hard and fast to keep the woman of his dreams from hitting the road right out of his life again.

TEXAS HUSTLE

WHISPERING SPRINGS, TEXAS BOOK 6 ©2015
CYNTHIA D'ALBA

Watch out for chigger bites, love bites and secrets that bite

Born into a wealthy, Southern family, Porchia Summers builds a good life in Texas until a bad news ex-boyfriend tracks her down. Desperate for time to figure out how to handle the trouble he brings, she looks to the one man who can get her out of town for a few days.

Darren Montgomery has had his eye on the town's sexy, sweet baker for a while but she's never returns his looks until now. He's flattered but suspicious about her quick change in attention.

Sometimes, camping isn't just camping. It's survival.

SADDLES AND SOOT

WHISPERING SPRINGS, TEXAS BOOK 8 ©2015
CYNTHIA D'ALBA

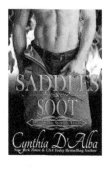

Veterinarian Georgina Greyson will only be in Whispering Springs for three months. She isn't looking for love or roots, but some fun with a hunky fireman could help pass the time.

Tanner Marshall loves being a volunteer fireman, maybe more than being a cowboy. At thirty-four, he's ready to put down some roots, including marriage, children and the white picket fence.

When Georgina accidentally sets her yard on fire during a burn ban, the volunteer fire department responds. Tanner hates carelessness with fire, but there's something about his latest firebug that he can't get out of his mind.

Can an uptight firefighter looking to settle down persuade a cute firebug to give up the road for a house and roots?

TEXAS DAZE

WHISPERING SPRINGS, TEXAS BOOK 9 ©2017
CYNTHIA D'ALBA

A quick fling can sure heat up a cowgirl's life

When a devastating discovery ends Marti Jenkins' engagement, she decides to play the field for a while. A ranch accident lands her in the office of Whispering Springs' new orthopedic doctor, Dr. Eli Boone. And yeah, he's as hot as she's been told.

Dr. Eli Boone is temporarily covering his friend's practice and then it's back to New York City and the societal world he's lives. He's not looking for a wife, but he wouldn't say no to a quick tumble in the sheets with the right woman.

Due to ridiculous challenge, Eli has to learn to ride before he leaves town. He turns to the one person who can help him win the bet, Marti Jenkins.

As he learns to ride a horse, Marti does a little riding of her own…and she doesn't need a horse.

Made in the USA
Monee, IL
14 November 2021